Praise for *You'd Look Better as a Ghost*

"A welcome addition to the burgeoning subgenre of darkly humorous female serial killer novels . . . *You'd Look Better as a Ghost* and its ilk are, I suspect, 'Marmite' books. If you're a fan, this one will be a treat."
—*The Guardian*

"This darkly comedic thriller turns serial killer convention on its head, mainly because you can't help but root for protagonist Claire. . . . Utterly unique and an absolute roller-coaster of a read."
—*Daily Mail*

"With echoes of Bella Mackie's bestselling *How to Kill Your Family* and TV's *Killing Eve*, this masterful debut is horrifying and hilarious in equal measure."
—*Woman and Home*

"This is a splendidly funny and buoyant, even jolly, novel . . . There are some deliciously ingenious twists. . . . It's first-class escapist entertainment—the most fun you're ever likely to have with a hammer-wielding maniac."
—*Daily Express*

"Refreshingly original and laugh-out-loud funny. This is a superb debut."
—Clare Mackintosh, #1 international bestselling author of *A Game of Lies*

"If you loved *Killing Eve*, Wallace's giddy dark ride will be your private Eden, filled with serpent-like twists beguiling you to bite! Her enticing wit had me enthralled and outwitted!"

bestsellin

"A pitch-black comedy horror . . . Roll up for your one-way ticket to the warped world of a glamorous psychopath and her relentless succession of hapless victims."
—Janice Hallett, international bestselling author of *The Appeal*

"Wallace had me at the title and kept me reading late into the night. Wicked, funny, and charming, a delicious combination."
—Sascha Rothchild, author of *Blood Sugar*

PENGUIN BOOKS

YOU'D LOOK BETTER AS A GHOST

Joanna Wallace studied law before working as a commercial litigation solicitor in London. She now runs a family business and lives in Buckinghamshire with her husband, four children, and two dogs. She was partly inspired to write *You'd Look Better as a Ghost*, her debut, following her father's diagnosis of early onset dementia.

YOU'D LOOK BETTER AS A GHOST

—

Joanna Wallace

PENGUIN BOOKS

PENGUIN BOOKS
An imprint of Penguin Random House LLC
penguinrandomhouse.com

First published in Great Britain by Viper, part of Serpent's Tail,
an imprint of Profile Books Ltd, 2023
Published in Penguin Books 2024

LIBRARY OF CONGRESS CATALOGING-IN-PUBLICATION DATA

Names: Wallace, Joanna, author.
Title: You'd look better as a ghost / Joanna Wallace.
Description: New York: Penguin Books, 2024.
Identifiers: LCCN 2023040098 (print) | LCCN 2023040099 (ebook) |
ISBN 9780143136170 (trade paperback) | ISBN 9780593512227 (ebook)
Subjects: LCGFT: Novels. | Detective and mystery fiction. | Humorous fiction.
Classification: LCC PR6123.A45455 Y68 2024 (print) |
LCC PR6123.A45455 (ebook) | DDC 823/.92—dc23/eng/20231011
LC record available at https://lccn.loc.gov/2023040098
LC ebook record available at https://lccn.loc.gov/2023040099

Printed in the United States of America
1st Printing

Set in Baskerville MT Pro
Designed by Cassandra Garruzzo Mueller

For my dad

YOU'D
LOOK
BETTER
AS A
GHOST

THEN

Half the people crammed into the hall have left their umbrellas at the back, by the door. The other half have closed their umbrellas and placed them at their feet. The people who left them by the door are settling into their seats, distracted. How do they know their out-of-sight umbrellas are safe, won't be stolen? Or forgotten? Maybe they shouldn't have left them at the door. Maybe they should have kept their umbrellas with them.

The woman seated in the middle of the front row puts her umbrella on the empty chair to her right. Whenever anyone approaches and asks whether the seat is taken, she smiles apologetically and tells them it is. The people unsettled by her seductive beauty look irritated when she says this. Everyone else stares transfixed. Music starts to play as the door at the back of the hall closes. Anyone still standing trips over umbrellas to find a seat. The show is about to begin.

The little children are dressed as mice. With cardboard ears attached to headbands, whiskers drawn across faces and long tails sewn onto leotards, they scamper across the stage and the audience claps. When one of the performers, a little girl, accidentally steps on the tail of the child in front, the audience laughs. When the tiny offender stops to pick up the tail, the audience cheers. When she taps the shoulder of the child ahead of her to return *the missing tail, the hall explodes into applause, obliterating the best attempts of the thunder outside. By the time the children scurry off stage, all those umbrellas placed by feet are the forgotten ones, crushed under the weight of a standing ovation.*

At the end of the show, the woman sitting in the middle of the front row retrieves her umbrella from the empty chair to her right and her daughter from the stage. As they hurry back towards the car, the little girl jumps over puddles as her mother smiles at every person they pass. "Wasn't it a wonderful show," the woman says to all the other parents hurrying through the rain towards their cars. "Didn't the children do well." Women smile uncomfortably when she speaks to them. Men just stare.

They drive out of the car park and the little girl watches the wipers move across the windscreen as they head towards home. Moving back and forth, back and forth, back and forth, until they don't. The rain doesn't stop but the windscreen wipers do. It's difficult to see the world outside but the little girl knows this isn't home. The woman switches off the ignition and turns towards her daughter.

"Who the fuck do you think you are?" she asks.

The little girl turns away and stares at each raindrop hitting the windscreen. Each one so free. Free to fall. Free to be.

The mother grabs the child's face. "Don't you dare look away from me. I'm talking to you." Her fingers are strong, her nails sharp. The little girl struggles to breathe. "All you had to do was be dainty." The woman tightens her grip. "That's what you're supposed to be. A dainty, delicate little girl. How dare you embarrass me like that? Stepping on that fucking tail. Everyone will be talking about you now. Talking about how useless and clumsy you are. And do you know what happens to useless, clumsy little girls?"

"*No,*" whispers the child.

"*You will,*" says the woman, slapping the child across her face. *The car starts and the windscreen wipers move again. Back and forth, keeping pace with her rage, back and forth, drawn-on whiskers and tears, back and forth, and that storm—it patiently watches.*

1

She looks about the same age as me, early thirties, and she's piling the plates precariously. I wonder whether she's in a rush or just enjoys the excitement of seeing how many she can stack before they fall. There are nine plates piled on the tray with a selection of cutlery on top. She turns towards the kitchen and hesitates. She's spotted another plate. Surely not. She reaches for the tenth plate and balances it on the cutlery. I take a sip of red wine and look away from the waitress. The serious-looking men in serious black suits are standing seriously too close and staring at me. Are they waiting for me to talk?

"Claire," one of them says, "like I was saying, I'm so sorry about your dad. He was a good man. One of the best."

One of the best? What a curious accolade. Out of how many? The whole world? This room?

"He was such a lovely man," someone else is saying now. Another solo voice emerging from a chorus of gentle agreement. They look like a depressed choir, all these men who used to work with my dad. The choir that charisma forgot.

"Always so calm," continues the soloist. "In fact, do you know something, Claire? I can't ever remember a time when I saw your dad rattled. Not once! In all the years I knew him, he never got rattled. No matter what was going on, he was always so calm."

"You're so right!" someone else is saying now. "He never got rattled, did he? It was extraordinary, now I think about it. I never saw him rattled. Not ever."

I stand here, watching their mouths move, and wonder about all the funerals in the history of the world. All the funerals that have happened since the beginning of time. How many billions of funerals must there have been? Hundreds of billions? Thousands of billions? Trillions? How many billions in a trillion? And has there ever been a funeral, I wonder, since records began, that has seen such a peculiar overuse of the word "rattled"?

"I remember one time, must be thirty years ago now," says another voice, "me and your dad, we were working together on this huge project and, let me tell you, the deadlines were unbelievable! Everyone—well, almost everyone—was panicking. The boss was panicking, the client was panicking, and I don't mind telling you, I was the most nervous of wrecks! But your dad, Claire, he wasn't one bit rattled. Nothing ever seemed to rattle him."

Maybe if the funeral was for a rattled young mother who died saving her infant from a rattling rattlesnake armed only with the child's rattle, maybe then I could understand the word "rattled" featuring so heavily in post-burial banter. Maybe.

"He was an extraordinary man," says a different voice. "Always so quiet. Peaceful."

The total opposite of the crash of crockery that now hits the floor. Everyone turns towards the waitress, who is almost at the kitchen door but not quite. That tenth plate, poised somewhere between precarious and reckless, lies smashed on the ground, to-gether with the other nine. The waitress is on her knees, picking up broken pieces of crockery, when another appears with a dust-pan and brush. They begin to giggle, shoulders shaking. Then, remembering the occasion, they become quiet and respectful again. But it's all an act. I know it is. As soon as they disappear into the kitchen their laughter will erupt.

"And how are you coping, Claire?" one of the men is asking me now. "It must be difficult for you, with no other family to support you through this difficult time."

I open my mouth to answer and then I hear my phone buzz. "Excuse me," I say, retrieving it from my bag. "I'd better check this." Staring at the screen, I see it immediately. New email alert. It's here. Finally. The news I've been waiting for. Taking a deep breath, I open the message.

Dear Claire,

Thank you for entering the Keiver Emerging Artist Prize. My colleague, Hannah, and I thought your entry was extremely compelling and we are thrilled to offer you a place on the short list . . .

"Is everything OK, Claire?"

I look up from my phone. They're still staring at me.

"Yes, everything's fine," I say, dropping my phone back into my bag. "It's good news, actually. Really good news."

"Oh?" The chorus of men quickly rearrange their expressions.

"I entered one of my paintings into an art competition a while ago. I've just heard that my entry's been short-listed."

"That's fantastic!" chants the choir in unison. "Well done, you!"

"Can I ask you something, Claire?" ventures the latest solitary voice. "What does it mean? To be short-listed."

"It means that my painting has made it into the top ten," I explain. "Only the top ten pieces of work are short-listed."

"Out of how many?"

"Hundreds."

"Wow! That's totally awesome," says a distinguished-looking man who looks and sounds like he doesn't say, "Wow! That's totally awesome" all that often. "Your father was always talking about how talented you are," he continues. "He used to say that he could see, right from when you were a small child, how brilliant you were at art."

I smile, which immediately feels weird. It's been a while since my face has been troubled with a smile. Then I think I'd better say something, as it's starting to hurt, cracking my face like concrete drying.

"I remember when he gave me my first sketchbook," I say, moving my wineglass towards my mouth. "I was dressed as a mouse at the time."

All their eyes are upon me. Suddenly I'm the choirmaster.

"Dad gave it to me on my fourth birthday. I'd been in a dance recital and when I got home, he was there with my cake. There was the biggest thunderstorm that day, I remember that."

That and more. Dad losing that famous calm of his when he

realized he'd missed the performance: "But it was in my diary for tomorrow. You told me it was tomorrow!" Rare that he ever challenged her. Mum then got one of her bad heads. She went up to bed and I opened my presents downstairs with Dad. And there it was. My first ever sketchbook.

"Is that when your love of art started?" one of the men asks, as I pause to sip my wine.

"I think so." They wait for more. I don't give it.

"You probably don't remember much from when you were four." What is it with these men? What's wrong with standing in silence?

"I remember everything."

All of it. The unwrapping of the sketchbook, how I grabbed a pencil straightaway. And typical Dad, once I'd finished, he'd declared my work a masterpiece. He said we should drive it to one of those fancy art galleries in town. We both laughed at that . . .

"Claire, are you OK?"

"I just remembered something about the competition. There's going to be an exhibition of the short-listed work. My painting's going to be displayed in a gallery."

"Wow! That's totally awesome," says the distinguished-looking man again, proving he still can't deliver that line, but his perseverance? Totally distinguished.

"Thanks," I say, taking another sip of wine, followed by another and another, until I'm not sure this constitutes sipping. "I just wish Dad was still alive to see it."

Another pause while they remember why they're here. And why that quiet, peaceful man they used to work with isn't.

A clearing of the throat. "I bet he's so proud of you, Claire. And you'll always have your memories . . ."

"Thank you," I say, taking another mouthful of wine. It's true. I'll always have my memories. Especially my favorite from that day, one I haven't shared. It happened after the sketchbook and the laughter. We'd just finished our second slice of cake and Dad was washing up plates at the kitchen sink when he told me to go upstairs and get ready for bed.

"Don't wake your mother," he said as I jumped down from the table. "Best be as quiet as a mouse."

I was standing on the stairs when the crash of glass made him run from the kitchen. "What happened?" he asked. "What was that noise?"

"It was an accident," I replied. A framed photograph of my mother lay at my feet, the glass broken.

"Don't worry," he whispered, glancing nervously towards the top of the stairs. "I'll clean it up. Just tread carefully and go quietly up to bed."

"I'M SORRY!" I shouted then, as loud as my four-year-old voice would allow. "IT WAS AN ACCIDENT."

"Sshhh," he hissed, panicking. "I told you. Quiet as a mouse!"

"Not all mice are dainty and delicate," I said, turning towards my mother who'd just appeared at the top of the stairs. "Some of them are useless and clumsy." And raising my foot, I slammed it down onto the image of her face, splitting the glass across that pouting smile. And that's when it happened, just before I scampered up the stairs towards bed. That's when I saw the flicker. Somewhere in her eyes between indifference and the arrival of rage, existing for less than a moment. But it was there. It was real. It was fear. And it was enough.

"I'm so sorry for your loss."

I look up from where I'm refilling my glass from one of the bottles on the table against the wall. The plate-smashing waitress is standing in front of me, not meeting my eye. She's holding a tray of empty glasses.

"And I'm sorry for all that noise earlier, breaking those plates . . . And for the giggling. We weren't being rude, it was just a nervous thing, you know?"

"Yes, I know," I say. "It's fine, I understand." Which is true. I do. What I don't understand is why she's still standing there. I hope she's not going to say sorry again. All this apologizing is getting embarrassing. It was less awkward when she was smashing plates.

She meets my eyes. Hers are a washed-out blue. "I understand what you're going through," she says, readjusting her grip on the tray. "When I lost my mum, everyone said waves would hit me out of nowhere. You know . . . grief. And they were right. A big one would get me, and I'd think, Mum's gone forever, she's never coming back. And that's when it would drag me right down, the feeling—like I was going to drown . . ."

Her voice melts away. Each thought starts to freeze, jagged icicles forming inside my mind. I think about the comfort of the Keiver Emerging Artist Prize. If I think about the exhibition, I don't have to think about Dad. Gone forever. All alone inside that small, cold box in the ground. Dad always hated the cold.

He always hated being alone, and he'd never been keen on confined spaces.

The waitress shivers now, almost as though reading my thoughts, and the empty glasses on her tray wobble, clinking together. She closes her eyes. Does that work, I wonder. As a strategy for dealing with life when things start to go wrong. Maybe if I close my eyes, all of this will disappear. Maybe when I open them, I'll be back at home, working on my painting. Dad will be sitting in his armchair, sipping whisky, and I'll feel safe. At peace. I open my eyes. The waitress is still standing there. So are the empty glasses, intact. She looks relieved. At least the eye-closing strategy worked for one of us.

Suddenly I'm exhausted, and my head is starting to hurt. The waitress stifles a yawn. She's had enough of this function. So have I. It's been a long day and I'm feeling a little . . . rattled. I turn and walk towards the door.

THIS MORNING, THE MORNING AFTER the funeral, I'm sitting in Dad's armchair, drinking tea, eating buttery toast and sketching ideas for my new painting when another email arrives.

Dear Claire,

I am terribly sorry, but I emailed you in error with an offer of a place on the short list yesterday. I'm ashamed to say that the message was meant for

another applicant named Claire and I clicked on your
email address by mistake. I am so sorry . . .

Carefully placing my tea and toast onto the coffee table, I
read the rest of the message. It goes on to tell me that I shouldn't
give up and that I should apply for other competitions in the future and that's when I notice my hand. Tense with the effort of
gripping, encasing the arm of the chair. Staring at the email, I
hold my breath as each word develops its own weaponry, moves
from the screen and hovers before my eyes. Taunting me, mock-
ing me, before fading into a place inside a fancy gallery that was
never there. Somewhere my painting will never hang. And now
the images appear. It's Dad. Lying alone in a box in the ground.
Has he begun to rot? When will the worms start to eat him? I
can't hold my breath any longer, but I'm far too scared to exhale. I grip the armchair tighter. The armchair where he used
to sit. I focus on the darkness rushing towards me. Is this what
she meant? Precarious piler of plates. Is this what it feels like
to drown?

2

When I exhale and the next breath is there, I run to the bathroom cabinet and empty every bottle of pills. There's enough here, I'm sure of it. Enough to transport my ears to his voice. And I need to hear his voice so much it hurts. I phone his number and a recorded message tells me it's not possible to connect my call at the moment and that I should try again later. This calms me down a little. The recorded message sounds so certain, so trustworthy. Maybe if I do what it says, maybe if I try again later, Dad will pick up the phone. The calm is illusory, dissipates as soon as the images reappear. Dad in the ground, lying alone in a small, cold box. I pick up a handful of pills, lift them to my mouth. Can I do this? Should I do this? I scatter the pills onto the floor and put my hands to my head. Try to squeeze the images out. How do I escape my mind?

I run downstairs and jump onto the treadmill in the corner of my living room. Maybe if I sprint as fast as I can for as long as I can, I will outrun all thought. Leave everything far, far behind. I run and I run and at the end, I'm exactly where I started. Desperate to hear his voice. Racing back up to the bathroom, I scramble on the floor to collect up each pill. But when I stand

and stare at my reflection in the mirror, I wonder what Dad will say when I see him. Will he be angry at me for ending my life? I don't want to make him angry. Hasn't he been through enough?

In any event, none of this is my fault. I'm beginning to see that now. All I did was enter a competition. The mistake wasn't mine. Dropping the pills onto the floor again, I reread the email.

Once again, I am terribly, terribly sorry for my mistake.

Yours,
Lucas Kane

Lucas Kane. A man so sorry for his mistake. Terribly, terribly so. I wonder whether that's true.

In the photograph I find of him on the internet, Lucas looks underwhelming and self-satisfied. Not sorry at all. But that doesn't mean he *isn't* sorry. He may be terribly, terribly sorry. And terribly, terribly unphotogenic. Photographs on the internet are about as trustworthy as that recorded message on Dad's phone. If I want to know for certain whether Lucas Kane is sorry, I need to find him and ask him. But first I need to decide. Do I want to know for certain whether Lucas Kane is sorry? Or do I want to forget about him and cram those pills into my mouth?

I decide to find out more about Lucas. It takes seconds on Google to discover he works in London. I live near London. Never takes me long to drive in.

• • •

WITHIN A COUPLE OF HOURS, I'm parking my car around the corner from his office. I get out and wait. It's perfect, the street opposite Lucas's office. The perfect place to pretend to be someone I'm not. I can be a person waiting patiently at a bus stop. Or a window shopper, never enticed quite enough to step inside. By six o'clock in the evening, I'm one of those people you see sitting on a bench, lost in thought with nowhere to be. And that's when I see Lucas Kane for the first time. I realize the photograph on the internet is unkind. In real life, he's surprisingly attractive, and I only recognize him when I hear someone shout his name. Someone else is waiting for Lucas Kane.

A skinny man, slouching in the smokers' area outside Lucas's office. He probably works there too. Dressed all in black, with a dour expression and the whitest of skin, he has the look of a reluctant vampire who's just learned to day-walk but would much rather be asleep in a coffin. Taking a long drag on his cigarette, Vampire Smoker calls out again, "Lucas!"

In contrast, Lucas looks like an ambassador of sunshine sent to welcome Vampire Smoker into the light. His body is toned, his skin is tanned, his smile is wide. And judging from the intricate pattern on that zany, designer-looking shirt, self-confidence isn't a problem. As Lucas exits the office and heads towards the smoker, I stand up from the bench and walk closer. From directly across the road, I stare at Lucas Kane in real life, and within moments I know. He doesn't look sorry.

Lucas swings his briefcase and talks nonstop as he and his friend amble along the street. I cross the road and follow. When the two men walk into a bar, my skin burns. Did Lucas just mention my name? I'm sure I heard him mention my name. What is he saying about me? Talking about my painting? Commenting on my lack of talent? Is that why he's laughing?

Vampire Smoker goes to the bar while Lucas finds them somewhere to sit. I buy myself a drink and settle into a seat nearby. Lucas removes a newspaper from his briefcase and flicks through it. His friend places drinks on the table. As Lucas points out something hilarious in the newspaper, he still doesn't look sorry. He sips his pint and talks to his friend and sips his pint and glances in my direction. His eyes meet mine. I don't look away.

When they've finished their drinks, Vampire Smoker leaves the bar to disappear into the night, but Lucas loiters behind. He glances at me again and makes his approach.

"Hi," he says. "Can I buy you a drink?"

"Sure," I reply. He returns from the bar, passes me my drink and pulls up a chair. I turn towards him and study his face. He looks about forty, with nice eyes, nice smile and cheekbones high enough to reach his self-esteem. All good. Sometimes I like conventional.

"So, what's your name?" he asks, and I'm impressed. It's valiant, his attempt to contain that leer.

"I'm Claire."

"Claire? You don't look like a Claire." His phone starts to ring. He ignores it.

"What does a Claire look like?" I ask.

"Hmmm," he says, taking a swig of his drink. "I guess I always imagined Claire being a dowdy kind of a person. A librarian, maybe. You know the type, an enthusiastic lover of tweed." This makes me laugh and he laughs too, his eyes sparkling as he leans forward in his chair. "Claire's the kind of person who goes to planning application meetings for fun."

I lean forward too, allowing my short dress to rise further up my thighs.

"And?" I say, drawing his eyes back up to mine.

"And what?" He is distracted, confused.

"What does librarian Claire do at these planning application meetings?"

"She sits at the back and makes notes."

I reach across the table for my drink, brush my hand against his, let it linger.

"She's a plain Jane," he adds, losing all control of that leer. "The total opposite of you."

"Surely plain Jane already has a name," I say. "Why would she be called Claire?"

"Good point." His smile and leer, by now, are expertly fused. "I'm Lucas."

"I know."

"What do you mean, you know?"

"You look like a Lucas."

"What does a Lucas look like?" he asks as his phone rings again. He glances at it this time before placing it back on the table, unanswered.

"Lucas is pretentious and arrogant." I pause to take a sip of my drink. "You know the type. Always veering the wrong side of smug. He works in the art world because he likes being around those with talent. Ever hopeful a little will rub off on him."

"Wow," he says.

"Wow what?"

"That's freaky."

"Freakily accurate?"

"Well . . ."

"You *are* pretentious and arrogant?"

"No."

"Just completely devoid of talent, then?"

"No! Not at all. But I do work in art."

"I know. I entered a competition you helped organize . . ." but he's not listening anymore. His phone is ringing again and this time he's staring at it. Distracted. Irritated.

"I'm so sorry, Claire," he says, shifting away from me in his chair. "I'm going to have to take this. Hello," he mumbles into the phone, addressing the female voice on the other end of the line. "Yes, I know . . . I'm sorry . . . I couldn't get to the phone. No, listen . . . I'm not going to make it tonight. I know what we agreed but something's come up and I need to work late. I'm terribly, terribly sorry . . . I'm not sure how long . . . hours probably. Look, I'll call you tomorrow, OK? Bye."

Switching his phone off, he places it onto the table and takes a swig of his drink. "Now, where were we?" he asks, smiling at me.

"Was that true?" I ask.

"What?"

"What you just said."

"What do you mean? When?"

"Just now. What you just said to that woman on the phone. I mean, obviously you lied to her about where you are, but when you said you were terribly, terribly sorry. Tell me, was that true?"

"Look," he says, leaning towards me, "it's not what you think. She's not my wife, or my girlfriend," he adds, reaching out tentatively to take hold of my hand. "I don't have either of those. That woman is nobody important. I'll admit we had loose plans to meet up later this evening but that was before—"

"Before what?"

"Before a stunning blonde called Claire," he says, pulling me gently towards him, "who doesn't look anything like a Claire, stepped into my life." He's leaning closer to me now, reaching out to touch my face. I breathe in his aftershave. Citrus. He smells good. And now he's looking into my eyes and telling me I'm beautiful, and that's when I notice something unexpected about Lucas. Something about the way he makes me feel. It's strange, this feeling. Nothing like I thought it would be. I expected to feel repulsed by him. And angry. But I don't. Sitting here with him now, looking into his eyes, I see the flickers of hope and it makes me excited. Fully alive. With my heart beating faster, I move my face closer. Close my eyes and we kiss.

He buys me another drink and tells me stories about himself that meander for ages around the point. Stories that really make him laugh. He speaks with a London accent but not an interesting one, just off-center on the scale between aristocrat and cockney. I try a couple of times to tell him about the art competition, but when he isn't talking about himself, Lucas is leaning forward to kiss me.

"Let's go back to your place now," he says as soon as I finish my drink, and I smile, my agreement immediate. Lucas likes being in control, and I like it too. I like his hand on my waist, guiding me. I like his voice in my ear, telling me all the things he wants to do with me. Stepping outside the bar, he pulls me towards him. One long, frenzied kiss before we start walking. No ambling anymore: Lucas is in a hurry. I have to quicken my pace to keep up. When he asks me where my car is parked, I love the urgency in his voice.

As I drive, he reaches across from the passenger seat, touches my face and my neck, tells me my skin is so soft. Whenever I stop at traffic lights, he shifts in his seat so he can kiss me. With his hand on my thigh, I don't want to mention the art competition. It seems crass to talk of his emails. We've moved far beyond that now. When we get back to my house, we stumble, kissing, through the front door, both of us desperate to get up the stairs. I lead him into my bedroom and that's when he becomes different, suddenly happy to let me take control. Pushing him onto the bed, I take my time as I start to undress him. Keep my eyes locked onto his, there's no need to rush. Once he's naked, I tell him to lie on my bed and be patient. I gather a selection of silk scarves. Choosing one, I tie his left hand tightly to my bed, and he smiles. He says he likes this, so I tie his other hand, just as tight.

"Don't forget my ankles," he adds, urgency returning. Once he's tied up beneath me, I tell him again that he needs to be patient. I'm going to take my time now. I like taking my time. He's excited and so am I. And so quiet. No more stories. Just the heaviness of anticipation in each labored breath. I look at him lying there, obedient and patient. Smile as I slowly run my fingers through my hair.

"What the . . . ?" he stammers as the blonde wig drops to the bed and onto the floor. He's staring, open-mouthed, as I shake out my long, dark hair.

"Why were you wearing a wig?" He sounds breathless. "You're even more fit as a brunette."

"Sssshhh." I place a finger to my lips, signaling silence. "From now on, I'll let you know when you have permission to talk." He nods in agreement as I slowly start removing my clothing. Both of us are smiling as I drop my dress to the floor. Leaning towards Lucas, I cover his face in gentle kisses. Breathe in the scent of citrus as I whisper gently, so gently into his ear: "How are you feeling?"

This is it. All he has to do is say "sorry." That's the only word I need to hear. But Lucas Kane isn't sorry. I've known that from the moment I read his email. So terribly, terribly insincere. When he sees the knife, he starts shouting but never once do I hear the word "sorry." I sit back and watch him wriggle. All that naked flesh. So pathetic and desperate to break free. He wriggles like a worm. A stupid, wriggling worm, and suddenly I think about the worms in the ground. When will they get to Dad?

I slice the knife into Lucas's belly, he screams, and my mind accelerates. Look at that! It *is* possible to outrun thought. Leave everything far, far behind. Removing the knife, I ask him to tell me one of his stories. Tell him I'll untie him if he makes me laugh. He's crying now, which I don't think will help his chances, and as soon as he starts talking, it's obvious—even he doesn't find himself funny anymore. Demanding silence, I slice the knife into his flesh and tell him he needs to be patient because I like to take my time. And that's when I notice it—his shirt, zany and designer-looking—screwed up in a ball on my bedroom floor. Such an intricate pattern on such a bold fashion choice. Such a perfect opportunity to try some new art.

His blood seeps eagerly as my knife gets to work, little red pools charting my progress, allowing thought to run free. It seems happy, his blood, to escape the routines of the mundane. Rushing excitedly from his body towards the unknown. Warm and sticky, it smells of possibility and sugar, congealing like toffee on apples, all the fun of the fair. And underneath the sweetness, that aroma of citrus lurks. Hijacked by the meaty stench of his fear.

It's exhausting and exhilarating, carving intricate patterns into skin—a canvas that is already fading. His translucency mesmerizes me, I can see straight through him, to the bloodied sheet he's lying on. I continue my work, pausing briefly to ask him questions. Watch intrigued as he transforms sobbing screams into words. Enhanced by terror, every utterance from his mouth sounds urgent. I do love that urgency in his voice. Loosening the restraints on his wrists, I stare deep into his eyes, so excited to see it. That beautiful dying flicker of hope. And that's when I retighten the restraints and plunge the knife deeper. Not deep enough to end his life yet, just enough to extinguish that hope. Lucas screams and closes his eyes. Opens them immediately upon my command, and I smile, enjoying my favorite part of the process. The part when I know one of my victims is going to die soon. The part when I can anticipate every moment of their deaths. The part when I already see them as ghosts.

Afterwards, I stand in the shower, close my eyes and think back to the silence that only exists beneath screams. So uncluttered, I live for that silence, allowing stillness to invade my mind. No images of Dad rotting in the ground, nobody expecting me to be someone I'm not. I open my eyes and notice the mud from my garden swirling around the plughole along with his blood. It's got to make a difference, the lack of a coffin. Nothing between Lucas Kane and the worms. Stepping out of the shower, my foot feels them immediately—the pills still strewn over the floor. Imagine if I'd swallowed them and never again savored that silence and stillness of mind. Clearing a line of steam from the mirror, I stare into my eyes and note the exhilaration. There's no anger there anymore. Deep down in his resting place, I honestly believe Lucas Kane is sorry now. Terribly, terribly so.

3

t's three weeks since Dad's funeral and my migraines are getting worse. The pain behind my eyes only used to bother me during thunderstorms, but lately it can strike at any time and be quite debilitating. I spoke about it with my GP, hoping for a magical prescription. Instead, he looked at me solemnly, drummed the tips of his fingers together and told me that sometimes it's good to think outside the box.

Convinced of a link between my headaches and Dad dying, the doctor suggested a bereavement counseling group. Why struggle with bereavement alone when you can grapple with grief in a group, he asked. At first, I hated the idea. If I wanted to surround myself with needy, self-pitying morons wittering on about their feelings, I'd join Facebook.

Funnily enough, after ten minutes at the first group session, I've decided there's a possibility I might enjoy it. Being around all this raw emotion is invigorating. Grief makes ordinary people infinitely more interesting, although sadly it doesn't appear to have the same effect on the venue. We're meeting in a boring church hall on a boring suburban street where the only issue of slight interest is how bizarrely busy someone's been with the Blu

Tack. There are handwritten notices all over the walls telling us what we can and can't do.

DO CHECK THE WINDOWS ARE LOCKED BEFORE LEAVING.

DON'T LEAVE PERSONAL BELONGINGS BEHIND.

DO STACK CHAIRS AWAY BEFORE LEAVING.

DON'T STACK MORE THAN SIX CHAIRS IN A PILE.

DO READ THE FIRE REGULATIONS PINNED TO THE NOTICEBOARD.

DON'T STACK MORE THAN SIX CHAIRS IN A PILE.

I wonder why the six-chair rule has got two notices. What happens when a seventh is added to the top of a stack? I can't be the only person tempted to find out. A circle of chairs had been positioned in the middle of the hall and we all chose one to sit on. Those first few moments were awkward, with obligatory smiles boomeranging around the group, but then everyone got their phones out and stared down at the screens and we all pretended we weren't sitting in a circle of strangers.

The group is run by an overweight woman in her sixties named Florence, but Lucas would say she should be named Claire. Wearing a shapeless tweed skirt that probably doubles up as a picnic blanket and a tired-looking blouse that could be mistaken for vintage if it wasn't so incredibly old, Florence looks like one of those inconsequential characters I see creeping around on the periphery of life—doing good deeds and saving for a rainy day. After dishing out sticky name labels to each of us, she sits back in her chair, introduces herself to the group and starts speaking about the need for respect between group members. My revulsion is complete. What the hell is that voice? She sounds like an annoying Christmas elf. On helium. The kind of sanctimonious, softly squeaking elf the other elves want to beat up.

She's speaking about the different stages of grief now, the first being denial. This has prompted a fascinating ripple of tears, shaking, and even a little shouting amongst my group mates who appear to be reading from a script no one told me about. The truth is, I'm not in denial about Dad's death. I knew he was going to die and part of me couldn't wait for it to happen. The Dad I knew left this world years before his heart failed. Early onset dementia, that was his fate, waiting for him after decades of kindness and hard work. A merciless disease, it disposed of his sanity fast, leaving behind confusion and psychosis inside the shape of my dad. I tried to care for him for as long as I could, praying every day that he would come back, read the newspaper, pour himself a glass of whisky, tell a joke, remember my name. Then one day he left the house with a knife, convinced all the demons inside his head were real. An interfering passerby called the police and my frightened, confused, brilliant father was taken away. He was detained under the Mental Health Act by a society that has lost its way. A society that allows us to destroy our pets as soon as they start shitting indoors but demands that humans be kept alive at any cost. A society that pretends to care about dignity and quality of life but no longer understands the meaning of either.

Florence is talking about feelings of isolation following the death of a loved one and when she asks whether anyone has any experiences to share, a nerdy-looking woman sitting next to me nervously raises her hand. I shift in my seat to take a proper look at her. Probably in her late thirties but she seems decades older than that. It could be the enormous dark circles under each eye, but I think it's the severe haircut that ages her the most. There's no way a hairdresser, even a drunk one, cut that fringe, and I would know. A drunk hairdresser once tried to cut a fringe into my hair, and then annoyed me by blaming her scissors and denying being drunk. Strangely enough, I didn't find anything wrong with her scissors and all that blood loss before death certainly seemed to sober her up.

The woman is wearing a tracksuit and a pair of open-toe sandals. She's fiddling with her phone.

"Hi, I'm Jemma," she says, briefly tapping her name badge.

"Hi, Jemma," everyone replies, and I acknowledge the inner onslaught of cringe. Why does this suddenly feel like an AA meeting?

"I recently lost my mother," stammers Jemma, her voice as shaky and weak as her physique. "She died of cancer."

This seems to be Florence's cue to squeeze out of her chair and waddle towards Jemma with a box of Kleenex. Jemma thanks her, takes a tissue and dabs her eyes. I take the opportunity to look around at the rest of the group. On the other side of Jemma sits a crumpled mountain of a middle-aged man. Crumpled name badge, crumpled T-shirt, crumpled tattoos, crumpled face. He smells of cigarette-scented body odor and there are broken capillaries all over his huge face, competing for space with a seemingly endless supply of beady sweat. Those jeans he's wearing must have been bought before he put on weight, and I've just noticed the red stain on his crumpled T-shirt. What is that? Ketchup? Blood? He's sitting there with his eyes closed, arms tightly folded, legs shuddering. Silently shaking his head, he looks like someone in the actual process of being chewed up by life and determined not to go down without a fight. Fascinating. I wonder whether he's about to start crying. Or a riot. Either look equally plausible.

"Mum battled cancer for four years," Jemma's saying now. "She was so brave. So incredibly brave. And I cared for her, of course I did. I loved her so much. I'd have done anything for her. Anything. I'd still do anything. Anything at all, if it meant I could have just one more day with my mum."

Cue Florence again. More squeezing out of the chair. More waddling. More Kleenex. Why doesn't she leave the box of tissues with Jemma, save herself the trip? The way this story's going, I predict Florence's going to be in and out of that chair and waddling across the room countless more times. She'll probably be thin by the time Jemma stops speaking. Maybe that's the plan.

"I wouldn't change a thing," Jemma's saying now, still dabbing at her eyes, "and I'd do it all again, but caring for Mum, day in day out, it didn't leave much time for anything else. I used to have loads of friends, but over the last few years they've all slowly disappeared. And I'm not criticizing anyone," she says. "I mean, people want to meet up to have fun, don't they? Who wants to meet up to listen to me cry or to hear about Mum's biopsies and chemo? I get it. I understand why all my friends disappeared. And the thing is, it didn't bother me so much when Mum was alive, but now she's gone it's all I can think about. This great big hole in my life. I've got nobody. Not one single friend. And I'm just so bloody lonely."

I wonder, as Florence squeezes herself out of her chair once again, whether anyone is pondering the same questions as me. Did Jemma's friends really disappear because they couldn't handle hearing about her mother's terminal illness? Or is it more likely that their disappearance coincided with Jemma's decision to start wearing open-toe sandals with tracksuits? But now I'm distracted by a different voice. Crumpled mountain of a man speaks.

"Fair-weather fuckers," he declares—which is a statement I don't think anyone was expecting to hear. Spoken robustly, in wonderful contrast to the jabbering of joyless Jemma. "That's what your mates are. Only wanting to spend time with you when life is good."

Jemma stops dabbing her eyes for a moment and looks at him, confused. We all do. And not just because he felt the need to explain the meaning of "fair-weather." Crumpled man speaks with the most remarkably strong accent. I wonder where he's from.

"And it's not just your mates," he's saying now, "the whole world is full of selfish pricks. That's the first thing you find out when someone you love dies. How fucking selfish most people are." Welsh! That's it! He's Welsh. With opinions and accent as robust as his physical form. If Aled Jones is walking in the air, this guy is stomping through the door.

"Excuse me," says a posh voice from the other side of the circle. We all turn our heads. It's Camilla Parker Bowles—or rather, Camilla's older, posher sister. "I understand emotions are running high for all of us and I don't like to cause offense but, please, would you mind your language?"

"I'm sorry, your majesty," says the Welshman, clearly picking up on the Camilla vibe too. "But if I'm going to get any benefit out of being here, I need to be myself. She," he says, pointing towards Florence, who appears to be frozen in time, standing awkwardly inside the circle, still clinging to her box of tissues, "said that we need to respect each other. Which means you need to respect my right to swear."

"And you need to respect my right not to listen to your profanities." Camilla sits even taller in her chair, demonstrating her impeccable posture. I wonder whether she glides through that country estate of hers with books piled high on her head, like they made her do in finishing school. "And she," she says, pointing towards Florence, "has a name. Florence. And I'd thank you to talk about her with a little respect."

"Fucking hell! Don't talk down to me like that." Welshman clenches his enormous right hand into a fist.

"OK, OK," says Florence, not exactly springing to life. But she is placing the box of tissues onto the floor, which I think for her constitutes a grand gesture. "I think we all need to take a few deep breaths. Let's try to remember, each of you is starting out on an individual journey of grief and the one thing I know about grief . . ." One thing? Shouldn't she know more than that? Isn't she running this group? ". . . is that everyone experiences grief differently. That's why it's so important we treat each other with respect," she settles her gaze on the Welshman, "and kindness," she adds, turning to face Camilla.

"I quite agree. I'm Christiana by the way," says Camilla, brushing the rows of pearls away so we can see her name badge. "Christiana, spelled with a C." I glance towards the Welshman just in time to see the smirk. No doubt thinking about another word spelled with a C.

"Hello, Christiana," says Florence, just as an elf would greet a child before leading them into the grotto to meet Santa. "Now, if it's OK with everyone, I'd like to get back to where we left off—"

"Sorry to interrupt you, Florence," says Christiana. She doesn't look sorry. "I'd like to say something else if I may?"

"Of course," says Florence. "Please go ahead."

"I just wanted to say that I think it's so true, what you just said—about all of us experiencing grief differently. And I suppose that's to be expected, given that we're all from completely different walks of life and different places. I mean, I'm from Wiltshire originally and you . . ." she says, gesturing vaguely towards the Welshman, "are from Wales and you, Florence, whereabouts are you from?"

"Croydon," says Florence.

"Oh, right," says Christiana, smiling. "But I mean, originally? Whereabouts are you from originally?"

"Croydon," repeats Florence. "Originally, I'm from Croydon."

"Oh," says Christiana, confused. "But you're . . ." She's floundering now, this woman who doesn't like to cause offense, as her individual journey of grief takes an unexpected early detour into racism.

"Thank you for your observations, Christiana," says Florence, breaking the silence with a smile. "And you're right, we all come from different backgrounds and have different life stories. But the one thing I know about grief . . ." not sure she should keep saying that ". . . is that it is one of the most common of human experiences." And I'm not sure that's the same as the other one thing she knows. "And the one thing you can be sure of with grief . . ." She's really confusing me now ". . . is that we can all learn from each other. So, getting back to where we left off—Jemma, I'm sorry to hear about your friends. Tell me, do you have any family to support you through this difficult time?"

"I have a sister," stammers Jemma, "but . . ." and now her whole body convulses with an alarmingly fast acceleration of tears and Florence is forced to intervene. No more waddling around with tissues, this is when we need her to step up and show us what she can do. Placing a hand on Jemma's shoulder, Florence urges her to concentrate on each breath and after a while the shuddering downgrades to a quiver.

"I'm so sorry," Jemma says, "I just get really upset when I think about my sister. You see, we used to be so close when we were younger but as we got older, we drifted apart and then . . ." and off she goes, veering dangerously close to hysteria again. Convulsing and sobbing and now she's flailing her arms around and . . . what the hell? Her bony hand reaches out and grabs hold of mine. What the hell is going on? Why is this woman holding my hand?

Florence is back with the Kleenex, urging Jemma to concentrate on every breath. Who cares about her breath? What about my hand? Who the hell are these weirdos and why am I here? How is any of this supposed to help my migraines? Bloody doctor. So much for thinking outside the box. What does that even mean? Stupid bloody box.

"My sister left me to care for Mum all on my own," splutters Jemma, still holding on to my hand tightly. "Even now, even after Mum's death," she sobs, "my sister still doesn't speak to me."

I look around at the rest of the group. Am I the only person who considers this weird? A grown woman, a complete stranger, is sitting here holding my hand and everyone else is just silently watching. Well, everyone except that peculiar little man over there, hunched forward in the seat opposite mine. Definitely too old for that earring/goatee combo. And what's he writing? I don't think he's stopped scribbling in a notebook since the moment we all sat down. Is he taking minutes of the meeting? Keeping note of Jemma's sobs? Is he allowed to be writing? What about confidentiality? Ordinary people love bleating on about privacy and data protection, I guess on the off chance they're not being boring enough, but no one in this circle seems bothered about any of that. They're just sitting in silence and staring at Jemma. I stare at her now too, and it's disgusting, the indignity of such a public display of self-pity. That's when I feel it: the most powerful urge to snatch my hand away and put her out of her misery. Strangulation would be my preferred choice, but Welshman would probably get involved, people like him always do, and I reckon he outranks me on strength. It needs to be quick. Sudden, blunt force to the head. Such a shame I didn't think to bring my hammer.

"I need you to listen to my voice, Jemma," says Florence, who is kneeling in front of her now. Just in case this scenario needed any more weirdness. "Try to concentrate on your next breath, and the one after that. That's it. In through the nose, out through the mouth. In through the nose, out through the mouth."

I close my eyes and listen to her voice. *In through the nose, out through the mouth. In through the nose, out through the mouth.* Start to refocus on why I came here. Not to kill but to explore that great big hole in my life. The enormity of my grief. *In through the nose, out through the mouth.* Dad's hideous death. After such a hideous illness. In that hideous psychiatric ward. *In through the nose, out through the mouth.* And now I'm thinking about that fish tank. Because my mind always goes there, every time I think about Dad's psychiatric ward. The fish tank I spent hour upon hour gazing into as I held Dad's hand, willing us to be anywhere else. The fish tank that nobody cared about or cleaned, in that little lounge at the back of the ward. *In through the nose, out through the mouth.* With water so murky, it was almost impossible to see any fish and, on the rare occasion I did spot one, I always wished I hadn't. Lifeless eyes, gasping for breath . . . did the fish know they were swimming through years of shit? Could they see anything through the filthy glass? Would they want to?

In through the nose, out through the mouth. It was two months ago, when it happened. When I walked into the ward and heard his voice. *In through the nose, out through the mouth.* Dad sounded raspy and transformed. Terrified. I followed his voice to the little lounge and peered through the gap in the door. Dad was sitting in a chair with his arms pulled out behind him. Sebastian, the male nurse, was sitting behind, holding my dad's wrists tight, restraining him. *In through the nose, out through the mouth.* I'd never paid much attention to Nurse Sebastian before, his lack of individuality rewarded with invisibility. He was just a vague presence on the ward, always seemed pleasant enough, always smiling at the right time. So it wasn't until that day, peering through that gap in the door, that I saw him. The real him. Smiling at the wrong time. *In through the nose, out through the mouth.* There were three other distressed-looking patients in that little lounge at the back of the ward, spooning filthy water from the fish tank. Dad was trying to move his face away, turning his head from side to side as spoons stabbed his cheeks and nose and chin. It must have felt so cold, that filthy water, trickling down his face and his neck.

Nurse Sebastian was smiling all the while, goading the three patients on, forcing them to do it, cheering when one of the spoons stabbed its way into Dad's mouth. *In through the nose, out through the mouth.* At this point, inconsequential characters such as Florence would have barged into the room aghast. They would have made official complaints, given evidence at tribunal hearings, shaken their heads in disbelief when justice wasn't served. But I'm not like Florence. *In through the nose, out through the mouth.* I quietly turned around, walked out of the ward and never told anyone what I had seen. On the way home, I bought a fish tank. *In through the nose, out through the mouth.* The next day I went back to the hospital and sat for hours with Dad. I sat for hours with him every day after that, making sure it couldn't happen again. Holding hands, we stared into the fish tank—the sight of which didn't even make him flinch. Memories of everything erased by that stage. He was dying and, in a strange way, it was comforting seeing Nurse Sebastian there too. It made those last few weeks easier, watching him move around the ward. Just as close to death as Dad. Just as blissfully unaware.

The week after Dad's funeral, I made my approach. Sebastian was walking away from the hospital, towards his bus stop. I'd been watching him from my car, he was slouching and drinking out of a can of Red Bull. A group of pedestrians were heading towards him as the pavement narrowed, and he stepped into the road, allowing them space to move past. Each of them smiled, no doubt clocking his NHS lanyard. He must be exhausted, that kind, underpaid nurse. What a saint. Where would we be without people like him?

He walked a little further and when he paused to look back, I wondered whether he could sense me, watching. But no—just checking those pedestrians were out of sight before chucking the can in the gutter. Hello, Sebastian. There you are. Pulling away from the curb, I drove along a road that was quiet enough not to draw attention and busy enough not to raise his suspicion. Then I slowly drew in beside him, lowered the car window, smiled.

"Sebastian! Hello, I thought it was you. What a wonderful coincidence."

Sebastian looked confused. I was out of context; he couldn't place me.

"It's me . . . Joseph's daughter. I met you when I used to visit Dad on the ward."

"Oh yes, of course." He took a step closer to the car. "I'm so sorry about your dad."

"Thanks. He'd been unwell for a very long time. At least he's at peace now."

Sebastian murmured in agreement and turned towards the bus stop.

"Actually, I'm so happy I bumped into you like this. I was going to phone the hospital tomorrow. Arrange a time to come and see you."

"Er, why?" He looked furtive suddenly.

"Well, I don't know whether you're aware, but my dad was an extremely wealthy man."

"That's none of my business," he said, stepping towards the car once again.

"Actually, Sebastian, it is. You see, Dad mentioned you in his will. He left you some money. Quite a lot of money. I guess he wanted to thank you for all the care you gave him during the last months of his life."

He looked confused again. He wasn't a stupid man. He knew that what I was saying didn't make sense. How could somebody as mentally incapacitated as my dad add new beneficiaries to his will? Such a shame for Sebastian that he didn't question me further. Such a shame he wanted my words to be true.

"I've been dealing with Dad's financial affairs. Your money's at my house, in fact. I could deliver it to you at the hospital to-morrow but, to be honest, I don't like driving around with that much cash. I don't suppose you'd mind coming back with me now to get it, would you? I can drop you back home afterwards. Save you getting the bus."

This was it. Everything hinged on what happened now. My hands felt clammy on the steering wheel as I watched his face. A man in conflict. Hundreds of years of instinct challenged in that one moment by the persuasions of greed. He knew something was wrong—how could my father's estate be paying out so soon after death? In cash? But I could see he was thinking about it, weighing up his options. When he looked into the car and stared at me directly, I knew I had won. Sebastian wasn't much older than me, but he was a lot bigger. Athletic-looking, and strong. I was a nine-stone woman who had just lost her father. Hardly a threat. He had nothing to lose and so much to gain. He got into the car.

FLORENCE IS TRYING TO STAND up from kneeling, but from the effort involved you'd think she's about to backflip into the splits. And now she's finally on her feet and declaring this a good time to break for coffee. People start moving around, and someone is asking Jemma whether she takes sugar in her tea. She says she doesn't usually, but she will today. She glances down at her hand, still clasping mine, and looks confused before loosening her grip.

"I'm so sorry," she stammers. "I don't even remember taking your hand. I'm so sorry."

"It's fine," I lie. "Don't worry about it."

"I'm Jemma." She taps her name badge, and a scurry of words stampede from my brain to mouth. I know you're called Jemma, you total freak! You introduced yourself to all of us before your monumental meltdown. Plus, you've got your name stuck on that hideous tracksuit.

"Hi, Jemma," I say.

"What's your name?" she asks.

"I'm Claire." I tap my own name badge, wondering what it is about the concept of name badges Jemma finds so difficult to understand.

"Thank you so much for your kindness, Claire," she says, tears collecting in the corners of her eyes.

"It's fine." I look away before she starts crying again. Nurse Sebastian cried. And he begged. Over and over again. Irritated the hell out of me by the end.

check my watch. Fifteen minutes until the end of this first group session, and robust-sounding Welshman is talking about his dead wife and crying like a baby. Utterly spellbound, I'm beginning to realize I've never given grief the respect it deserves. Drawing no distinction between strong, weak, rich or poor, it plows through everyone's lives the same, leaving identical mounds of emotional debris behind. Florence is loitering by the Welshman, dishing out tissues and speaking words of comfort I have no interest in. I think about something else.

I'd put fifteen fish into my tank and no filter. The water started to discolor within days and, after three weeks, the darkness was almost complete. Some of the weaker fish died along the way and I left them in there to be fed on by the strong. The association with death was good. It felt right. As soon as Nurse Sebastian walked into my home, I mentioned a new carpet, politely asked him to remove his shoes then aimed my hammer with precision at the back of his head. He was unconscious before the front door closed behind us. When he came to, the first thing he saw was the fish tank. His eyes darted this way and that as he tried to move the rest of his body, without success. As he sat in a chair with his arms tied behind him, struggling to get free, I thought about Dad and plunged Sebastian's head into the filthy water. Yanking it out, I waited for the choking to stop before asking my questions.

"What was it like in the tank? Could you see anything through the glass? Were you aware of the fish? How did the water taste?"

"Crazy bitch!" he shouted, no doubt hoping someone would hear. "I'm going to kill you when I get out of this chair!"

"Do you think I'm crazy, Sebastian?" I asked him, removing my hand from the back of his head. "I mean, you would know, wouldn't you? You're the expert. That's your job, isn't it? Caring for the mentally ill. So, I guess you know crazy when you see it."

"I mean it, bitch! I'm going to kill you! You've no idea who you're messing with."

"I thought I was messing with a mental health nurse who abuses vulnerable patients in his care," I said, putting my hand on the back of his head again. "But please, do tell me if you have another persona I should know about. I hope, for your sake, it's someone with gills."

"I'm gonna fucking kill you—!" he managed to scream before I slammed his face back into the tank, his efforts to resist resulting in a lot of unnecessary splashing. It was so annoying that first day, having to refill the tank the whole time. So much water ended up on the floor. Fish too. Which was unfortunate and led to a ponderance of one of the many curiosities of life. How can I feel pity for a goldfish flipping desperately across my living room rug, yet nothing but irritation for the man I'm drowning?

On day two, there was less splashing, and I learned Sebastian couldn't see anything through the glass—although ironically I could see straight through him because he looked like a ghost already and kept telling me he wanted to die. On the third day, he got his wish. It satisfied my sense of justice that at the moment of his death, he understood what life had been like for those poor, neglected fish on the ward. Even after his death, I found that I wanted this understanding to continue. His head looked like it belonged in the fish tank. It felt good to keep it there.

Chairs scraping on the floor bring me back to the hall, where the bereavement session seems to be at an end. People start to leave but Jemma stays behind to speak to Florence who probably offers extra counseling for the incurably tragic. I walk home and think about the not-so-robust-sounding Welshman. Will he return to an empty house and spend the evening in tears? Walking into my own, I glance at Nurse Sebastian's shoes, neatly placed on the doormat where he left them. I really need to get rid of those shoes, can't believe I haven't done so already. Hopping onto the treadmill in the corner of my living room, I think about grief and the impact it has had upon me. I may not have cried, drunk to excess or wrung my hands in disbelief since Dad died but I've definitely become more reckless with my kills. I guess not all mounds of emotional debris are the same. Two miles run; I increase the speed. I'm sprinting now, my chest feels tight and, when my legs start to burn, I increase the speed again. I'm at the point I always get to, where I fear I may fall but still I run. My body is screaming at me to stop but I increase the speed again because I have no choice. This isn't a hobby or something I do for fun. This is essential to my survival. People fighting for their lives can be surprisingly strong, and the element of surprise only gets me so far. At some point it always comes down to strength.

Running done, and I'm sweating so much I open the window. Mrs. Davis, my only neighbor on this most secluded of streets, is walking past the house with her ugly black dog. As usual it growls and barks at me, and as usual she smiles apologetically while reprimanding the dog, telling it to "be nice." As usual I return the smile and wait for Mrs. Davis to engage me in small talk that I know will be as inevitable as it is pointless.

"What about the weather earlier?" she asks. "All morning long, raining cats and dogs!"

"I know. I hope it will stay dry for the rest of the day. Only time will tell."

"Yes, we both got soaked on our morning walk, didn't we?" she directs at the snarling dog. "There were muddy paw prints all over the house when we got home! Still, at the end of the day, you have to laugh."

"It's the best medicine."

The dog suddenly tries to lunge at me through the window and it takes all of Mrs. Davis's septuagenarian strength to get him back under control. I watch her shout and yank on the lead and wonder whether the pathetic, people-pleasing Mrs. Davis will ever do anything worthy of that dog's unwavering loyalty and protection.

"Oh my, I'm making heavy weather of this!" she declares, trying to untangle the lead from around her dog's back legs. "The problem is, he's as fit as a fiddle and strong as an ox." Mrs.

Davis loves clichés almost as much as she loves her dog, and for this I'm grateful. As soon as she introduced me to these curious little phrases, I realized they would be an invaluable tool in my interactions with ordinary people. Whenever I'm unsure of how I'm expected to respond, I use a cliché. Even if I'm not sure what it means, even if I use it incorrectly, no one ever seems to mind.

"We'd better get home now," she says, glancing up towards the sky, "just in case the rain starts again."

"Of course, Mrs. Davis. Always good to think outside the box."

"Yes, you're right," she says with a smile, before turning and walking away. Beautifully proving my point.

Weights lifted and chin-ups complete, I notice my sketchbook on the coffee table and absentmindedly flick through it as I wander into the kitchen. There are some decent sketches in here, lots of good ideas, but I haven't been able to focus properly on my new painting for weeks. Emptying a tin of soup into a saucepan, I turn on the stovetop, drop my sketchbook onto the work surface and run upstairs for a shower. Ten minutes later and I'm back—hair washed, clothes clean, soup bubbling, sketchbook gone. This is the moment when inconsequential characters such as Florence and Mrs. Davis would doubt themselves. Maybe they didn't leave the sketchbook on the work surface. Maybe they took it upstairs. I don't doubt myself. I know. Somebody is in my house.

Removing the saucepan from the heat, I pour the soup into a mug and open the living room door. She's sitting in my armchair. Dad's chair. The sketchbook is obscuring her face, but I know immediately who she is. I sit on the sofa opposite, sip my soup and wait for her to speak.

"I'm impressed, Claire," she says. "These drawings are really good." When she lowers the sketchbook and smiles, she looks different from how I remember her. There's a confidence that wasn't there before. She knows she has my full attention. Crossing her legs, she drops the sketchbook onto the floor and sinks further back into the chair. She's still wearing the open-toe sandals and tracksuit, but every last trace of victimhood has gone. This woman has followed me home, broken into my house and is now behaving like an invited guest. I sip my soup and watch her, trying to decide whether she is mad, dangerous or a combination of both.

When it becomes clear she is not going to speak again, I place my mug on the coffee table and try to imagine what an ordinary person in my position would say. "Jemma," I say, keeping my voice low and gentle, "I understand that you are going through a tough time grieving for your mother but—"

"I hated my mother," she spits, springing forward in the chair. "Nasty witch always preferred my sister."

The room is silent again as Jemma settles herself back and I silently acknowledge that the woman is completely insane. At least this explains the hideous outfit. And that fringe.

"That must be really difficult for you," I say, adopting the delicate tone I perfected during all those visits to the psychiatric ward. "All those unresolved issues with your mother must be very hard and I understand your anger, I really do. But no matter how much you may be struggling with your grief, it doesn't give you the right to break into my home. You do understand that, don't you?"

My question hangs in the air for a few moments before she gets to her feet. "I'm so sorry." She sounds cold. Not sorry. "I remember thinking that I wanted to speak to you after the group meeting, so I followed you home. I felt like we'd made a connection, you and me, especially when you held my hand." Her eyes drop to the ground. "But then I found myself standing outside your house, too scared to knock on the door. I remember seeing the open window and the next thing I know—I'm sitting in your living room." Her eyes slide back on mine. "Do you think I'm mad?"

"Of course not," I say, rising to my feet. "You're obviously experiencing intense feelings of grief and—"

"But I broke into your home," she says.

"It's fine," I say, stepping towards her, mentally calculating the best way to guide her towards the front door.

"It isn't fine," she says, but her tone still isn't right. She seems almost amused. "I broke into your house. I'm a criminal. You should call the police."

With my hand on her elbow, I gently steer her across the living room. "Please don't worry, I don't want to call the police. I think you just need to go home and get some rest."

We've reached the living room door when she turns to face me once again. "Why don't you want to call the police, Claire?"

When I meet her eye, my hand falls away from her elbow as I experience something approaching shock. There's calculated menace in Jemma's eyes. I think about the whereabouts of my hammer.

"I told Florence I was coming here," she says quietly, reading my mind.

"What did you say?" My voice is even, calm.

"I told her you and I really hit it off over coffee and you invited me to your home."

"Why did you say that?" I ask, despite already knowing the answer.

"Insurance," she replies simply. "If I go missing, Florence will know I was here. And something tells me you really don't want the police turning up at your door asking questions."

I can smell her breath on my face, but I know it's the unexpected surge of adrenaline causing my lightheadedness and nausea. Two undetectable deep breaths later and I'm smiling sympathetically. "Oh, Jemma, I don't know what you're talking about. I feel desperately sorry for you, I really do. You're obviously finding it difficult, you know, not having any friends, but it's time for you to go home now."

She stares unblinking into my eyes and I find myself thinking about Mrs. Davis's dog. The dog that always growls and barks at me, the one and only living creature who can see I'm not like everyone else. Is it possible that Jemma sees me too? As we walk towards the front door, I calm myself by focusing on facts. Jemma knows nothing about me. I only met her today. She is clearly deranged and doesn't know what she's saying.

"Goodbye." I smile, opening the door. "Look after yourself."

"Goodbye, Claire," she says sweetly. "I'll see you at the next meeting."

Before I can shut the door behind her, she turns back to face me. "Oh, and Claire?"

"Yes?"

"There appears to be a rotting human head in your fish tank. It might be time to clean it out."

And with that, she turns and walks away.

I stand at the door and watch her leave. A solitary raindrop falls and bounces off my garden wall. Followed by another. And another. The sky has turned dark, and from somewhere far away I hear something that sounds like thunder. Mrs. Davis was right to hurry home.

Storm clouds are gathering.

THEN

W ow! Look at that lightning," says her father, staring out through her bedroom window. "I wonder whether this storm is ever going to end." He pulls the curtains closed and turns away from the window, then crosses the room and kneels by the side of her bed. She's snuggled up underneath the blanket, her favorite cuddly toy clutched tightly in her arms. "You two look cozy." He smiles, tucking the blanket around her. "Sleep well, beautiful birthday girl. You too, Bambi," he adds, placing one kiss on his daughter's forehead and another on the nose of her toy.

"Goodnight, Daddy," the little girl says as he rises. He blows her another kiss before turning towards the woman standing just outside the bedroom door.

"How are you feeling now?" he asks, going over to her. "How's the migraine?"

"Much better," the woman replies, smiling bravely. "I just feel terrible about missing Claire's cake. I should have been there when she blew out her candles. No wonder she hates me." Her voice drops to a whisper and her eyes slowly fill with tears.

"Hey," says the man, putting his arms gently around her. "What are you talking about? Claire doesn't hate you. She knows it wasn't your fault you got one of your bad heads."

"If she doesn't hate me, why did she smash my photograph?"

"Ssshh," whispers the man, pulling her closer. "She didn't do it on purpose, that was an accident. I'll buy a new frame in the morning. No big deal. Hey," he says again as the woman starts sobbing into his shoulder. "Please don't upset yourself. Claire doesn't hate you. She loves you. You're her mum. Her wonderful mum."

"How do you do that?" asks the woman, raising her face to look at him. "How do you always know the right thing to say?"

"Because I love you," he says, smiling.

"And I love you," says the woman, wrapping her arms around him. "Let's go to bed," she whispers, before kissing him. "Just give me a minute to say goodnight to Claire."

They kiss again and then the woman walks into the bedroom. "Claire," she whispers, approaching the child's bed. "I'm so sorry I wasn't there when you blew out your candles. Daddy said you really enjoyed your cake."

"It was delicious, wasn't it?" says the man from the doorway. "I can't remember, did we save Mummy a slice?"

"Yes," comes the voice from under the blanket.

"Well, thank you for saving me some, you two," laughs the woman, kneeling by the side of the little girl's bed. "I'll look forward to eating my slice. My goodness! Listen to all that rain at the window. Let's make sure you're all cozy," she says, tucking the blanket around the child. "There's something lovely about being snuggled up in bed when it's stormy outside."

The woman glances over her shoulder towards the child's father who smiles and gives her a thumbs-up before turning and walking down the hall.

"That rain sounds quite spooky, doesn't it?" says the woman, tucking the blanket in even tighter. "Makes me think about ghosts and monsters and *other terrifying things, scuttling around in the shadows." The little girl moves further down under the blanket and closes her eyes.*

"Daddy said you liked the presents he bought you for your birthday," says the woman. "Aren't you lucky? The way he spoils you. You really have a way with Daddy, don't you? I can see why you think he loves you. Can I tell you something about Daddy, Claire?" she says, moving her face closer.

"What?"

"He doesn't see the truth about people," the woman whispers into the child's ear. "He doesn't see the truth about you. But I do," she adds, retrieving something from her pocket. "Happy birthday," she says, holding her closed hand out towards her daughter. Her fingers clenched tightly around an object hidden in her palm.

"What is it?" asks the little girl, peering out from under the blanket.

"It's this," smiles the woman, uncurling her fingers. "The key to the lock on your bedroom door. I found it! Although, it's more of a present for me, I suppose, as you don't get to keep it. I do." The woman places her hand on the child's head and gently runs her fingers through the little girl's hair. "While you were downstairs eating cake, greedy piglet, I was searching through that box of keys left by the people who used to live here. From now on, whenever Daddy's at work, I can lock you away and won't have to look at you. I won't have to be reminded of the thing I'm always trying so hard to forget.

"I'm going to bed to cuddle with Daddy now," says the woman, standing up. "You see, I have a way with him too." She stares at the child, unblinking. Then she walks out of the room and closes the door. There's a moment of silence before the little girl hears it. From somewhere deep within those shadows inside her mind. It's terrifying and there's no escaping the sound; it scuttles. That's when the scuttling starts.

5

'm not sure whether it's real or inside my head but I'm grateful for the scream when it comes, casting me out of sleep. I walk to the kitchen to get a glass of water, the image still imprinted on my eyelids every time I blink. Pain, dying, none of that scares me but the image of a key, turning slowly in a lock, is enough to leave me claustrophobic and struggling for breath. The thought of being locked away has always terrified me, the solitary neural pathway I've never been able to divert. It's the one thought that always reminds me—I can be ordinary, inconsequential, weak.

Jemma. Who is she and what does she want? Everyone wants something. Mrs. Davis's dog wants to protect Mrs. Davis and relies on instinct to know the truth about me. But I don't believe for one moment Jemma shares that dog's insight, so how does she know? *What* does she know? Why hasn't she gone to the police? How much trouble am I in?

I've never aroused the slightest suspicion before and I don't think it's coincidence this has happened now, weeks after I buried my dad. His death triggered something in me, a recklessness I've never known before—years of killing experience washed away in an instant by those enormous waves of grief. I've killed twice since his death, and neither was planned well. Nowhere near my meticulous standards. Did I make a mistake? Overlook something in one of those kills? Is that how Jemma caught a glimpse of who I really am?

I've replayed the moment with Sebastian over and over, hundreds of times inside my mind. There was nobody sitting at the bus stop when I pulled my car over to the curb and those smiling pedestrians were way out of sight. A couple of cars drove past while I was talking to him but why would that have aroused anyone's suspicion? A grown man speaking to the driver of a parked car in the middle of the day. He didn't call or text anybody when he got into my car, and I know I wasn't followed home. I can't be certain, but I don't think it was Sebastian who put me on Jemma's radar. I think I was already there. Which brings me to the person I killed a week earlier. Lucas Kane.

I should never have followed him from his office to that bar. What the hell was I thinking? Where was the groundwork? The weeks of planning that always go into each kill. And it could have been so perfect, beyond perfect—it could have been a work of art. Seamlessly lost to invisibility within the folds of time. Instead, here I am, standing in my kitchen at four o'clock in the morning, forced to revisit all the clunky, ill-fitting fragments of that night.

Lucas Kane left his office alone but then walked to the bar with a skinny vampire-looking man, waiting for him in the smoking area outside the office building. At the time I'd assumed Vampire Smoker was a colleague, but I see now that's not necessarily the case. After all, I never saw him walk out of the office building.

What was the nature of the relationship between Lucas and Vampire Smoker? Were they friends, colleagues or both? I'm not sure whether this is important, but the fact I never even considered it is appalling. I know I should never assume anything. I know assumption is the mother of all fuck-ups. I know this and yet I let assumption be my guide.

After that, the two men—friends, colleagues, whatever they were—headed towards the bar. I remember watching them walking along the street, talking, and laughing. Shame burns me now as I recall how distracted I'd been at the time. Honestly believing they were talking about me; I'd been unable to focus on anything else. Now I think about it properly, the truth hits me hard. Lucas had been animated that night, chatting, and laughing, but Vampire Smoker? That guy never spoke a word.

I take a sip of water to distract myself from the seed of a thought, germinating somewhere inside my mind. It doesn't work. As distractions go, sipping water is almost entirely ineffectual. It's so glaringly obvious to me now, why didn't I see it at the time? Even before I made eye contact with Lucas in the bar, even before I let him buy me a drink, even before I drove him home and carved him up into pieces, something about that night had been very, very wrong.

6

I t's the second meeting of the bereavement group and Welsh-man is robust again. He's talking about his wife's tumor, the one the bloody doctors kept saying wasn't there. If only they'd done their jobs properly and found it sooner. His knuckles are white as he tightens his right hand into a fist, the volume of his voice increasing all the time. He's shouting now about all the tax he and his wife paid over the years, calling it a fucking waste. All that money plowed into the NHS, only to be rewarded with misdiagnosis after misdiagnosis. As his anger reaches its peak, I wonder why he doesn't march down to the hospital and put that fist to good use. Instead, he starts to cry and apologize to everyone for raising his voice. Florence tells him that anger is normal, in fact, it's to be expected, being the second stage of grief. She reassures the group that this room is a safe place for anger to be expressed. I think about the Welshman's anger neatly contained within this place that is safe. That's what I call a fucking waste.

Jemma is wearing a kilt with wellies and she trembles slightly as she raises her hand to speak. Her voice is a whisper and the group lean in closer to hear what she has to say. She brushes away a tear, pauses for a moment and then starts to talk.

"I know it probably sounds strange, but I'd love to feel angry," she sobs. "I'd love to feel anything. Anything would be better than feeling nothing."

Florence is nodding her head as she squeezes herself out of the chair and I find myself thinking about Jemma's kilt. Somehow it manages to be too short and too frumpy at the same time. Where does a person go to buy something like that?

"Jemma," squeaks Florence, holding out the box of Kleenex, "can I share something with you? It's four years since my husband died, and I still feel that nothingness. Not all the time, but sometimes."

Why are they talking about nothingness like it's a bad thing? For me, nothingness is a perfect state. My mind flicks back to the nothingness I felt when killing Lucas. If only I knew then what I know now, I think I would have enjoyed that nothingness even more.

"There's a book I read, which I found useful. What was it called . . . ?" Florence looks up at the ceiling as she tries to recall the author and title. "No, I can't think of it," she squeaks, waddling back towards her chair. "But as soon as I remember, I'll let you all know." Shouldn't she have this information at her fingertips? Isn't she running this group?

Jemma glances in my direction and her eyes glisten with something I know is not tears. To her credit, Jemma plays the role of victim to perfection, fooling almost every person in the room. They see the kilt, wellies and tears and their minds reliably fill in the gaps. Because that's what minds do—forever telling us stories we feel compelled to believe. If you see two men drinking together in a busy bar, your mind will tell you they're friends. Even if it occurs to you to question the truth, there's probably no time. Your mind will have already moved on.

Jemma is crying again, and Florence looks torn. She wants to rush over and provide comfort, but she's worried about bereavement group protocol. The leader of the group should always remain neutral, impassive—everybody knows that. In the end Florence throws protocol out the window and moves her considerable bulk with remarkable speed. She crouches in front of Jemma, throws her arms around the hysterical woman's shoulders and lets her sob. The rest of us study the floor or our fingernails as Jemma smears snot onto Florence's oversized navy-blue cardigan and reaches the pinnacle of any decent crying journey—the part where sharp, staccato breaths override a person's ability to listen, to reason or to speak.

After monopolizing far more of Florence's time and cardigan than could ever be considered decent, Jemma begins to calm down.

"Thank you for the hug, I needed that." She's smiling bravely. "I'm so sorry I keep getting upset. It's just this nothingness. It feels like there's no point in anything anymore."

"Oh, Jemma, I understand," says Florence, in her most understanding Christmas elf voice. "I felt exactly the same way, four years ago, when my husband died."

And there's another mention of the dead husband. Florence's really making this all about Florence today. And she's still talking.

"I'm going to share something with the group now. I'm going

to be honest with you all. Four years ago," she says, "I thought about ending my life. My husband was my soulmate, we did everything together, and when he died, I thought if I didn't kill myself, the loneliness would. But what you have to remember," she says, taking Jemma's hands into her own, "what we *all* have to remember," she adds, turning to look around at the rest of the group . . .

What? What do we all have to remember?

"Time heals," she says, hugging Jemma again.

Time heals? Is that it? I wonder if she got that from Mrs. Davis, at a convention for tired old clichés. Is Florence qualified to be running this group?

Jemma and Florence continue to hug without speaking and while I can't see Florence's face, the gentle quiver of her back fat suggests she is crying too. Bereavement group protocol has well and truly taken its last breath. Something else for us all to mourn.

Welshman slams his hands onto his knees and clears his throat.

"Well, this is a load of depressing bollocks, isn't it?" he proclaims. "I know, why don't we all go out for a curry later? Cheer ourselves up."

The room falls into silence and even I feel awkward. Florence has returned to her seat and is looking flummoxed. What would the recently deceased protocol have to say about this?

"You must come along too, Florence, love," adds the Welshman. "Wouldn't be the same without you."

Florence's barely concealed pleasure at being invited out is so pathetic, it makes me feel sick but seems to have an adverse effect on the rest of the group. As more and more strangers express an interest in eating a meal together, I feel my nausea grow. And when Jemma giggles that she is always up for anything hot and spicy, the vomit I taste inside my mouth is real. The mood in the group verges on happy hysteria as arrangements are made to meet at the Old Bengal tonight at eight. There's no doubt about it. I definitely prefer these people when they're crying.

I'm just about to stack my chair away at the end of the meeting when I turn at the sound of my name. Jemma is talking to Florence and appears to be calling me over.

"Claire!" she says, smiling as I approach. "I've just been telling Florence about how close we've become. It's amazing, isn't it? How quickly grief builds a bond."

I smile and nod, wondering where this is going.

"And I was telling Jemma how pleased I am that you've found one another." Florence is staring at me. "I know you don't say much during group discussions, Claire, which is fine. Some people are more comfortable sitting and listening. But it's important you have someone to talk to about your grief. I know you have Jemma, and you can always talk to me in private if you'd prefer. Tell me, who was it who died?"

"My dad." Her eyes are too intense. I stare over her shoulder. The Welshman, Christiana with a C and that peculiar little man who writes everything down are standing by the stacks of chairs. They're talking to each other. It looks heated. Are they having an argument?

"And were you very close to your dad?"

What do you think, Einstein? Why else would I come to a bereavement counseling group? Ignorant elf.

"Yes," I reply.

"We can talk about your dad later, Claire." Jemma's piping up now. "When I come round to your house. Four o'clock this afternoon. That's what we agreed, wasn't it?"

No.

"Yes," I say, with a smile.

"Perfect!" says Jemma. "And I'll come pick you up later, Florence. Just before eight? We can go to the restaurant together."

"That's so kind." Smiling elf. "Let me give you my address."

Jemma makes a note of it on her phone, and I start to understand. If Jemma is collecting Florence at eight o'clock, and Florence knows that Jemma is visiting me at four o'clock, Jemma has to walk out of my house alive.

Florence is saying her address out loud, spelling her address out loud, repeating the spelling of her address out loud and giving directions too, just in case Jemma gets lost. "You shouldn't, though. It's easy enough to find, the second road on the right after St. Matthew's Church. Do you want me to send you a map?"

"Don't worry," says Jemma. "I've got sat nav, I won't get lost."

When Florence starts her next sentence with the words "The funny thing is . . ." I stop listening. When ordinary people feel the need to announce how funny a thing is, the only thing you can be sure of is that the thing will not be funny at all.

I glance over again at the three people standing by the stacks of chairs. Christiana with a C is speaking, and she sounds angry. And posh. So incredibly posh.

"I know you've recently suffered a loss, same as the rest of us," she says, "but that does not give you any right to break the law."

"Break the law? Are you insane?" Welshman sounds angry too. And even more Welsh. "Stacking seven chairs in a pile is not breaking the law."

"There are two notices, clearly displayed, both expressly prohibiting the stacking of any more than six chairs in one pile." It's the first time I've heard the peculiar little man speak. And he sounds exactly as I would expect. Peculiar and little.

"My Derek, he never trusted sat nav." I'm listening to Florence again. Who's Derek?

"We were married for forty-two years . . ."

Ah, the dead husband.

". . . and in all that time, I don't think I ever saw him so much as look at a map. He always had the most amazing sense of direction. He never got lost . . . Oh!"

Florence stops talking suddenly and claps her hands together. What's this? Some kind of banality-induced seizure?

"I've just remembered the name of that book I mentioned earlier. The one I read shortly after Derek's death. It's called *Peace at Last.* Jemma, make a note of the title. Definitely worth a read."

As Jemma stares at her phone and starts typing on the Notes app, I watch Florence's mouth move, marveling at the deplorable depths of dullness ordinary people are always so determined to descend to.

"Bye, Claire," calls Jemma, as I make my excuses and turn to leave. "See you at four."

I put my chair away and walk out of the hall. I wondered what would happen if a seventh chair is added to the top of a stack. I guess I'm about to find out.

7

There's twenty minutes until Jemma is due to arrive and I'm drinking tea and staring at the object on my coffee table. I know I should have disposed of it immediately after the kill, but I'm so pleased now that I didn't. Everything got tangled up in my mind for a while, but this object sets it all out straight. Dull looking, ridiculously ordinary—the object sitting on my coffee table tells me everything I need to know about Lucas and Vampire Smoker.

I'm still not sure why I got it so wrong at the time, I normally never make mistakes when it comes to the behavior of others. You can't watch people as much as I do without becoming an expert. I know that friendships come in all shapes and sizes because I see it all the time: extroverts hang out with introverts, the chic and scruffy love to trade views, hopeless optimists often spend time trying to cheer up the depressed. In this inclusive world in which we find ourselves, it seems anyone can become friends with anyone as long as the key ingredient of friendship exists. Mutual respect. That's what was missing that night.

On the evening of his death, Lucas sauntered along the street, swinging his briefcase with the exuberance reserved solely for the carefree. Beaming, laughing, radiant—his manner was almost celebratory in nature. In contrast, Vampire Smoker shuffled silently, slouched and dejected, never once joining in the joke. Even in the bar when Lucas pointed out something funny he read in the newspaper, the smoker's expression remained the same. So, why was he there? Why go out to a busy bar if you have no intention to engage? And what about Lucas? Why did he seem so oblivious to his companion's dour mood?

I pick up the object from the coffee table and place it on my lap. Lucas's briefcase. Boring on the outside, fascinating within. There's tough competition for the most surprising item inside the briefcase but I think the prize goes to the first one I retrieve: a loaded gun. How the hell did a wuss like Lucas, with his zany shirt and job in the art world, get a gun? They're really hard to get hold of and why did he need one? I can only think of two categories of people likely to slip a loaded gun into their briefcase and I'm fairly certain I can rule out the first. If Lucas was an assassin, I'm sure killing him would have been more of a challenge. This means that Lucas belonged to the second, much less select category of gun-carrying folk. Someone who pisses people off. A lot.

The second item is a fat envelope stuffed with £20 notes. Light is beginning to shine on the relationship between Lucas and the smoker but it's only when I study the third item that I know for sure. Hidden between the pages of Lucas's neatly folded newspaper are a number of photographs, each one more disturbing than the last. From the slight blurring of the images they are obviously stills from a video recording. I think back to that night in the bar, remember Lucas laughing as he pointed out something hilarious in the newspaper. I'd assumed he was pointing to a news article. Now that I know Lucas was pointing at the stills, everything makes sense. It's pitiful really, how focused I'd been on Lucas, barely glancing at Vampire Smoker. A nondescript, pale, skinny bloke smoking outside an office—who's going to pay much attention to him? But people are so much more than the image they project to the world, a fact beautifully illustrated by these disturbing pictures. I pick up the first one. He may not have been smiling in the bar, but Vampire Smoker certainly looks happy here. His face contorted into a sadistic grin, nothing normal or nondescript about him.

There are other items in the briefcase, including Lucas's wallet and a couple of work files, all disappointingly dull in comparison. It's the gun, cash and video stills that tell me everything I need to know because they all point towards the same thing. Blackmail.

Putting everything back into the briefcase, I think about Lucas Kane and fate. If he hadn't clicked on my email address by mistake, our paths would almost certainly never have crossed. It's hilarious to me that a simple error cost him his life, especially considering everything else he was up to. Moonlight excursions into the murky world of blackmail must have kept Lucas Kane very busy indeed. No wonder he made mistakes in his day job.

At the sound of repeated knocking, I return the briefcase to its hiding place, remove my gloves and open the front door. It's hard to know what offends my vision more. The wellies, the kilt or the sickening smile.

"Hello, Jemma," I say, stepping aside to let her pass. She walks straight through to the living room, making no offer to remove her boots or even wipe them on the mat. I follow and take my place on the sofa; she's already sitting in Dad's chair. We stare at each other for a moment as I focus on controlling my breath. When I open my mouth to speak, she raises her hand to silence me, fishing her phone out of her bag. She dials a number and moves the phone towards her ear, watching me all the time.

"Hello, Florence," she says when the call connects. "It's Jemma. I just wanted to check we're still on for tonight. Great, I'm really looking forward to it too." She crosses her legs before speaking again. "I've been thinking about it," she says into the phone, "and you know what, Florence? I think I'm going to order a chicken jalfrezi later. Have you never had one? Oh, Florence, you should try it. No, it's not too spicy at all and I always ask for it to be served with a slice of lime. A tiny bit of lime juice really seems to bring out the flavors."

I watch her, fully aware of what she's doing—babbling on about nonsense and making me wait, letting me know she's in control.

"Florence, I've just arrived at Claire's," she continues, "so I better go. I'll see you at eight o'clock tonight. Bye."

She returns the phone to her bag and clears her throat.

"So," she says, sitting back in the chair again. Dad's chair. "Have you worked it all out yet? Do you know why I'm here?"

When I fail to respond, her left foot starts tapping gently on the floor, but the smile never leaves her lips.

"OK," she says after a while. "I've got an idea, let's play a game. It's called 'Let's tell each other what we know,' OK?"

If she's expecting a response, she doesn't wait for one.

"I'll go first," she continues, leaning forward. "I know that you killed my friend."

I contemplate giving her a few moments to enjoy her dramatic pause before deciding against it.

"I don't know what you mean," I say simply. "I didn't kill your friend."

"Yes, yes you did," she says. "I know that Lucas walked into this house on the night he disappeared." She pauses for a moment. "And I know he never came out."

"I think you might be a little confused," I say kindly, destroying yet another pause that was no doubt intended to be dramatic. "I'm not disputing that I killed Lucas, I'm disputing that he was your friend."

She watches me in silence for a few moments before laughing. "I don't know what you think you know about my relationship with Lucas, and frankly I don't care. Our relationship is completely irrelevant to the fact that you killed him."

"What I don't understand," I say, ignoring her last comment, "is how you knew about the bereavement group? Bit of a coincidence, isn't it? Turning up at the same one as your 'friend's' killer." My sarcasm is probably wasted on her, but I can't help myself. "How did you manage that? More importantly, why did you want to?"

"Have you forgotten the rules of this game already?" she asks.

"We're supposed to be telling each other what we know. Not asking questions."

"I'm not interested in playing games, so I'll get straight to the point. Why haven't you called the police?"

"I've thought about calling them," Jemma says, her left foot tapping slightly faster. "I've thought about it many times."

"And yet here we are," I say, gesturing towards the living room window and the world outside. "No flashing lights or sirens."

"I could call them right now," she spits, uncoiling in the chair and grabbing her phone from her bag in one fluid movement. "All it takes is a hysterical woman saying she hears screams from this address, and you'd have the police bursting through that door. And what do you think would happen then? Because I think it would be all over for you very quickly, Claire. Christ only knows what the police would find in this house. This room alone would probably keep a forensics department busy for years."

"So, call them," I say, keeping my eyes locked onto hers.

"I might do," she says, glancing briefly towards the phone in her hand before returning her eyes to mine. "But first I want to talk to you about my friend, Lucas. The man you killed."

"It's funny," I say, running my finger along the frayed edge of the sofa. "Lucas wasn't very friendly about you that night in the bar. I assume that was you, Jemma, wasn't it? Phoning him over and over again."

She stares at me unblinking, her left foot going into overdrive.

"He was very dismissive of you in fact," I continue. "Told me that you were no one important."

Her smile doesn't flicker although when she speaks, her voice is slightly tense. "Don't flatter yourself," she says. "Lucas never could resist a skinny brunette with long legs."

I cross my long legs and give her the silence I know she craves. I can tell she wants to talk and, for now, I'm happy to listen.

"Lucas was supposed to call me that night," she says, "and when I didn't hear anything I phoned him. I could hear background noise from the bar, so I knew where he was. I needed to speak to him, so I drove down, arriving just in time to see him leaving with you. Now I understood why he wasn't answering his phone, but I still needed to speak to him, so I followed and parked a little way down your road, waiting for Lucas to shag you and leave. But he never left."

"Which brings us back again to the curious question of why you haven't called the police," I say, twirling a loose thread from the edge of the sofa around my finger. "It wouldn't have anything to do with Lucas's briefcase, would it?" I ask, pulling the loose thread free. "Or, more specifically, the photographs in Lucas's briefcase? Stills from a rather nasty film, I think. I can understand why you wouldn't want those falling into the wrong hands. You don't look very good in those pictures, Jemma."

"Do you still have the briefcase?" she asks, suddenly direct.

"No," I lie. "I got rid of it."

"I don't believe you. People like you always keep souvenirs."

"People like me?"

"Serial killers. I'm assuming that Lucas and the head in the fish tank aren't the only ones."

"Well, I don't know how many serial killers you know, Jemma, but I can only speak for myself, and I don't keep souvenirs. Keeping souvenirs is a surefire way to get caught."

"No, Claire," she smiles. "An anonymous phone call to the police is a surefire way for you to get caught so go and get me the briefcase."

"I can't go and get you something I no longer have," I state calmly. "But if you don't believe me, please feel free to search my house. I'm sure you know your way around, don't you? I assume you've broken in at least a couple of times."

"What else did you expect me to do?" she shouts. "I was trying to work out what you'd done with Lucas. And let me give you some free advice, Claire, you really need to get a life. I kept coming back here after he disappeared, and it was days before you went out. And yes, when you finally did, of course I broke in and searched for Lucas and the briefcase, but I got a bit distracted when I found the dead man tied up with his head in your fish tank."

"And still you never called the police."

"No, because I saw an opportunity. The leaflet about the bereavement group was in your kitchen and finally I worked out a safe way to get to know you."

"But why?" I ask, sensing we are finally nearing the point of her visit. "Why do you want to get to know me?"

"Because you owe me," she says simply. "Lucas and I—we'd just started working together."

"Oh, Lucas was your colleague, was he? I thought he was your friend."

"He introduced me to a new source of income," she says,

ignoring my last comment. "And we had a good system. I supplied him with the video recordings, and he did the meet and greets. The people we . . ."

"Blackmailed?"

"Yes, well, they don't know I'm involved. It wouldn't work if they did."

"Get to the point, Jemma," I say, aimlessly pulling at another loose thread; this conversation is becoming tedious. "What are you trying to say?"

"Lucas and I, we'd just started on something big. I'd given him the details the day before and that's what I was calling to talk to him about the night you killed him."

"So?" I ask.

"This is a really big job, Claire. Chance to earn some decent money."

"So?"

"But I'm new to all this. Lucas was the expert."

"So?"

"I can't do it on my own."

"So?" I say for the fourth time.

"*So*, now that you've killed Lucas, somebody else needs to take his place and I can't exactly advertise the position. To pull off a job this big, I need someone threatening. Someone really nasty." She pauses and smiles. "I need someone like you."

My laughter shatters the silence in the room, but Jemma never once moves her eyes from mine.

"Let me get this right," I say, composing myself. "You want

me to work with you in your grubby little start-up blackmailing business?"

"Don't be silly," she smiles. "I want you to work *for* me in my grubby little start-up blackmailing business."

"I don't know," I say. "There's just so much to think about. Will I get health insurance? What about a pension plan?"

"You're funny, Claire," says Jemma. "As a matter of fact, you remind me of Lucas. He had a good sense of humor too. He was always making people laugh. I think it helps, in our line of work."

"That's the thing," I say, thinking about Lucas's sense of humor. How he wasn't raising many laughs at the end. "Blackmail isn't my line of work. I'm grateful for the offer—really, I am. It sounds like a fantastic opportunity, but I just don't think it's for me."

"Why not?" snaps Jemma, her smile suddenly gone. "Blackmail not good enough for the high and mighty murderess?"

"Horses for courses," I say. "Personally, I think blackmail is too good for the people I saw in those video stills, present company included. I'd prefer to kill them all."

If I've unsettled her, she doesn't show it. "Well, that's lovely for you," she says. "A killer with a conscience. I'm sure you never kill innocent people, only the ones who do really bad things, the ones who deserve to die. But here's the thing, I can't make money out of corpses and frankly I don't give a fuck whether you're cut out for blackmail or not. The way I see it, you don't have a choice. One phone call to the police, Claire, that's all it will take."

I've twirled the loose thread so tightly around the tip of my finger, the skin is turning red. I'm wondering how long before circulation is cut off altogether when Jemma stands up. She takes a step towards the sofa and looks down at me, back in control. When she speaks, her voice is clipped, businesslike—the time for small talk has passed.

"So, this is what's going to happen," she begins. "Tonight, I'm going to tell Florence about the lovely time we had today. So lovely we decided that you will visit me at my home tomorrow." She throws a piece of paper in my direction. "That's my address. You'll meet me there at ten thirty exactly tomorrow morning. I'm your boss now, Claire, I'm not running around after you anymore. You'll bring Lucas's briefcase with you, and I'll give you your first set of instructions. If you deviate from this plan in any way, I will call the police. If you're late, I will call the police. If you don't have the briefcase, I will call the police. Do you understand?"

I'm oblivious to the loss of feeling in the tip of my finger when I nod. My mind consumed solely with one image. It's a key. A rusty key. Turning slowly one way in a lock.

AFTER JEMMA LEAVES, I SIT down in Dad's chair and think back to kissing Lucas Kane outside the bar. I'd checked the position of the CCTV cameras on my way in and ensured we stood somewhere we wouldn't be filmed. With Lucas no longer thinking with his head it had been easy to remove his phone from his pocket and chuck it over a wall as we walked quickly towards my car. I never once noticed we were being watched and followed, clearly a mistake. So too was keeping the briefcase for so long, although at least I hid it well. There's a fluttering in my stomach I don't recognize and, reaching for the piece of paper on the floor, I wonder whether I'm experiencing stress. I stare at Jemma's address—a place I really don't want to go to tomorrow. But what choice do I have? If she calls the police, it's all over for me. Jemma is right, this house would keep a forensics department busy for ages, and what about my vegetable garden? They'd discover it's not just cabbage heads out there.

The fluttering in my stomach intensifies and when I taste vomit I run upstairs to the bathroom, stand at the sink, look into her eyes in the mirror. She's there, my mother—every time I stare at my face. Her eyes, her hair, her cheekbones and now I hear a voice. His voice—measured and calm, telling me he loves me, and he'll always be there. As I splash water onto my face, the nausea subsides but I'm still not sure what I should do. Blackmail isn't my style, it's not who I am. But with Dad in my corner, I'm sure I can adapt. Learn to play by new rules as required. I close my eyes now and when the image appears, it's as sudden as it is unexpected. A waitress's tray. My freedom piled high. Balancing somewhere between precarious and reckless. Opening my eyes, I stare into her face and, as the glare withers, that's when I know.

I know what to do.

8

The road she lives on is exactly as I expected. Neat lines of semi-detached houses, cars parked outside each, a uniform pattern of identical wheelie bins and a random scattering of satellite dishes. Nothing to give any indication of the type of person who lives behind each door. Her paved driveway is gray and matches the front of her house, a solitary hanging basket providing the only spot of color. Velvet red pansies, yellow begonias and purple fuchsias—all working overtime to inject some character into a backdrop of suburban sludge. As I reach for the doorbell, my hand brushes gently against the flowers and I'm not surprised to discover they're fake.

She answers the door after a few moments and looks a little surprised. I'm early. She checks her watch, notices the briefcase in my hand and forces a smile.

"Claire!" she says. "How lovely to see you. Please, do come in."

I follow her into a warm, cluttered living room. Every surface is covered with two objects that serve absolutely no purpose: doilies and ornaments. I place the briefcase on the floor and keep my eyes locked onto hers. She tries to engage me in small talk, but I remain silent and, when she offers me tea, I can tell she can sense it—something's wrong. She closes the living room door behind her and pretends to walk to the kitchen. Instead, she heads upstairs and is standing in her bedroom, jabbing at her mobile phone, when I speak.

"Put the phone down, Florence."

When she hears my voice, she's so startled she drops the phone. She didn't expect me to follow her up here. She knows that I *shouldn't* have followed her up here. She knows I shouldn't be standing in her bedroom doorway. She knows I shouldn't be wearing gloves.

"Claire!" she stammers, forcing another smile, desperate to regain composure. "I was just about to phone Jemma . . . just wanted to check the plans for tonight. You see, I thought Jemma was picking me up at eight, I didn't realize you were coming earlier. Still, no matter. I'm sure it's my mistake, I'm always getting things wrong. Typical me!"

She's gabbling now, pretending everything is normal.

"Shall we go and have that tea?" she asks. "Wait for Jemma downstairs?" There's still hope, I see it in her eyes. If she can just pretend long enough, maybe this strangeness will end.

I'm momentarily distracted by three shapeless dresses hanging on the door of her wardrobe and I'm trying to decide which is least hideous when she speaks again.

"Claire?" she says gently. "Shall we go back downstairs? Why don't you let me make you that cup of tea?"

"Which one were you going to wear tonight?" I ask.

"What?"

"Which one of those dresses were you going to wear tonight?" I repeat.

She glances towards the dresses before speaking. There's panic in her eyes.

"I'm not sure," she says in a broken half whisper. "I don't look good in any of them."

"Why do you do that?" I ask.

"What?"

"Put yourself down like that. You're a good person, Florence. Why don't you treat yourself with respect?"

"And you're a good person too, Claire," she says, misreading something into my last comment. Her eyes are huge, staring directly into my own. What is it she thinks she sees?

"Why don't we go back downstairs?" she says again.

"No, Florence. I want to know which dress you were going to wear."

"But why?" She's attempting to hold her nerve. I'm deciding that I quite like Florence. "Why does someone like you care what I wear?"

"What do you mean, 'someone like me'?" I ask, confused.

"You're young, Claire," she says, "and attractive. Most young women like you, they don't see people like me."

"Is that how you feel?" I ask. "Invisible?"

"Yes," she answers simply. "I think that once you pass a certain age, the world stops looking at you. Until one day, nobody sees you at all."

I think about this for a minute, wonder whether that's how Dad felt towards the end. In those final, fleeting moments of lucidity, in addition to the fear and loneliness, did he feel invisible too?

"Do you think everyone feels like that?" I ask.

"I don't know," she replies. "I think it must be fairly common."

There's something about Florence. It makes me do something I never do. It makes me tell her the truth.

"My dad was never invisible to me," I say.

"I know," she says.

"I didn't want them to take him away," I say. "I pleaded with them to let him come home."

"Oh, Claire," she says, and her arm is reaching out towards me now. "It must have been so difficult."

"I missed him so much when they took him away," I say, allowing Florence to put her arm around me. "I still miss him so much." I lower my head onto her shoulder. "I wish I could speak to him. Just one more time."

"What would you say?"

"I'd ask him if he's OK."

"I'm sure he is. I'm sure he'd tell you that he wants you to be happy. I'm sure all your dad wants is for you to get on with your life."

"I think you're right." We stand in silence for a few moments, and I breathe in the scent of Florence. She's so kind, so caring, I feel safe in her embrace. Peering over her shoulder, I notice a framed photograph on the bedside table. A man's face stares out at me, he's laughing; he looks kind and caring too. Rosary beads are draped over the frame.

"Come on," she says after a while. "Let's go downstairs. I think we could both do with a nice, strong cup of tea."

"Thanks, Florence," I say, raising my face to look at her. She smiles and I smile too.

"Florence?"

"Yes?"

"You're not invisible."

"Thank you, Claire," she says, "that means so much to me."

"The world does see you. And it listens to what you say."

The pillow is on her face in less than a second. She's heavy but has no real power. It's easy to push her huge ghostly form onto the bed and deflect her flapping arms. The translucency of her navy-blue cardigan is fascinating but reminds me of something revolting. She's going to die covered in Jemma's snot. When all movement stops, I remove the pillow and look at her face. I thought it would be difficult killing someone as pleasant as Florence, but it turned out to be just as easy as killing all those people I didn't like. I lie next to her for a while and look again at the three dresses hanging on her wardrobe door. I wonder which one she would have worn. She never did tell me. I wonder whether she's been reunited with her Derek already. I wonder whether soulmates reconnect instantaneously or whether they have to search for each other all over again. At least that shouldn't be a problem for Derek and his navigational skills.

After that I place the pillow back on her face, her phone on the bedside table and go downstairs to wait. I've counted seventeen doilies and fifty-three ornaments when the doorbell rings. It's eight o'clock exactly when Jemma pushes open Florence's front door.

"Florence! It's me, Jemma," she calls, stepping into the house. "Your door was on the latch, so I've let myself in."

She's standing in the hallway, looking from left to right when she calls out again.

"You really should keep your door locked, Florence, there's some nasty people about."

I rise from my seated position behind the door and slam it shut. She turns quickly and screams.

"Where's Florence?" she asks. She's wearing blue dungarees over a brown polo neck and what appear to be ballet shoes. Where the hell does she buy her clothes?

"Where's Florence?" she repeats and, when I glance towards the stairs, she turns and runs. She doesn't have much choice; I'm blocking her exit. I follow her up the stairs and hear her scream for a second time when she reaches Florence's bedroom. She's holding the pillow, having removed it from Florence's face as I hoped she would.

"What have you done, Claire?" She sounds angry. "Why did you kill her? You don't kill people like Florence, you only kill people who deserve to die."

"Those were your words, Jemma. Not mine."

She squeezes both ends of the pillow before dropping it on the bed. "Look," she says, raising her hands submissively. "I'm sorry, Claire. I know I should have treated you with the respect you deserve. But it's not too late. Together, we can do anything."

She runs her fingers through her hair then clenches her fists, preparing for the most important sales pitch of her miserable life.

"We can be partners, Claire. Just like Lucas and me. There's more money in this new job than you'd ever believe, Claire. You can be part of something big, Claire. No more aimless killing. A chance to put your talents to proper use."

The contrived flattery, repeated use of my name, short, breathless sentences—there's no doubt Jemma knows she's in trouble. Yet she's still able to multitask at an impressive level. Pleading for her life, attempting to read my mind and wondering what the hell I'm holding behind my back, all at the same moment.

"We have an amazing opportunity, Claire," she continues. "Don't throw it away. We're not like other people, you know that. You and me, Claire, we're the same."

"No, we're not."

"Yes, yes we are," she insists. "We're much more alike than you realize."

"No, we're not," I repeat. "You're a sociopath. I'm . . ."

"What? A psychopath? Is that it?"

"I'm . . . nothing like you, Jemma."

"So, what are you then?" The outline of her body is starting to flicker. "Because I don't think you're a psychopath, Claire. Not a proper one, anyway. Psychopaths don't go to bereavement groups and grieve for their dead dads."

"Don't you dare mention him!"

"I'm sorry, I'm sorry." She's disappearing in front of my eyes. "I'm just saying if I'm a sociopath, Claire, maybe that's what you are too. We could be an unstoppable team."

"I'm—"

"What?"

"I'm fucking sick of looking at that outfit!" Such a ghastly—and now ghostly—fashion choice. "Blue dungarees over a brown polo neck? Seriously? That's what you wear to a restaurant? And what the fuck are you wearing on your feet? Are they even shoes? What the fuck is wrong with you?"

If she starts to answer, I don't hear because I'm moving too quickly. Crossing the room in an instant, slamming Lucas Kane's gun into her mouth. Pulling the trigger.

It only takes moments to arrange the scene in Florence's bedroom and then I leave through the back door, using my long legs so admired by Lucas to hop over the garden fence. I have no way of knowing what Florence's neighbors are like. They might be the kind of people who hear a gunshot and assume it's a car backfiring or fireworks. Alternatively, they might be hammering down her front door at this very moment. Either scenario makes no difference to me. Within five minutes of firing the gun, I'm walking past St. Matthew's Church and heading towards the Old Bengal. I can't wait to get there because I haven't eaten all day and I know exactly what I'm going to order.

Chicken jalfrezi with a slice of lime.

THEN

The little girl is hungry, but she knows there's no point telling the woman sitting on her right. There's no point telling that woman anything. The doctor calls her name and the little girl and her mother rise from their seats in the waiting area and follow the doctor into a room. He shuts the door behind them.

"Hello, hello," he says as they all sit down. "Now, what can I do for you two?"

"It's Claire," says the woman. "There's something wrong with her, doctor. She's not right."

"Oh dear, I'm sorry to hear that," says the doctor, flicking through a file of notes on his desk. "Let's see, how old are you now, Claire? Ah, look at that! It's your birthday! Five years old today. Happy birthday, Claire. How miserable to be feeling poorly on your birthday. What seems to be the trouble?"

"There's nothing wrong with her physically, doctor," says the woman, slowly unbuttoning her coat. "It's her head. She's not right in the head."

The doctor sits back in his chair and stares at the woman. Transfixed. He reddens and coughs before speaking again. "What do you mean?"

"She got into trouble at school again today," says the woman, leaning forward. Her dress under the coat is tight. And short. "She cut another girl's *hair. In the middle of an art lesson, by all accounts. She got up and snipped the poor girl's ponytail off."*

"Oh dear," says the doctor, coughing again. "That sounds most unfortunate."

"It was unfortunate, doctor," says the woman, absentmindedly tracing the seam of her dress with a red, pointed manicured nail. "And that's not all. Because of her behavior, Claire doesn't have any friends. Not one single friend. She doesn't even try to make friends. I see the other children playing together but Claire just stands there. Watching. It's weird. Like I said, there's something wrong with her. She's not right in the head."

"Have you spoken to Claire about this?" asks the doctor, glancing towards the little girl.

"I've done everything I can to help her fit in," says the woman. "I take her to dance classes and piano lessons, but nothing works. She acts like she doesn't want to be there."

"Maybe she doesn't want to be there," says the doctor.

"What do you mean?" asks the woman.

"Have you asked Claire whether she wants to do dance classes and piano lessons?"

"Of course she does. What little girl doesn't want to learn to dance and play the piano?"

"If you have serious concerns about Claire's emotional well-being, I can make a referral to a child psychologist," says the doctor. "They usually like to meet the whole family when making their assessment."

"I don't think there's any need for all that," the woman says, smiling as she sits back in the chair again and slowly crosses her legs. "Can't you just prescribe something, doctor? Give her a pill to make her nice? More manageable?"

"*I'm sorry,*" laughs the doctor, "*I'm all out of niceness pills.*"

"*Well, what if I ask you really, really sweetly,*" says the woman, staring at him, "*could you get some more?*"

"*No,*" says the doctor, shuffling the papers on his desk into a pile. "*I'm sorry for any misunderstanding but there is no such thing as a niceness pill. Now, would you like me to make that referral?*"

"*No,*" says the woman, after a moment of silence, before standing and buttoning her coat. "*Thank you for your time.*" She smiles as she turns to leave the room. "*Come on, Claire.*"

They drive home and, as soon as the car pulls up outside the house, the front door opens and he's there.

"*Where have you two been?*" he asks.

"*I took Claire to see the doctor,*" says the woman.

"*Why? Is she ill? Claire, are you OK?*"

"*She got into trouble at school again today,*" says the woman. "*She cut another girl's hair.*"

"*What? Why did she do that?*" asks the man. "*And why did you take her to see the doctor?*"

"*Did you hear what I just said? She cut another child's hair off.*"

"*I know and that's terrible. Why did you do that, Claire?*"

"*She did it because you spoil her,*" mutters the woman, locking the car and walking into the house.

"*What did you say?*" asks the man.

"*You spoil her,*" says the woman. "*See!*" she says, pointing towards the kitchen table—to the chocolate birthday cake, the card and the present waiting there. "*Look how you spoil her. Is it any wonder she's out of control?*"

"*It's just a cake and a present,*" says the man. "*It's her birthday.*"

"She cut another child's hair off!" the woman shouts. "And you're rewarding that behavior."

"I'm not rewarding her behavior. And I feel awful for the other child, of course I do. Obviously, we need to speak to Claire and try to understand what happened, but I think it would be cruel not to celebrate her birthday."

"I give up," says the woman, turning back towards the front door, the car keys still in her hand.

"Where are you going?" asks the man.

"Somewhere where I don't feel quite so unheard."

"I hear you," says the man, blocking her path. "Talk to me. I want to listen."

"No, you don't. You're just like him."

"Who?"

"That bloody doctor. Sitting there behind that big desk, talking down to me like I'm the stupid one—revolting man. Who the hell does he think he is? Fucking ridiculous. I tried to tell him there's something not right with her but he didn't listen to me. Just like you never listen to me."

"I do listen. Please talk to me. Don't walk away. Please. I love you."

"If you love me, why do you always take Claire's side?"

"I don't! I love both of you. Please stay," he says, reaching towards her. "I love you so much."

"You say that, but do you mean it?" asks the woman, suddenly still. "Do you really love me?"

"Of course I do," replies the man, taking a step closer.

"How much? How much do you love me?"

"I love you with all of my heart."

"If that's true," says the woman, staring into his eyes, "why don't you want me to be happy?"

"I do," says the man, pulling her towards him. "Your happiness means everything to me."

"But you know I'm not happy living here!" she cries, pushing him away. "You've known that from when we first moved in, and you said it was only temporary. You said we'd move somewhere bigger, and I could have all those things I've dreamt about—the sweeping staircase, the walk-in wardrobe. You said I could have it all."

"We will move to a bigger house. I promise you," says the man, reaching out towards her. "You just need to give me a little more time."

"How much more time?" asks the woman, swatting his hand away. "It's been years. I've been waiting for years."

"I know and I'm sorry," says the man. "I'm doing everything I can to get the money together."

"Are you?" she asks. "Are you doing everything you can?"

"Of course I am. I've taken on more hours at work—"

"You didn't take that promotion," she says, interrupting. "It would have meant more money. Enough money to move."

"But that would have meant working even more hours. It would have meant never being here. Never spending any time with you and Claire."

"It always comes back to Claire, doesn't it? She's the real reason I'm still living in this dump."

"This isn't a dump," he says quietly. "And none of this has got anything to do with Claire. We will move to a bigger house, I promise you. Just as soon as I've saved enough money."

"How can you save when you're buying cake and presents for her?"

"It's her birthday. Please," he says, reaching out towards her again. "Please don't go out."

"You have no idea how much the pair of you upset me," she says, pushing past him. "I need to clear my head."

The man watches the woman drive away and then walks into the kitchen. He sticks five candles into the chocolate cake, makes a sandwich and pours a large glass of whisky. Placing the food and his glass on the table, he sits down next to the little girl.

"Happy birthday."

"Thank you," says the child, biting into the sandwich.

"So, tell me," he says, taking a large gulp of his drink, "why did you cut the girl's hair? Was she being mean to you? Is she bullying you?"

The little girl laughs and takes another bite of sandwich. "You're funny," she says with a smile.

"So, she isn't bullying you?"

"Of course not."

"So, why did you do it?" he asks. "I don't understand."

"The art teacher said we could take whatever we needed from the craft table to make our pictures," says the little girl.

"Yes?"

"The girl with the long hair was standing at the craft table."

"Yes?"

"I needed hair for my picture."

Silently the man stares into his glass for a few moments. Swirls the liquid for a while before taking another swig. "Cutting someone's hair off is very wrong," he says after another moment of silence. "You do understand that, don't you?"

"It didn't feel wrong," says the little girl. "It felt right. The girl with the long hair—I mean, the girl who used to have long hair—she's very annoying. She was pushing everyone out of the way and grabbing all the best things from the craft table. After I cut her hair, she didn't grab anything. Can I have my cake now?"

"Oh, Claire," says her father, reaching towards his daughter and pulling her close. "You remind me so much of my mother. Your grandmother. Such a shame you never got to meet her. She was just like you. Quiet and strong, always doing things her way. You look a bit like her too."

"Why don't we have any photographs of her?"

"I don't think Mummy would like that," says the man, smiling.

"Why not?"

"Your grandmother was a strong woman and Mummy is a strong woman and sometimes strong women don't always get along."

"They didn't like each other?"

"No, they didn't."

"Why not?"

He thinks about the question for a few moments and takes another drink before answering. "Truth is," he says slowly, "I think your grandmother scared Mummy."

The little girl laughs. "Mummy was scared?"

"Yes, sometimes."

"And I'm like her?"

"Yes," he says. "You're very like her. Now, let's light these candles so you can have your cake."

The man sings "Happy Birthday," and the little girl blows out the candles and makes a wish. They eat cake and later the man tucks the little girl into bed where she snuggles up with her favorite toy.

"Goodnight, beautiful birthday girl."

"Goodnight, Daddy."

He walks towards her bedroom door and turns back towards her before leaving the room. "I'm sorry this hasn't been a great birthday," he says. "Next year will be better, I promise."

The little girl laughs. "You're funny," she says. "This has been the best birthday ever."

9

At the third meeting of the bereavement group, we meet a woman called Star—our new leader. She has dark skin, long dark hair, and is wearing colorful, flowing clothes with lots of jangly jewelry. Star is one of those rarities you occasionally meet in life who appear to be flourishing, her facial features shrouded in such syrupy serenity it's impossible to guess her age. She looks about fifty, but I wouldn't be surprised if at any moment she starts reminiscing about the good old days of the Blitz. She's listing her qualifications and in addition to completing specialist training courses in anger problems, anxiety, depression and bereavement, she's also an expert in something called mindfulness. I'm not sure what this is but it seems to involve Star closing her eyes and thinking carefully before uttering each and every word. I'm not disputing any of her credentials but, to me, Star looks like someone out-of-her-bloody-mind-fulness.

After the bodies were discovered, the police came to speak to each member of the group. I looked into the prepubescent face of an overexcited policewoman and told her I didn't know either woman very well, but I did know that Jemma was devastated at the recent death of her mother. After this the police child thanked me and went on her way, probably via the swings in the park. I'm interested to hear what the others told the police and robustly reliable Welshman doesn't disappoint.

"I just can't bloody believe it!" he hollers, slapping his thighs while Star closes her eyes and nods. "I told the copper I thought she was odd. I knew something wasn't right about her. She was always wailing at the top of her voice, you see," he says to Star's eyelids. "Always going on and on about her poor, dead mum. But now we find out the truth," he adds before rummaging in the tatty rucksack at his feet, retrieving a local newspaper and violently pointing at the photograph of Jemma on the front page. "Now we find out that Jemma's mother is alive and well and living in Bognor," he exclaims. "Bognor Regis by the sea!"

I'm wondering whether there is a landlocked Bognor Regis when a clipped, posh voice pipes up.

"According to the report in the newspaper," says Christiana spelled with a C, "Jemma lived miles away. I wonder why she drove all the way here each week, pretending that her mother had died."

"Because she was obviously bonkers!" shouts Welshman. "Not right in the head," he adds, as if further clarification is required. "One of those nutty types always looking for sympathy and attention." And no longer bothering me. Such a relief.

Star's eyes are still closed but she raises her hands and asks for silence. While she mindfully works out what she's going to say, I look at Christiana. The epitome of an organized, high-functioning ordinary person, Christiana has clear skin, a neat bob, clothes that match her handbag and a trim figure. She must be well into her seventies, and I imagine she plays bridge, enjoys walks in the country and probably cooks a Sunday roast every week when her children and adult grandchildren come to visit. If it wasn't for one small detail, Christiana would take the definition of normal to a horrifying new level. Pinned to her crisply ironed pink blouse, just below her creamy string of pearls, is Christiana's name badge. The sticky, paper name badge that was given to her by Florence at the beginning of the first group meeting two weeks ago. Everyone else in the group disposed of theirs after the first session and Florence never gave out new ones. But for some reason, Christiana has kept her name badge and, as it presumably no longer sticks to her clothing, she chooses to pin it back on at the beginning of each meeting.

I stare at Christiana's name written in Florence's handwriting and wonder where Christiana keeps the flimsy paper sticker. Is there a special drawer in her kitchen, opposite the stove perhaps? Or maybe it's kept up on a bookshelf, amongst Mary Berry's recipes and P. D. James's crimes. And why does she keep it anyway? No one else is wearing one anymore. Maybe Christiana is more interesting than she seems. Maybe she doesn't play bridge or enjoy country walks after all. Maybe she's never given birth or even attempted to cook a roast. I wonder who the real Christiana is and whether she meets the crude threshold of mental illness so delicately set down by the Welshman. Is she one of those nutty types? Or is she just lost?

Talking of nutty types, Star has started to speak.

"I really don't think we should speculate about Jemma's state of mind," she says, opening her eyes. "Clearly the poor woman had problems but it's not our place to—"

"That *poor woman* killed Florence!" shouts Welshman. "And frankly, I couldn't care less about her problems. We've all got problems," he continues, looking around the group for support. "But we don't use that as an excuse to start suffocating people."

A few people are nodding and murmuring in agreement, which seems to spur Welshman on.

"I've got no problem with Jemma killing herself, no problem at all," he says, the embodiment of reasonableness and charm, "but why did she have to kill Florence? That makes no sense at all."

"As I said," begins Star, closing her eyes again, "I really don't think we should speculate; it's far too early to know for sure what happened. I know what has been reported in the newspapers," she continues, opening her eyes, "but I think we need to let the police do their job and establish all the facts before jumping to any conclusions."

When Star closes her eyes again, I think about the police doing their job and the conclusions that will be reached, not jumped to, after a thorough forensic investigation. I think about Jemma's fingerprints on the pillow. The position of the gun next to her limp, dead hand. The blood splatter on Florence's wardrobe, adding a welcome level of interest to three dresses of competing drabness. I think about Lucas's briefcase that will be found next to Jemma's body together with her phone, the Notes app open, displaying the title of that book Florence found so useful and Jemma's last communication with this world. Three simple words. Her suicide note. PEACE AT LAST.

My thoughts are interrupted by Christiana, who suddenly seems unable to keep her voice within appropriate parameters of excitement.

"I agree with Star, we shouldn't speculate," she gushes before speculating. "I mean, how do we know that Florence didn't ask Jemma to—"

"Kill her?" finishes the Welshman. "You think Florence asked Jemma to kill her?"

"Well, we all heard Florence talking last week," says Christiana, leaning forward in her chair. "About how she wanted to end her life after her husband died."

"That was four years ago!" exclaims Welshman. "That's how she felt then, not now."

"But how do we know that?" asks Christiana, pushing her glasses further up her nose, channeling her inner Miss Marple. When Welshman doesn't immediately respond she starts counting off facts on her fingers.

"First of all, we know that Florence never fully recovered from losing her husband. She told us so last week. Secondly, we know that she entertained feelings of suicide because she told us that too. Thirdly . . ."

I have no idea how long this list is going to be nor any interest in its content so I stop listening and glance around at the rest of the group. Star has adopted her default position—eyes closed, head nodding. Welshman is clenching his fists and looks like he's about to explode. Peculiar little man is sitting next to Star, listening to Christiana and making notes, and everyone else is staring down at the floor. When the explosion happens, it's as underwhelming as it is predictable.

"Florence wasn't suicidal!" shouts Welshman, slamming both hands down so hard that his thighs will surely be bruised tomorrow. "I really won't sit here and listen to this," he snaps, sitting there and listening.

"I'm sorry," says Christiana quickly. "I don't mean to upset anyone." Her hands are raised in submission and my mind flicks to Jemma in the last pathetic moments of her life.

"What we are all experiencing here," says Star, appearing to take control, "is a layering of grief. We have the grief that initially led each of you to this room and now we have the grief for your former group mate and counselor."

Star's eyes remain open as she demonstrates the meaning of layering—her right hand moving above the left followed by the left hand moving above the right—and I'm wondering how long a person can keep doing this when she finally speaks again.

"I think it would be useful if we all take a few moments to try to reconnect with what's in here," she says, tapping at her chest. "So, I'm going to walk you through a brief meditation. Please bear with me," she adds, as Welshman grimaces and shifts uncomfortably in his seat. "I know this may be unfamiliar to some of you, but I also know it will help. First, I'm going to ask everyone to please sit upright, no slouching, and when you feel ready, please lower or close your eyes. Now I want you to concentrate on your breathing. The rise and fall of your chest. The cool air exiting your nostrils. I want you to think of each and every breath as a refuge—a safe place to return to. No matter what else is going on, your breath is always there."

"Unless Jemma is suffocating you with a pillow," says Welshman, without sarcasm.

I open my eyes and note that a few other people do too. But Star's eyes remain closed.

"Return your focus to your breathing," she says, ignoring Welshman's comment, "and when your mind becomes distracted by outside noise or internal thoughts, gently bring it back to the next breath."

I close my eyes and enjoy the black silence of nothingness. After a while, Star's voice fills the room again. She talks about the busyness of our minds, the endless stream of thoughts dragging our attention this way and that. She suggests that we picture our thoughts as passing buses; we can decide which bus we get onto and how long we stay on board. I find myself thinking about the peculiar little man sitting next to Star. Is he meditating? Fighting the urge to make more notes? Or, if I open my eyes, will I see him manically scribbling in his notebook? I let this bus pass me by. When the next bus turns up, I know I'm going to jump on board and I'm not going to get off until the other passenger is dead. Star is telling us to slowly open our eyes and, as I do so, I picture the bus disappearing down the road, the stench of vampire smoke still heavy in the air.

"So, how did everyone find that?" asks Star.

"I'll be honest with you, Skye, it was a waste of time," replies Welshman. "Didn't relax me at all."

"My name is Star, not Skye, and relaxation isn't the primary objective. The purpose of meditation is to try to bring stillness to busy minds."

"I rather enjoyed it," says the peculiar little man, "and I didn't think I would. I've always been wary of hypnosis."

"This isn't hypnosis," says Star, "it's—"

"Thank goodness for that!" he laughs. "I was worried I'd start strutting around like a cockerel!"

"Oh, Will," giggles Christiana. "You do make me laugh."

"Meditation isn't about losing awareness of who you are," says Star, forcing a smile. "On the contrary, it's about *developing* awareness."

"I found it useful to imagine my thoughts as buses," says Christiana. "It helped me realize that I don't have to become absorbed in every single thought."

"Good, that's really good," says Star, her forced smile transforming into a genuine one.

"By letting some thoughts pass me by, I found I had more time to concentrate on the thoughts that matter," continues Christiana, her inner Buddha unceremoniously displacing poor Miss Marple. "One thought I focused on—or should I say one bus that I decided to get on—concerned Claire."

I blink at the sound of my name but keep my facial expression neutral. "It occurred to me that Jemma's death must be particularly difficult for Claire," explains Christiana. "Because she and Jemma had become so close."

I'm aware of people looking at me but keep my eyes fixed on Christiana and my mouth shut. I have no idea what Christiana knows or thinks she knows but I am aware how much ordinary people hate silence, how they always feel compelled to fill the void with words that don't need to be spoken.

"I chatted to Jemma last week during the coffee break," continues Christiana, "and she told me how much time she'd been spending with Claire. How grief had enabled them to develop an amazing connection. I'm ashamed to say it now, given what's happened since, but it made me quite jealous."

"Can you elaborate on those feelings, Christiana?" asks Star, nodding before closing her eyes. Again. I wonder if narcolepsy is a by-product of professional mindfulness.

"Well, as we all know, grief can be a really lonely place," says Christiana, looking slightly uncomfortable. "I suppose I was jealous because I wished I had developed such a closeness with someone in the group."

"You know you can always talk to me, Christiana," says the peculiar little man.

"Thanks, Will," smiles Christiana, "I do know that. Ever since we all had that lovely meal last week, I feel so much closer to everyone. But I also feel guilty about my stupid jealousy now because Claire has lost that special connection. Jemma's death must be hitting her really hard."

Everyone is looking at me and waiting for me to speak but I'm not sure what I'm expected to say. Should I comment on Christiana's pathetic need to be liked? Her odious envy of a phony friendship? The silence proves too much for Will, who starts stammering before forming words properly in his mind.

"Er, yes, Claire. Jemma mentioned it to me last week too. All of this must be very upsetting for you."

"Of course it's upsetting for her, they were proper friends," snaps Welshman. "When I spoke to Jemma last week, she told me she'd been to Claire's house and that they had arranged to meet up again."

Bloody hell, how long was this coffee break?

"You stayed behind last week, Claire, talking with Florence and Jemma," says Christiana gently. "Did you get any sense of Jemma's state of mind?"

"Did she happen to mention that she was going to suffocate Florence with a pillow and then shoot herself in the head?" asks Welshman, sarcasm definitely present this time.

"I'm just wondering whether this was as much of a shock to Claire as it was to the rest of us," declares Christiana, directing everyone's thoughts in a direction I don't want them to go.

"Of course it was a shock to Claire!" says Welshman. "What are you getting at?"

"I'm just curious, that's all. If Claire and Jemma spent so much time together, I'm wondering whether Jemma ever gave anything away. What did you and Jemma talk about, Claire?" she asks me directly.

"Yes, what did you talk about?" repeats Will. "Did Jemma talk about a dead mother or admit the truth?"

"Yes, and if she did keep up the pretense, how does that make you feel, Claire?" asks Christiana. "Knowing that the grief that connected you two was based upon a lie?"

I don't know which question I'm supposed to answer first but I am certain of something. This isn't the first time these thoughts or buses have run through the busy minds of Christiana and Will. From the way they're both looking at me I can tell they've spoken about this before. Which means they've spoken about *me* before. Which places them both on my radar.

Having exhausted my modest share of silence that society allows in any given situation, I clear my throat before speaking.

"It's nice of you to be so concerned about me," I say, coughing slightly, "but really there's no need. Yes, I did get on very well with Jemma, but we'd only known each other for a couple of weeks. She never said anything to me or even hinted at what she went on to do. I guess we'll never know for sure why she did what she did." Turning towards Star, I add, "For me, I just want to focus on coming to terms with my grief so that I can move on with my life."

"Of course," says Star, nodding. I expect her to close her eyes but instead she keeps them open, wide open, unblinking. "I think this discussion has been very rich, very rewarding," she says, "and I thank you all for sharing but Claire's right, we're here to concentrate our minds on moving through our journeys of grief. Now before we begin, would you like to do another brief meditation?"

"No!" shouts the Welshman, catching my eye and giving me a wink.

As Star closes her eyes and waits for a different response I think about the Welshman and Christiana and Will. I always picture myself in the shadows of life, silently observing ordinary people and their ridiculous ways. Today has reminded me I'm not invisible, they see me too.

No one has requested meditation, but Star appears to be doing one anyway. She asks us to close our eyes and when I do, I think about the plan I've been formulating for the last few days. I know it won't bring Dad back and probably won't even take away my pain but it's the only thought that gives me any comfort. Star is telling us to concentrate on each and every breath, reminding us that our breathing will always be there, a safe place that we can call home. I listen to Star's words and think about the people in the video stills I found in Lucas's briefcase; each one so unaware of the limited number of breaths they have left. Smiling, I open my eyes for a moment and see the flick of a head, eyes shutting, and wonder whether I was being watched. The next bus to arrive is unexpected. I hesitate for a moment and then let it pass me by.

10

The vanishing of Nurse Sebastian is all over the news and I'm not entirely sure why. There must be far more important events going on in the world but for some reason we keep being told about the devoted, God-fearing husband and father of three who finished his shift at the hospital thirty days ago and disappeared off the face of the earth. There's been so many family photographs printed in the newspapers, I feel like I know his wife and children. I know that at one point they all stood in front of a Christmas tree, on another occasion they sat in a boat on a lake and at some stage over the last few years they visited the London Eye. I've seen images of his wedding day and various shots of him and his wife perched on hospital beds, cradling newborns. Sebastian looks quite good in all the photographs, but the maternity shots aren't very flattering of his wife. I'm surprised she agreed to the publication of those.

All the photos are accompanied by plea after plea for information. What happened to Sebastian Sinclair? Does anybody know anything? Did anybody see anything? Where is he? Has he suffered amnesia? Been abducted by aliens? Or worse still, run off with another woman? I know from experience that in a couple of weeks this level of interest will dissipate. People get bored quickly when a body isn't found, and it won't take long for a middle-aged nurse to disappear into yesterday's news. But for now, Sebastian is everywhere, and I'm so used to seeing his image that I almost expect to spot it in the newspaper I'm unfolding on my living room floor. The headlines on the front page scream of human suffering—the teenage girl killed in a hit-and-run is described as being "everyone's friend," the drug-addicted young mother recounts her torment after awaking to find her baby gone. That must have been some bender. And of course there is the obligatory photograph of the latest household name, who is accused of putting his hand up young girls' skirts forty years ago and just can't fathom why anyone cares. There are no shots of Sebastian here, however, because this is all old news. This is the newspaper Lucas Kane had with him on his last evening on earth. Back in the days when Nurse Sebastian was still alive. Albeit on borrowed time.

I take a sip of coffee and start removing stills from between the pages of the newspaper. I place them into two piles. Tall Woman. Vampire Smoker. I wonder which one is worse. I wonder whether it matters. I wonder which one I'll enjoy killing more.

I pick up one shot and study it. Really study it. I want every detail committed to memory, it's those details that will enhance the experience of the kill. Whoever filmed the video this frame was taken from must have been standing outside a bathroom, looking in. An old lady is sitting on the floor of the bathroom naked. Standing over her is Vampire Smoker, laughing. He's wearing a uniform. He looks like a nurse or a caregiver. His trousers are around his ankles and he's naked from the waist down. He's cupping his penis in his hand and urinating over the old lady. Over her face. Into her mouth.

I pick up another shot. It shows a bedroom, and from the position of the shot I think the camera or phone must have been concealed somewhere high. On top of a wardrobe perhaps. A different old lady is sitting up in bed with arms outstretched, and it looks as though she's screaming. Jemma—wearing the same uniform as Vampire Smoker—is standing on one side of the bed and a tall woman, wearing her own clothes, is on the other. An object is mid-air between them; it looks like a doll. They're throwing it to one another and laughing.

The third shot shows another bathroom, and this time features an old man. He's naked and on his knees with his head in the toilet bowl. Vampire Smoker is standing beside him, urinating over the old man's head. Whoever took this footage has managed to capture Tall Woman in the bathroom mirror. She appears to have scraped her hair back into a headband and is watching Vampire Smoker and smiling. The image repulses me. It's never OK for a grown woman to wear a headband.

The other stills follow similar themes—Tall Woman is shown mistreating the old lady's doll in more and more ingenious ways while Vampire Smoker seems content to urinate over naked, old people. Which is a strange hobby, even for such a creepy-looking bloke. My preferred hobby is art but, lately, I haven't been able to focus on my painting—I haven't been able to focus on anything at all. Until now.

Stacking the pictures into a pile, I think about ordinary people and their ridiculous ways. What's with all this abuse of the elderly? Why is it so popular? What's the appeal? Nurse Sebastian, Jemma, Vampire Smoker, Tall Woman—that's four abusers I've stumbled across in the last couple of months. How many more would I find if I went out looking? And why isn't anyone, other than me, doing anything about it? They're so fucked-up, ordinary people—so busy posting opinions and selfies, what about the protection of their weak?

I pick up my notebook and pen now, flick through it until I get to a blank page. The report in the local newspaper mentioned Jemma's place of work, so my next two victims will be easy to find. From now on I shall be methodical, thorough and organized. From now on, there will be no more mistakes. Because from now on, I shall be watching Vampire Smoker and Tall Woman. I shall be studying every aspect of their routines and miserable lives. An idea starts to form and when it makes me smile, I jot it down. It feels so nice to have something to do.

11

Waterbridge Oak Care Home isn't just an impressive building, it's an imposing one. Beautiful grounds, endless driveway, pillars either side of the grand entrance—if the structure could speak, its voice would be one laced with arrogance. It knows it's the most magnificent building for miles. The inside is spectacular. Surfaces polished until they shine reflect ornate furniture and flawless, velvet carpet. The grandeur of the place is almost as breathtaking as the hypocrisy. What's that saying? Never judge a book by its cover. Nor, it would seem, a care home by its carpet.

The receptionist speaks with an Eastern European accent and wears too much makeup and a fake smile when she asks me to sign the visitors' book and directs me to room twenty on the third floor. I push the door open and think back to the first time I walked into Dad's room on the psychiatric ward. I could see straightaway the too-small bed, the too-cracked wall, but what really caught my attention was the narrow object that had once been a wardrobe. Stripped of doors, shelves and rails, the wardrobe in Dad's hospital room was no longer fit for purpose but that didn't seem to matter. Nor did the fact that a man who had always kept his clothes so neat and organized was now denied the small dignity of using a hanger. Wherever my dad was during the last two years of his life, be it lost within the depths of insanity or enduring a terrifying moment of lucidity, the first and last thing he saw every day was an object resembling an open, upturned coffin. An accelerant for nightmares? Probably. A grim reminder of the only way he was ever going to leave? Definitely. But at least some idiot got to tick a box and deem the pointless wardrobe safe.

The wardrobe in room twenty on the third floor of Waterbridge Oak is most certainly fit for purpose, along with the oversized bed, coffee table, plasma TV and en suite bathroom. Sinking into an obscenely comfortable armchair, I note that the ivory-colored tassels on the curtain tiebacks are matched perfectly to the bases of the ceramic table lamps. Of course they are. Opulence doesn't just happen when a load of expensive items are thrown together; it's created by the detail. The sleeping figure in the bed is beginning to stir and I turn my attention to the framed photographs on the walls. The adorable baby with beautiful blond curls became a cheeky-looking schoolboy, an awkward, gangly teenager and then an underwhelming, self-satisfied man.

"Where's my baby? What have you done with my baby?"

The shrillness of the voice surprises me, containing none of the grogginess I would expect from such recent sleep. Then I remember the overriding power of madness and the only thing that surprises me is the fact I was surprised.

"Where's my baby?" she repeats, and I stare at her, marveling at what age can do to a person given enough time. An intricate web of wrinkles is spun over a face that was probably once quite beautiful. I recognize her from Lucas's video stills, but she looks smaller and more delicate in real life. I glance back towards the top of the wardrobe, to where the recording device must have been concealed. It certainly captured the distress etched amongst the wrinkles on this old lady's face but didn't do justice to her fragility.

"Where's my baby?" she says again. "What have you done with my baby?"

The door opens and a man in his twenties appears at the side of the bed. He has black skin, brown eyes, is wearing a caregiver's uniform and acknowledges my presence with a brief nod of his head before focusing attention on the occupant of room twenty. Rearranging pillows, he helps her sit up before retrieving something from the floor.

"There you are, Kathleen," he says gently, placing a doll into her ancient arms. "Here's your baby. All safe and sound."

The woman rocks the doll and silently moves her lips. Lullabies and lunacy. How thoroughly depressing.

"I see you've got a visitor, Kathleen," says the man, pouring a glass of water from a jug on the bedside table. "That's nice, isn't it?"

No response from Kathleen although she does turn her head towards the glass when he offers it and sips water through a straw.

"I'm Ben, one of the caregivers," says the man, replacing the glass onto the table and approaching me with an outstretched hand.

"Nice to meet you," I smile, standing up and shaking his hand. "I'm Claire."

"Hi, Claire," he says, returning my smile. "So, are you related to Kathleen?"

"No, no I'm not," I say, making a split-second decision to answer honestly. "Actually, I don't know Kathleen at all," I add. "This is the first time I've met her."

"Oh, right," he says, looking confused. "So why . . ."

"I knew Jemma," I say, answering his unspoken question with a baffling reply.

"Jemma? Jemma Williams?" he asks. "Jemma who used to work here? Before . . ."

The air is becoming heavy with Ben's unspoken words.

"Before she had her . . . funny turn," he says finally.

"Yes," I reply, deciding I quite like Ben. Anyone who describes murder and suicide as a funny turn gets my vote.

"Oh, right," he says again. "But I still don't understand why you're visiting Kathleen."

I open my mouth to speak and then shut it again. I need a moment to rethink my response because something about Ben has caught me off-guard. Most people I meet, especially the good ones, are insecure. They playact fake personas and measure their fake worth by the fake validation of other fakes. The man staring at me isn't like that. He's authentic, still connected to the person he was always meant to be. I wonder what life is like for someone like that.

"Ben, can I be honest with you?" I ask.

"Of course," he says, "I'd prefer that to the alternative."

Smiling, I glance towards Kathleen. She's still rocking the doll and looks happy. Or at least content.

"Is there anywhere we can speak in private?" I whisper. "I don't want to say anything that may upset her."

Ben looks unsure for a moment before checking the safety guards on both sides of the bed and ushering me into the bathroom.

"So, what's this all about?" he asks, keeping his voice low, leaning against the wash basin and eyeing me with suspicion.

Catching sight of my reflection in the mirror, I avert my eyes and note that Kathleen uses lavender-scented soap and the same night cream as me. It's expensive stuff and promises to ward off wrinkles. I make a mental note to try a different brand.

"I only met Jemma a couple of weeks before she died," I begin, quietly. "But even though I didn't know her long, I can't get her out of my head. I keep asking myself whether there was anything I could have said or done to change what happened. The Jemma I knew was a completely different person to the Jemma in the papers."

"Bloody newspapers," says Ben with sudden irritation. "We've had journalists hanging around here pretending to be visitors, upsetting residents and asking questions about Jemma. Hang on a minute . . ." he adds, irritation abruptly giving way to accusation.

"I'm not a journalist, I promise you," I say quickly but Ben doesn't look convinced. "I recently lost my father," I add, trying a different approach, appealing to the abundance of empathy I know is there. "I met Jemma at a bereavement group a few weeks ago. She told me her mother had recently died."

"I didn't know that," says Ben, confused again.

"No, well, according to the newspapers, her mother is alive and well."

"So, what was she doing at a bereavement group?"

"I don't know. The other lady who died—Florence—I knew her too. She was the group leader."

"I don't remember reading anything about that," says Ben.

"You will," I say. "Now that the nationals have picked up the case, the whole story will come out. I'm telling you the truth."

"But I still don't understand why you're visiting Kathleen."

Sensing I've gained a fraction of his trust, I take a step closer and lower my voice even more. "A couple of days ago I read that Jemma is now being linked to the disappearance of a man who vanished weeks ago. A man she met here. Apparently Jemma met Lucas Kane here while caring for his elderly mother, Kathleen."

Ben keeps his eyes on the bed and remains silent.

"It's also been reported in the papers that Kathleen suffers from dementia and Lucas is her only child."

"So?" he says eventually.

"My father died of dementia," I say. "I know what an awful disease it is, how confused and terrified my father was."

Ben is staring into my eyes, trying to decide whether I'm telling the truth. "Dad's friends couldn't handle seeing him like that," I continue. "They stopped visiting after a couple of weeks. In the end it was just me. I was the only link my father had to the outside world."

"I'm sorry to hear that," he says in such a way I know he believes me. "But I still don't understand why—"

"Since her son disappeared, how many visitors has Kathleen had?"

"I'd have to check the visitors' book."

"How many visitors have *you* seen?"

"You're the first."

"I keep thinking how awful it would have been for Dad if something had happened to me, if I had vanished into thin air like Kathleen's son. If I hadn't been able to visit Dad, I would want someone to spend time with him—"

"But you don't know Kathleen," Ben interrupts. "And more importantly, she doesn't know you."

"But I could *get* to know her," I say, "and she could get to know me. I mean, at least as much as her illness allows."

"I don't know," says Ben, looking unsure. "As you yourself said, dementia is a confusing, terrifying disease. I'm not sure whether visits from a stranger is what Kathleen needs."

"But surely it's better than no visits at all," I say, placing my hand gently on his arm. When he shakes it off, I realize I'm down to my last chance.

"I understand your concerns, Ben, I really do," I say, stepping back. "I can see how much you care about Kathleen and I fully respect your opinion. Thank you for listening to me." I turn away, then pause. "It was selfish of me to come here; I see that now."

"I wouldn't say that," says Ben. "I don't think visiting an elderly lady is selfish."

"Isn't it?" I ask, turning back to look at him. "The truth is, ever since Dad died, I feel lost. It was horrible seeing him so ill but at least when he was alive, my life had some purpose. Visiting him every day—it gave me something to do, somewhere to go."

"Don't you have any family?" asks Ben. "A husband? Kids? Friends?" he adds as I shake my head. "Don't you have a job?"

"No," I reply, pulling a tissue from my pocket and dabbing at my eyes like Jemma used to do. "Dealing with Dad's diagnosis more or less took over my life. It's all I've spoken about for the last few years and, let's be honest, who in their right mind wants to listen to me drone on and on about terminal illness? I don't blame them, of course I don't, but all my friends just seem to have disappeared." I think I might actually be using Jemma's exact words now.

"It broke my heart to think about Mrs. Kane suffering the same horrible fate as my dad and having no one come to visit," I say, blinking away a tear. "But I also wanted to come because, in all honesty, Ben, I don't have anywhere else to go." My voice actually splinters during the last few words to coincide with a crescendo of frenzied eye-dabbing. Move over, Jemma, there's a new Queen of Fake Martyrdom in town.

I pick up my bag from the floor by the armchair. "Goodbye, Kathleen," I say quietly before staring at the carpet and heading slowly towards the door.

"Good afternoon, Kathleen!" The voice is pretentious, and the soft-soled shoes walking into the room look vintage. I raise my head and the Tall Woman is there—her headband nearly scraping the ceiling as she ducks through the door frame. She's wearing purple flared trousers with a green patterned shirt but the strangest thing about her is her head. It's disproportionately large and a peculiar shape, like a deformed pumpkin left unsold at Halloween. She must be in a constant fight with gravity, keeping that enormous thing all the way up there—balancing on such a long, elegant neck and slender physique. And what's with the night fever outfit, has 1977 kicked her out? Slung her into the present day, bashing that misshapen head on every year in between? It's hard to see what she's eating from below, but she seems to be enjoying it—shoveling slimy-looking food from a plastic tub straight into her mouth.

"Hello, I'm Deb. I'm the manager," she declares, staring at me like a bouncer who has just discovered an underage drinker in a nightclub. "Irina on reception told me Kathleen had a visitor, so I thought I'd come up here to introduce myself."

She shoves her right hand out towards me, and I feel my stomach turn. Her fingers will be covered in that slimy food juice. We shake hands and now that giant head is descending towards me, the stench of anchovies arriving at the exact moment I spot slimy deposits of food lodged between her teeth. With this assault on my senses, my stomach turns again—every single part of me finds this woman repulsive. And I'm speaking as someone who once sliced open a flasher and unraveled his small intestine, just to see how long it really was.

"Hello, Deb," I say, fighting the urge to wipe my hand on the leg of my jeans. "I'm Claire."

"And how do you know Kathleen?" she demands, scooping more anchovies from the tub.

"Claire is an old family friend of the Kanes." Ben's voice is slightly different now, containing a nonchalance that wasn't there before.

"Really?" asks Deb, still staring at me.

"Yes," replies Ben, going over to Kathleen's bed and pouring her another glass of water. "Claire was just telling me about her father. He worked with Kathleen years ago."

"At the law firm in Mayfair?" asks Deb.

"Yes," Ben and I say at the same time. "Sorry," I add, giggling nervously.

"It's OK," smiles Ben. "I know you can answer for yourself. Just thought I'd save you going through the whole thing again. Kathleen worked as a secretary for Claire's dad many, many years ago," he says to Deb, "and the two families have been close friends ever since."

"Was your father a solicitor or a barrister?" Deb asks.

"He was a solicitor," I say with confidence. Barristers work in chambers; solicitors work in law firms. Even I know that.

"Was?"

"Sorry?"

"You said he was a solicitor."

"Oh yes," I say. "He passed away recently."

"I'm sorry to hear that," she says.

"Thank you."

"At least he achieved a lot in his life," she adds. "I mean, being a solicitor at a top London firm, he must have been a well-educated man."

And there it is. Not her only insecurity, I'm fairly certain of that, but it's an easy one to exploit.

"Yes, Dad went to Oxford," I say. "It used to get quite competitive actually," I add, raising my eyes upwards, pretending to remember, "especially during the boat race. He would be supporting Oxford while I always made a point of wearing my Cambridge scarf and cheering them on."

I smile now and keep my eyes fixed on something high up on the wall, lost in memory.

"We were always very close," I say after a moment or two.

"That's nice," says Deb. "It's nice you have good memories. Has Ben offered you a cup of tea?"

I look at her face and register the change. Minutes ago, I was an underage drinker who needed to be escorted off the premises. Now I'm a celebrity being ushered into the VIP area. And all because of an imaginary Cambridge scarf.

"A cup of tea would be lovely, thanks."

"Of course," she smiles. "Ben, get Claire a cup of tea and see if you can find her one of those good biscuits. It's a shame the weather isn't nicer today," she says to me, "you could have your tea out on the sun terrace."

And there's an awkward moment now as she glances down towards her hands. Notices the empty, plastic tub in her grasp.

"Get rid of this immediately," she snaps at Ben, chucking the tub towards him, which is strange because it's her tub and she's standing next to the bin. "I'm always so busy, Claire," she says, turning back to me. "Always rushing around, that's why I have to eat on the go. I literally never sit down." She runs anchovy fingers through hair that looks like it's already hitting its target for grease. "Sometimes the staff, they say to me, 'For goodness' sake, Deb! Stop rushing around. You literally never sit down!' That's what you always say to me, isn't it?" she directs at Ben who shrugs noncommittally and looks confused. Too authentic to do anything else. "This place is my life. I give my heart and soul to the staff and residents here. And do you know something?" she says again, moving that enormous head closer. "All my hard work is starting to pay off because we've just been nominated in this year's Care to Join Us Awards!" Her smile is wide; that's a lot of anchovy breath. "Care to Join Us is the company that owns this place, amongst others, and every year an award is presented to the best-run home. As you can imagine, competition is fierce and winning would be quite the achievement."

Returning the smile, I breathe through my mouth; still thinking of an appropriate cliché in response when she speaks again.

"I'll leave you now to spend some time with Kathleen and please feel free to explore while she's sleeping. This being our dementia floor, you'll see we have a separate sitting and dining room up here for the ease and convenience of our residents. There will be a quiz starting shortly which you're welcome to join. If you need me, my office is on the ground floor. Not that you'll ever find me sitting at my desk. I mean, I literally never sit down, do I?" she directs at Ben, but he's already left the room and, ducking through the door frame, she follows.

Standing in the middle of room twenty I congratulate myself on a job well done. My assumption that the management of this place would be unfriendly and suspicious had been correct. So too had been my decision to be honest with authentic Ben. Now I can come here as often as I like to perfect every last detail of my plan. No more rash decisions. No more mistakes.

Settling myself back into the armchair, I glance around Kathleen's bedroom and my mind flits back to Florence's. I can still picture it so clearly. The three dresses hanging on the wardrobe door, the neatly made bed, the rosary beads draped over the photo of her husband Derek's beaming face. I wonder what that bedroom looks like now. I think about the police officers and forensics experts and cordons and evidence bags. I picture the police discovering the bodies, the gun and the suicide note. I see them opening the briefcase, carefully removing the wallet and work files—objects linking Lucas Kane to the dead women forever. Minimal detective work will have led the police to this room and a confusing collection of facts. The police know that Jemma cared for Lucas's mother and that Jemma met Lucas in this care home. They are aware that Lucas is missing, they think that Jemma killed Florence, they know that Jemma killed herself and they suspect that Jemma is somehow involved in Lucas's disappearance. What the police don't know is that Jemma was abusing Lucas's mother and that Lucas knew about it.

I glance at the wardrobe, where the recording device must have been concealed. I wonder what happened. Did Lucas suspect abuse and set up a secret camera? Did he confront Jemma with the evidence? If so, what happened then? How did Jemma go from being his mother's abuser to Lucas's partner in the blackmail of Vampire Smoker? And why did Lucas keep his mother here if he knew she was being abused?

There's a thud and I look up to see Kathleen's doll back on the floor.

"Where's my baby? What have you done with my baby?" she says, sounding upset.

I walk over to the bed and stare into her old, dark blue eyes. "Where's my baby?" she repeats, her voice louder than before. "What have you done with my baby?"

I glance at the photograph of Lucas as a baby, notice the blueness of his eyes and consider telling his mother the truth.

"Where's my baby?" She's shouting now. "What have you done with my baby?"

I pick up the doll and place it back into her arms. She quiets down immediately, madness appeased for a while. Disease has already obliterated this woman, telling her the truth would be unkind. Glancing again at the photo of Lucas, I listen as his mother sings lullabies to an inanimate object and feel confident that my decision is the right one. I may have cut up her baby and buried him in my garden, but there's no need to be cruel.

sip the tea and survey my surroundings. More fucked-up microcosms of society must surely exist but there can't be too many. We've moved into a little sitting room on the third floor of Waterbridge Oak. I'm sitting on a hard-backed chair that I think has been brought in from the dining room. Ben has expertly transferred Kathleen into an armchair and he's now guiding an elderly gentleman out of the room. Vampire Smoker is here, slouched in a chair up against the wall, looking disconnected and bored. Or is he tired? Nearing the end of a shift? I need to find out what hours he works. Two old ladies are sitting together on the sofa, each refusing to look at the other. Have they had a row? The man gazing out of the window must be in his seventies. He's wearing a smart suit and looks like he may have been crying. A toddler with curly blond hair keeps walking over to the tea trolley, chubby fingers reaching up for a biscuit. His mother repeatedly pulls him back onto her lap, her olive skin much darker under each eye—she looks tired, nervy, apologetic. Her chair is from the dining room too. Pumpkin-Head Deb who literally never sits down is sitting on the other sofa and smiling at the toddler. Her eyes are cold—she's probably concerned about him pulling over the tea trolley. Doesn't want him getting burnt. Definitely doesn't want him getting any of the good biscuits.

We're all gathered in a semi-circle, staring at the man sitting in the center. His name is Jeremy, "But everyone calls me Jez." He's in his mid-thirties and wearing a *Sesame Street* T-shirt, blue jeans, red socks and brown moccasins. He's the question master and the only person remotely interested in this Monday morning quiz. One of the old ladies starts to cough and the other turns away in disgust. The suited gentleman dabs at his eyes with a handkerchief, Vampire Smoker drops further down in his chair, Kathleen whispers to her doll and the toddler makes a break for the biscuits. If invading aliens landed now, they'd take in this snapshot of life on earth and hurry back to the spaceships. Some things just aren't worth the trouble.

"Anyone?" asks Jeremy, optimistically. "Anyone at all? I'll accept answers from anyone. You don't have to be . . ."

Demented? Knocking on death's door?

". . . a resident," he concludes. "So, who would like to hazard a guess at what is the largest island in the world?"

"Is it Australia?" asks the mum of the toddler, frantically emptying building blocks onto the floor.

"Good guess, Miranda," says Jeremy. "But Australia is actually defined as being a continent rather than an island."

"Oh right, sorry," says Miranda, dragging her son away from the biscuits and setting him on the floor. He immediately starts banging building blocks together.

"Come on, someone else must have a guess," says Jeremy, raising his voice slightly.

"Is it Ringo Starr?" asks one of the old ladies.

"Of course it isn't Ringo Starr!" shouts the other one. "Why do you always say Ringo Starr?"

"OK, OK, Janet," soothes Ben, returning to the room and squeezing himself in between the two women on the sofa.

"Good guess, Edith," smiles Jeremy. "But no, it's not Ringo Starr."

"That's not a good guess," snaps Janet. "It's a stupid guess."

"Is it Ringo Starr?" asks Edith again.

"I think the largest island in the world is Greenland," says Ben quickly, taking Janet's clenched hand into his own.

"That is the correct answer, Ben," says Jeremy, suddenly serious. "Although please remember that this quiz is for residents and their guests. Not staff."

"Yes, Ben," sniffs Pumpkin-Head Deb. "Stop showing off."

"Sorry," says Ben before pulling a face that makes Janet squeal with laughter.

"Right, this last question is all about history," says Jobsworth Jez. "More specifically it's about an event I'm sure all you residents know about . . . the Gunpowder Plot of 1605."

Bloody hell. How old does he think they are?

"So, the Gunpowder Plot of 1605," says Jeremy, looking excited, "was a failed assassination attempt on which king?"

For fuck's sake. Why are all these questions so hard? Can't he see his audience?

The suited man looks away from the window and clears his throat. Miranda perches on the edge of her chair and pulls her son onto her lap. "Yes, Dad?" she directs at the man in the suit.

"Do you know the answer, Dad? You were always so good at history."

The man in the suit looks towards the ceiling and gently brushes the tips of his fingers together. He stares at Jeremy. There's a moment of silence before he speaks.

"Why are you wearing such horrible shoes?"

At last. A decent question.

"Dad!" exclaims Miranda. "Don't be so rude. I'm sorry, Jeremy."

"It doesn't matter," says Jeremy, attempting and failing to hide his horrible shoes by awkwardly pulling his feet further back under his chair.

"Who's wearing horrible shoes?" asks Edith.

"You. That's who," snaps Janet.

"The answer is James the First," says Jeremy, shuffling his papers together, indicating the end of the quiz. "Well done, everyone."

"Who's James?" asks Edith. "Is *he* wearing horrible shoes?"

"James is the king, you stupid woman!" shouts Janet.

"We have a king now, do we?" asks Edith. "What happened to the queen?"

There's a sharpness on my leg and my attention is diverted away. The toddler is standing directly in front of me, smiling. One of the building blocks is clutched in his plump little hand and he's banging it over and over again against my shin. His beautiful bright blue eyes are sparkling behind blond curls bouncing in front of his rosy face. He's an attractive child but he needs a haircut. And he definitely needs to stop hitting my leg.

"Oscar! Stop it," scolds his mother. "I'm so sorry," she says to me, looking scared. I wonder why she's scared. Does she think I'm going to shout at her child for hitting my leg? Is that what ordinary people do these days? Shout at little children and their exhausted mothers? And she looks really exhausted, this woman. Her eyelids are heavy and her unwashed hair, almost black with grease, is tied up in a messy bun.

"Don't worry," I say, mentally scanning my memory bank of stock statements used by ordinary people. "He's a gorgeous little boy," I decide to say.

His mother looks at her child and smiles. "Yes," she says, following the toddler with her dark, mesmerized eyes. "He is a gorgeous little boy. He's amazing."

In that moment I wonder what life is like for little Oscar and all those like him, enveloped from day one in their mothers' limitless love. But I'm distracted by movement elsewhere in the room—Ben and Vampire Smoker are helping the two old women get to their feet. Once they're standing, I can't tell which one is Edith and which is Janet. I imagine that Janet is the angrier-looking of the two but could be wrong. Vampire Smoker glances over in my direction and, just for a second, I hold my breath—wondering whether he recognizes me from that night in the bar. Then I remember he's a sadist and I breathe comfortably again because sadists rarely notice anything outside their own vile orbit.

"I'm Miranda by the way," says the mother of the small child. "My father, Frank, he lives here," she adds, as though living here is Frank's choice. "He has Alzheimer's," she continues. "Sudden onset. He's not even that old."

I scan the bank once again for a suitable response and wonder whether she's finally stopped talking. What is it with ordinary people and their need to cast information out into every conversation? Don't they appreciate its power? The ease with which information is transformed into ammunition?

"That must be so difficult for you."

"Yes, it is," she agrees, staring at her father.

"Dementia is a truly awful disease," and as I say the words, I'm vaguely aware that I didn't need to scan my memory bank that time before speaking.

Oscar has stopped banging the building block against my leg and now hands it over to me.

"Wed," he says. What's he talking about?

"Yes, Oscar!" says his mother. "It is red. Well done!" Now she's looking at me and smiling and I realize I'm supposed to react.

"Thank you," I say, taking the block, although I have no idea why they think I want it, what possible use I could find for a red plastic cube. Giggling, he turns around, picks up another block and passes it to me.

"Gween," he says this time.

"Yes, Oscar!" exclaims his mother. "It is green. Clever boy."

"Thank you," I say again. He giggles and runs to pick up another block. There are about fifteen different-colored blocks on the floor. This could go on for ages. When is his mother going to tell him to stop? Or at the very least correct his pronunciation?

"Good boy, Oscar," she says, as though I asked for all these stupid blocks. Maybe that's the cornerstone of motherly love—a belief that the happiness of a child overrides everything else, even the truth. No wonder people like Oscar choke when they take their first bite of reality.

I accept two more blocks from Oscar and then tell Miranda I have to go. She says it was nice meeting me and I reply with one of my favorite words and one I try to use often.

"Likewise." No need to scan the memory bank when using "likewise."

As I stand up, Pumpkin-Head Deb feels the need to butt in and tell me she's rushing downstairs for a meeting, but it's been nice to meet me, and she hopes to see me again soon. She can depend on it. I say goodbye to Ben and then approach Kathleen. She's completely focused on the doll and muttering words I can't hear. I wonder whether I can get away with merely patting her on the head but then I notice that Miranda and Ben are watching. Miranda with detached interest, Ben with genuine curiosity. I lower my face towards Kathleen, breathe in the scent of lavender and gently brush my lips against her papery skin. I think she's whispering something about her baby sleeping soundly but can't be sure.

"Goodbye, Kathleen," I say as I stand up. "I'll come back and see you again soon."

"Right then, Kathleen." Ben's voice reaches me as I leave the room. "Let's get you ready for lunch. Shepherd's pie and sticky toffee pudding are on the menu today—your favorites."

Deb is waiting for the lift, and I smile and say goodbye to her as I head for the stairs. The smell of lunch being served in the dining room is incredible and reminds me I need to eat. The receptionist caked in makeup and insincerity wishes me a nice day as I head into the world outside.

Walking through the car park, I notice a bright red Mercedes with a sticker in the back window: YOUR ANGELS ARE WATCHING. I think about Frank who used to be good at history and Kathleen who used to work in a law firm and Deb and Vampire Smoker who have no idea how much danger they're in and wonder when their angels are going to realize. Watching may not be enough.

13

t's the fourth meeting of the bereavement group and a special guest has joined us: Jemma's sister. Her name is Helen, and she reminds me of a heron. Long, elegant neck, small beady eyes—there's a twitchiness and intense energy to her that seems to be unsettling the rest of the group.

The Welshman is shifting awkwardly in his chair and looking at Star for answers. Christiana is wearing her name badge again, which is noticeably less creased than last week. Is it possible she ironed it? Will is scribbling in his notebook. What on earth is he writing? The meeting has only just started. Star has introduced Helen to us and is now sitting with her eyes closed, seemingly oblivious to the uncomfortable silence. Helen is crying softly and keeps dabbing at her eyes with a tissue. Robust Welshman shifts in his chair again and raises his eyes briefly to the ceiling. In one fluid movement Will removes a pencil sharpener from his briefcase, sharpens the pencil in his hand and then returns the sharpener and shavings. I wonder whether he does this throughout the day and, if so, how often he empties the shavings out of the briefcase. Every evening? Only at weekends? I'm trying to decide whether this is more or less odd than Christiana keeping her name badge safe each week when Star finally starts to speak.

"Helen is here today because she recently suffered a bereavement, the tragic loss of her sister Jemma. Given the sudden, unexpected, shocking nature of Jemma's death," Star is emphasizing each adjective slightly more than the last, "Helen feels that she is stuck in the first stage of grief. Denial."

Everyone stares at Helen, hoping perhaps that she will demonstrate what a person stuck in denial looks like. She obliges, to a certain extent, by keeping her eyes low and squeezing the tissue in her hand into a tight ball.

"It was felt that if Helen came and met you all, it might help her begin her journey through grief. That said," Star adds, sitting upright, suddenly brusque, "I am aware that every member of this group has their own unique journey of grief; one person's experience should not overwhelm or diminish another's."

There follows a long-winded masterclass on how to overthink things that aren't worth thinking about, during which I count the words "boundaries," "respect" and "closure." Within seconds I've reached double digits and stop listening.

"So, if nobody has any objections to Helen being here, I think we will begin," concludes Star, sitting forward in her chair. "Helen?" she directs at the sad heron in the corner. "Would it be OK if we start with you? If you have any questions for the group, it might be a good idea to deal with them now."

"Thank you, Star," sniffs Helen, "and thank you, everyone, for allowing me to join you today." She unravels a tiny piece of tissue from the ball in her hand and wipes her nose. "I guess I'm just hoping that if I can retrace some of Jemma's steps in the week or so before her death, I might be able to gain some understanding of why she did what she did." She starts rolling a new tissue into a ball. "I'm ashamed to say that Jemma and I, we haven't seen very much of each other over the last few years. We were inseparable as children," she adds, dabbing at her eyes, "but somewhere along the line, things changed."

"Jemma spoke about having a sister." Christiana is leaning back in her chair and eyes Helen with suspicion before adding, "She also told us that you used to be close as children."

"Really?" asks Helen, dropping her latest tissue ball into her lap. "What else did she say?"

"Hmmm, bear with me," says Will, flicking through his notebook. "Ah, yes, here it is. During the first meeting of this group, Jemma told us that her sister left her to care for their dying mother alone and even after the death there had been no communication between the siblings."

My God. He really does write everything down. What a bizarre little man.

"I don't understand why she would say that," says Helen, staring blankly at Will. "I mean, it's just not true, any of it. Jemma didn't care for Mum on her own because Mum didn't need any care. She's alive and well—"

"And living in Bognor!" exclaims Welshman robustly. "Bognor Regis by the sea!"

Why does he keep clarifying that?

"And even if Mum did need care," continues Helen, "there's no way I'd leave Jemma to deal with it on her own. She knows that I wouldn't." The latest tissue is squeezed into a ball before she adds, "I mean, she *knew* that I wouldn't." Maybe it's the emphasis on the past tense but something renders Helen suddenly mute. Even the tissue rolling stops. "At least I hope she knew that I wouldn't," she says finally, staring sadly at the floor.

The silence that follows proves too much for the Welshman.

"So, Helen," he says, "was Jemma always nuts?"

"Sorry?"

"Was she always, you know, a bit bonkers?"

"I don't understand," stammers Helen.

"Oh right, sorry," he says and for a moment it seems as though he is going to stop talking. But he can't do it. "I was just curious to know," he continues, "whether you think Jemma was always crazy or whether you think she killed Florence and then committed suicide in a one-off episode of craziness?"

Helen is leaning forward and openly sobbing now. She's surrounded by tissues but all of them are rolled into balls, not really fit for purpose. Everyone looks towards our leader, but she's got her eyes closed and seems immune to the tsunami of emotion. I sit back in my chair and think about Florence. She may have been irritating and a lover of doilies but to her credit I bet she'd be over there with Helen the heron now, dishing out Kleenex and hugs.

"Good, good," says Star eventually. "This is really good."

Is it?

"This level of honesty is exactly what is needed."

Really?

"Denial is what we cloak ourselves in to protect us from the truth."

Do we?

"In order to slice through denial, we need to be confronted with the truth."

What are her qualifications again?

"It must be very difficult for you, Helen, to be confronted with the enormity of what your sister did," continues Star. "But until you accept the truth, it's going to be impossible to move forward."

"What's difficult for me," says Helen, "is accepting that my sister is a killer. I know that she had her faults, but so does everybody."

She pauses and looks around the room. I expect her to retrieve another tissue from her bag, but she doesn't. For the first time I notice that there's something else simmering under all those tears. Something that reminds me that herons are predators.

"Jemma wasn't perfect," she continues, "but she would never hurt anyone. It just wasn't in her nature. She was a caring person. She worked as a caregiver, for heaven's sake!"

There's a muttering from somewhere and everyone turns towards Will.

"Sorry," he says, looking embarrassed. "I was just saying to Christiana that having the word 'care' in a job title is not necessarily indicative of a caring nature."

"I agree," says the Welshman. "That's like saying all fishermen only eat fish."

"Hmmm, I'm not sure it is like saying that," says Will, furiously scribbling in his notebook.

"I've got one!" says Christiana excitedly. "It's like saying a composer is always composed."

"Yes! That's it," says Will.

"I think we're veering off course a little now," says Star. "So, Helen, you were talking about your perceptions of your sister."

"They're not just my perceptions," says Helen too quickly, exposing her anger. "That's how Jemma was. She cared for people. She wouldn't hurt anybody."

"But how do you know that?" asks the Welshman. "You said yourself that you hadn't seen much of Jemma over the last few years. How well did you really know her?"

"She was my sister!" says Helen, so loudly it makes Will jump and drop his pencil. "You lot only knew her for a couple of weeks. I was there when her first tooth fell out, I plaited her hair every day before school, tied it with red ribbons. Red was her favorite color. I cried with her when our dog died, comforted her when she got her heart broken for the first time. No, she wasn't always crazy. The Jemma I knew was strong and funny and kind. I knew her like only a sister can and that's why I know she wasn't capable of murder."

If life was a film, we'd all sit chastised at this point, guiltily regretting all those cruel misconceptions about Jemma. But life isn't a film and in the real world people listen carefully to rhetoric but are rarely persuaded to change their minds.

"That's all well and good," says the Welshman without emotion, "and of course your loyalties lie with your sister. But don't forget, we knew Florence. She was a lovely lady with a lifetime of experiences. I've no doubt she had her hair plaited and lost teeth too."

"I don't think coming here was a good idea," says Helen, collecting tissue balls and dropping them into her bag. "I wanted to understand more about my sister's last few weeks, but I don't think I'm going to learn anything here."

"Well, as you yourself said, only a few moments ago," says Will, referring to the previous page of his notebook, "we hardly knew Jemma at all. I'm not sure any of us is able to tell you what you need to know."

"One of us might," says Christiana, leaning back in her chair as I register the shift inside my body. Adrenaline is kicking in. I'm on red alert. "Isn't that right, Claire?"

"What do you mean?" The heron is confused.

"Claire spent much more time with your sister than the rest of us did," says Christiana. "Jemma visited her at home a couple of times. They were friends."

Everyone is staring and now that Helen is facing me, I can see the family resemblance. She's more attractive than Jemma despite her nose being slightly too big and pointed for her face, beak-like. Her small, dark eyes are darting this way and that as she attempts to get her thoughts into order.

"What did you talk about? Did she seem depressed? Did she say anything about our family? Please, I'm begging you. Please tell me what you know."

I watch her mouth twitching, firing out question after question, and close my mind off to the noise. Why are ordinary people so revoltingly needy? Life is so easy for them, yet still they find reason to complain. No wonder I'm constantly disgusted. How do they think I cope? All I want is to be left alone in the shadows. Not sitting here, with people looking at me, demanding answers.

"Grief." The word comes from somewhere deep inside. Even I'm surprised when I say it.

"Sorry, what?" asks Helen.

"That's what we talked about. I'm grieving for my father. Jemma told me that she was grieving for her mother. I had no reason not to believe her. I don't understand why anyone would lie about that."

"Neither do I," says Helen. "It's so completely out of character for Jemma."

"I'm no expert," I say, glancing towards the person who supposedly is, "but if you want my advice, I'd stop focusing on the person Jemma was when she died and concentrate on the person you knew. You're lucky to have so many wonderful memories of your sister. I'd use them to help you work through your grief."

"Good, good. This has been very rich, very rewarding," says Star. "I hope you've found this helpful, Helen."

"No, not really," she replies. "I still don't know—"

"I'm sorry," says Star, raising her hand to indicate silence, "but we really need to move on now. Right," she says, sitting up straight, "I think this is the perfect time for a brief meditation, so I'd like to invite you all to close your eyes and take a couple of deep breaths."

I lower my gaze and listen to Star's voice. By the time she starts talking about buses I'm aware of Helen gathering her things.

"This is a load of bollocks," Helen says, marching towards the door, a trail of tissue balls left in her wake.

Star acts as though nothing has happened, invites us all to return our attention to the next breath and the one after that.

When I hear a car revving up outside, I open my eyes and look towards the window. A red Mercedes is pulling out of the car park, and I don't need twenty-twenty vision to read the sticker in the back window. As the car drives away, I lower my gaze once again but not before I register the unwanted interest. The eyes flicking away can't conceal the knowledge held behind them—the instinct that something about me isn't right.

Angels are watching. And they're not the only ones.

14

She's waiting at the end of the road to swoop. Of course she is. People like her don't give up that easily. The passenger door of the red Mercedes swings open as I approach.

"Claire! Please talk to me. I'm going out of my mind trying to work out what happened. Please, I'm desperate."

I peer into the car. The heron is sitting at the wheel leaning across the passenger seat. She must have been sitting here for ages, waiting for the meeting to end. The skin on her long neck is pulled tight; I can see a vein twitching near the surface. She's shading her eyes against the sun. The light is unflattering. I can see the area of skin near her jawline where her foundation hasn't been blended properly. Mascara and eyeliner look as though they've been applied in a hurry. She certainly *looks* desperate. A woman in need of a face mask and a few early nights. She brushes her hand briefly across her eyes and I revise my appraisal. Maybe it's the mascara-stained crow's feet or the shaking hand but something about Helen tells me she needs more than sleep and an improved skin-care routine. This is a woman on the edge. I'm marginally intrigued.

"Please, Claire," she repeats. "I really need to talk to somebody who spent time with Jemma before she died. They all seem so odd in that group," she adds, disapproval now added to an already weighty frown, "apart from you. You seem like the only normal person there." Either the heron is an appalling judge of character or Welshman and co. really need to rethink their public personas. "Let me buy you a coffee. Just twenty minutes of your time, that's all I ask."

Twenty minutes. That's an interesting figure. Must be an ordinary person's estimation of how long it takes to fathom the unfathomable. Seems a highly unrealistic estimation to me, especially factoring in all the unknowns. Where are we going to have this coffee? Are we going to walk there? Drive? Does the clock start ticking as soon as we head off? Or only after the first sip of coffee? And what happens once the twenty minutes are up? Can I leave straightaway regardless of how much coffee is drunk or do I have to wait until the mugs are empty? Taking encouragement from my silence, Helen pats the passenger seat.

"Please get in," she says, "I don't know this area at all. You can direct me to the nearest coffee shop." She smiles. "Don't worry, I'm not a serial killer."

Returning the smile, I get in the car and wonder how many serial killers in the history of serial killing have used that line. I might try it.

We drive into the town center, and I direct Helen to a car park. She pays and I glance at the ticket. Two hours. That's how long she really thinks it will take to fathom the unfathomable. We walk to a coffee shop and as we pass the town's war memorial, I notice Helen study it for a moment before bowing her head.

A sign of respect? Genuine or for my benefit? Queuing at the counter in silence, scones, flapjacks and cookies compete for my attention but it's the cakes that remind me I've forgotten to eat today. Each oversized slice is priced at eight pounds. Helen asks whether I want anything to eat. A slice of chocolate cake. That's what I really want. But I'm mindful of the fact that I killed this woman's sister fairly recently and the cake is ridiculously overpriced. So, I order a shortbread biscuit instead. Feels like the decent thing to do.

We sit at a table in the corner and the heron runs her finger around the rim of her coffee cup for a while before speaking. Her words, when they come, have been given some thought.

"First of all, Claire," she says, keeping her eyes fixed on the table, "I just want to thank you for agreeing to come. Secondly," she says, flicking her eyes up to meet mine, "I want to tell you how sorry I am for your loss. I really don't want to add to your distress. I hope you believe me when I say that."

I bite into my biscuit and silently count down the seconds of inevitability until her next word.

"But," she says as I knew she would, "the thing is, I'm at a complete loss trying to understand why Jemma did what she did. Anything you can tell me would be a great help."

She pauses and takes a sip of coffee. I think she wants me to start talking but I'm content to listen. Besides, I'm enjoying the shortbread far more than I expected.

"I went to Jemma's workplace the other day," she says. "Jemma worked in a care home. I spoke to the manager and a few of Jemma's colleagues. They were friendly enough, don't get me wrong . . . well, all except the manager. She wasn't very friendly at all, to be honest. I got the impression she didn't want me talking to the others."

She pauses again and takes another sip of coffee. Swallows too much, coughs then grimaces. That last sip probably burnt the roof of her mouth but still she raises the cup to her lips to take another. I sit perfectly still and watch her in silence. Stillness and silence. The most underrated weapons in any given armory. People will do anything to avoid the discomfort created by stillness and silence. Gulp their coffee, burn their mouths. Reveal everything they know. And suddenly I'm interested to know what the heron knows. Because if she spoke to all the staff in the care home, she would have spoken to authentic Ben. Did he mention someone from the bereavement group showing up to visit Kathleen? Does the heron know more than she's letting on? Does she already know I'm involved somehow? Is that the real reason for this coffee and biscuit? Maybe I should have asked for that cake.

"In particular, I wanted to know about Jemma's relationship with Lucas Kane," she says. "I don't know whether you've read about it in the newspapers, but Jemma is being linked to his disappearance."

More silence. More stillness.

"Jemma cared for his mother in the home," she continues. "That's where she met Lucas. I asked her colleagues whether anyone had noticed anything odd about their relationship, but nobody had, not really. One guy mentioned that Jemma always seemed keen to spend time with Lucas and his mum, volunteering to accompany them on day trips and so forth. But he stressed that there was nothing strange about that. I mean, it was Jemma's job after all. It just made me wonder . . ." She pauses and runs her finger around the rim of her coffee cup again. "It just made me wonder whether there was anything more between Lucas and Jemma. Whether they had become friends." She moves the cup to her lips and stares at me. "Or lovers," she adds.

I know she's waiting for me to confirm or deny her suspicions, but I stay silent and register her irritation.

"Did Jemma ever mention Lucas to you?" she asks, and I know I'm going to have to answer. It's a direct question after all and the rules of direct questions are clear. One-word answers are permitted but there will be no moving on until an answer is supplied.

"No," I reply.

"Are you sure?"

"Yes."

"So, she never mentioned Lucas Kane to you?"

"No," I repeat.

"Did she ever mention his mother?"

"No."

"Did Jemma ever talk about her work? What she did for a living?"

"No," I reply, wondering vaguely why the heron felt the need to clarify the definition of work.

"I'm sorry, Claire," she says, although I don't think she is, "I just don't understand what you and my sister talked about."

It isn't direct, not even a question, but I need this to end. The truth is, I'm bored. Really bored and have been ever since I finished the biscuit. It's quite clear the heron doesn't know anything about me, I don't think she knows anything at all. This has become very dull very quickly and I can't wait to get home to my painting. Ever since I started hunting Deb and Vampire Smoker, I've been able to focus on it again. Another coastal scene—acrylic on canvas with an effortless fluidity to the water that looks really good. Funny how I always work better when I'm planning to kill someone.

"I'm sorry, Helen," I say, reflecting her insincerity with my own, "but as I mentioned to you in the meeting, Jemma and I talked about our grief."

"That's all? Are you sure my sister never mentioned Lucas Kane?"

"She never mentioned him."

"OK," says the heron, placing both hands palm down on the table. She's silent for a moment, trying to collect her thoughts. Desperate to control her frustration.

"How did Jemma seem," she asks, "when you spoke to her?"

"What do you mean?"

"Did she seem happy? Sad? Excited?"

I think about two women talking about grief. See them in my mind, imagine how they would feel.

"She seemed sad," I say.

"All the time?" asks Helen. "Did she seem depressed? Or lonely?" she adds, before I have a chance to reply. "Did Jemma seem lonely, or did you get the impression that she was in a relationship?"

I wait for the talking to come to a definite stop and think about this relentless need for information. What's the driving force behind it, I wonder. Guilt, perhaps? Nosiness? Boredom? Maybe it's the heron who is lonely and depressed. She's looking at me in silence and I realize I'm supposed to respond.

"Helen, can I be honest with you?" I ask, as I often do when I'm still trying to decide what to say.

"Yes," she replies as I knew she would. No ordinary person has ever answered that question in the negative.

"I don't want to upset you and I hope you don't take this the wrong way but Jemma, she seemed to me to be rather . . ."

"Yes?" she prompts, perched on the edge of her chair, eager to devour any scrap of information I chuck her way.

"Unhinged," I say.

"Unhinged," she repeats, exploring the word in her mouth. "Unhinged," she says again, staring off into the distance, contemplating this one word as though it holds the key to unlocking the secrets of the universe.

"In what way?" she asks, returning her focus to me.

"Well," I begin, shuffling in my chair and flicking my eyes around the room, mimicking all the awkward reactions I've seen Welshman deploy every time Star mentions meditation.

"It's OK, Claire," soothes the heron. "Nothing you say can make me feel any worse than I already do. I just want to know the truth."

"OK," I say, sitting more upright in my chair, pretending that any of this matters. "To me, Jemma always looked a little . . ."

"Yes?"

"Odd," I decide to say.

"Odd? In what way?"

"The clothes she wore," I say. "They were quite unusual."

"Yes, well, that was Jemma," smiles the heron. "She always had her own unique sense of style."

"Really?" I ask.

"Oh yes," she says. "I remember when she was at sixth form college, Jemma went through a stage of matching full goth makeup with paisley shirts and jodhpurs!"

The heron is smiling at the memory and I'm beginning to feel sick. I'd assumed Jemma's appalling dress sense was part of the fake victim act. The realization that she liked wearing open-toe sandals with tracksuits is rather upsetting.

"When I look back now," says Helen, "and think about some of her outfit choices, it's surprising our parents ever let her leave the house!"

Yes, that is surprising. Almost as surprising as the fact Jemma survived long enough to graduate to the wellies/kilt-wearing stage of her life. I can't have been the first person who wanted to kill her. The heron is smiling at something above my head, and I've got a horrible feeling she's reminiscing. If there's even the slightest chance of her sharing more of Jemma's crimes against fashion, I need to jolt her out of memory and back to now.

"I guess Jemma's 'unique sense of style' combined with the frequent emotional outbursts," I say, "led to her appearing . . ."

"Unhinged," Helen says quietly, completing my sentence.

"Yes."

With that she slumps forward in the chair, lowers her face into her hands and sobs. Mission accomplished. Sad heron is back in the room.

"There's just so many unanswered questions," she says, wiping her eyes then running a hand through her hair. Her roots are gray. And greasy. She needs highlights. And a hair wash.

"Firstly, why was Jemma traveling so far from where she lived to attend a bereavement group? Secondly . . ." She's counting the questions on her fingers, her nails are bitten and stained with remnants of dark red nail polish. Reminds me of something. "Why was Jemma attending a bereavement group anyway? Why was she pretending Mum had died?"

What do her nails remind me of? It's irritating that I can't remember.

"Why did Jemma spend so long talking about grief when she wasn't grieving?" she continues. "Thirdly, I know that she met Lucas Kane at the care home but what kind of relationship did they have? Why did she have his briefcase? And why did she take it to Florence's house that night?"

Florence's dress! The one hanging in the middle. I'm sure it was salmon-colored. Speckled with Jemma's blood. That's what I'm reminded of when I look at Helen's nails.

"And where is Lucas?" she asks, sitting up in the chair. "He's been missing for weeks by all accounts. If Jemma did something to him, where's the body? If Jemma knew she was going to kill herself, why leave the briefcase at the scene but no note explaining his whereabouts? It doesn't make sense. And fourthly, why did she kill Florence?"

Fourthly? I lost count and interest a while ago but I'm sure there's been more than four unanswered questions.

"I'm sorry I can't answer any of your questions, Helen," I say, keen to bring this to an end. "None of it makes sense to me either. The Jemma I met was a woman torn up by grief. When I found out that grief wasn't real, it crossed my mind that maybe the woman I met had been suffering some kind of . . ."

Funny turn? Too glib.

Psychotic episode? Too extreme.

"Nervous breakdown," I decide.

"That crossed my mind too. Of course it did," she says, somewhat aggressively. "But when I spoke to the care home manager, she told me Jemma had always been a conscientious employee right up until the day of her death. Never turned up late for a shift, never took any time off sick. She certainly didn't appear to be having a nervous breakdown. I don't know," she says, slumping forward once again in the chair. "Is it possible that a person can present an image to the world that is so completely at odds with who they truly are?"

Yep.

She's staring at something on the floor and appears lost in thought. I do the same. The rules of rhetorical questions are fairly relaxed. Silent pondering is well within the accepted parameters of responses.

When she sits upright and meets my eye, she seems more determined.

"Maybe Lucas's colleagues can shed some light," she says. "I'm meeting some of them tomorrow."

"I hope so," I reply, wondering again where this drive for information comes from. Doesn't the heron work? Doesn't she have a family, kids? Why does she have all this time to peck through the remains of this mystery? Why does she want to?

She retrieves a notebook from her bag and opens it on a page of writing. Her handwriting is neat and well-spaced—easy to read upside down. She's underlined the title, *Jemma's colleagues*, and written the names in a list. I read *Deb (manager)*, *Ben*, *Linda*, *Tim* and *Gary* before she speaks again.

"Claire, can I give you my phone number?" she asks, already writing it down. "If anything else occurs to you, anything at all, please don't hesitate to contact me."

"Of course," I say, wondering whether Vampire Smoker is called Tim or Gary.

"I feel so bad about losing contact with Jemma," she says as I try to decide which name suits him best. "I keep wondering why I never picked up the phone. Four years went by and in all that time I never reached out to her. Why didn't I pick up the phone?"

Another rhetorical question. More time for silent pondering during which I decide Vampire Smoker looks more like a Gary, which probably means his name is Tim.

"It wasn't even a big argument," she's saying now. "The reason why we fell out."

She's looking at me. Is she expecting a response? Does she think I care?

"This has been so nice," she says, forcing her mouth into an awkward smile. "Spending time with someone who knew Jemma before her death. I don't suppose we could meet again, could we?"

Why, heron? What's the point? You've sat here for ages with me and learned nothing. One split second of mental calculation later and she's passing me her notebook. I agree to meet up with her again because agreeing to another pointless meeting means that this pointless meeting will end. I turn the page of her notebook to write my phone number and read more of her neat, well-spaced handwriting. Tomorrow's date is written at the top and then there's the underlined title, *Lucas's colleagues*. She's so organized, the page is already prepared—ready and waiting for a new list of names. I wonder whether any of those names will provide answers to her long list of questions; whether this time tomorrow she'll be any closer to the truth. I think about what I'm like when I'm working on something—the lengths I will go to, the understanding that the thing is not done until it is done. I hand the notebook back and register something new. Not with her. With me. Practically imperceptible but I know it's there. Unease.

We stand to put on our coats, and she offers to drive me home. I thank her but decline, telling her that the walk will do me good. She smiles and compliments me on my figure—tells me I don't need any exercise, pats her rounded stomach and says she wishes she was so lovely and slim.

We walk out into the street and I catch sight of our reflections in the shop window. She's there, my mother, lovely and slim—her eyes, her hair, her cheekbones. Helen's staring at herself now, wiping the skin under each eye, saying she looks like she's aged two decades in the last two weeks. I think about her need for a face mask, hair wash, highlights, manicure, diet and a few early nights and tell her I think she looks great. Packaging the words in my mother's insincere smile.

We say goodbye and then she turns to head back towards the car park. Back to her red Mercedes and unanswered questions and new life as an only child. I watch her drive away and will her to get on with that life. Silently plead with her to leave all of this alone.

Curiosity killed the cat. It will make mincemeat out of a heron.

THEN

The meaty stench from downstairs is so bad, it almost distracts her from her writing. Almost. She's six years old today, creating her best story ever and the little girl can't wait for her father to read it. All she has left to write is the ending. It won't be happy because happy endings don't exist, but it will be the perfect ending for this story. A cat the color of honey emerges from its favorite sleeping place under her bed and jumps up next to her. The little girl strokes the cat's head.

"Honey! Get out of her bedroom," shouts the woman who has just appeared at the bedroom door. The cat ignores her. So does the little girl.

"Honey! Come here to Mama," the woman says now, walking into the room and lifting the cat up from the bed. "Look at you," she says, gazing down at the cat in her arms, "Mama's perfect little girl. Mama loves you so much, Honey. Mama's best little girl."

The little girl continues to write and doesn't look up until the woman says her name.

"Claire, come downstairs. I need your help in the kitchen."

The little girl puts her story and pencil to one side and follows the woman down the stairs. In the kitchen, there's a large pot bubbling on the stove and a thickening of the disgusting, meaty smell.

"Claire, I'm cooking a special meal for your birthday," says the woman. "You can help me by chopping the meat."

"You're cooking?" says the little girl. "You never cook."

"Well, I'm cooking today," says the woman, slapping a pile of red, slimy meat onto a chopping board.

"What's that?" asks the child, wrinkling up her nose. The meat smells rotten. It smells like death.

"Liver," says the woman with a smile. "I'm cooking you a birthday liver stew."

"Daddy said he was going to take us out for dinner," says the little girl.

"Well, now he doesn't have to, does he?" says the woman. "Now he can save his money and have more to spend on me. You should see all the things he buys me, Claire. Ever since he got promoted, he's always buying me lovely little gifts. Expensive bubble bath, perfume, lingerie. And when we move into the new house, he'll buy me even more things to fill all that extra space. That's why he's always working," she says, smiling. "So he has more money to spend on me."

Still smiling, she points towards the chopping board.

"The meat is quite gristly, so it might take a while to chop," she says. "You'd better make a start. I'm going for a bath. Oh no, Honey!" she smiles as the cat starts to meow. "Don't worry, this isn't for you. This is all for Claire. A special birthday treat."

The woman leaves the kitchen and when she returns, she's wearing a short black satin nightdress and her hair is wrapped up in a towel.

"Right, Claire," she says, "put the meat in the pot and give it a good stir."

The front door opens and suddenly he's there.

"Hello, Claire," he says. "Happy birthday. Sorry I'm late. What the hell is that smell?"

"Mummy's cooking," says the little girl.

"Cooking what, exactly?" asks the man, peering into the pot.

"Liver," says the woman. "I'm making Claire a liver stew."

"I said I'd take us all out for dinner tonight," says the man, turning away from the stove.

"Well, now you have more time to spend doing other things," says the woman, putting both arms around the man's neck and pulling his mouth towards hers. "With me. Upstairs."

They kiss for a moment before the man pulls away.

"We shouldn't be doing this in front of Claire," he whispers, glancing towards the little girl. "It's her birthday. I want to spend time with her."

"Later," says the woman, leading him from the kitchen.

"Daddy, can I read you my story?" asks the little girl. "It's my best story ever."

He looks from his daughter to his wife and back to his daughter.

"Of course, Claire," he says, "I'm just going to spend a little time with Mummy and then you can read me your story. You can read it to both of us."

"I don't think Mummy will understand my story," says the little girl, turning back towards the stove. "It's got big words."

"Keep stirring the stew, Claire," says the woman with a smile, leading the man away.

After a while, the woman reappears in the kitchen. She's still wearing the short nightdress, but the towel is in her hands now, no longer wrapped on her head. Approaching the stove, she pushes the little girl out of the way.

"Right, I just need to add the finishing touches," she says.

The little girl runs up to her bedroom to find her story but it's not there. She searches the bed, under the bed, everywhere.

Running back to the kitchen, she watches the woman ladle stew into a bowl.

"What have you done with my story?" she asks.

"What would I want with your stupid story?" says the woman. "Sit down and eat the meal I made for you."

The man reappears in the kitchen now and the woman turns towards him with a smile.

"Why don't you pour yourself a glass of whisky and me a glass of wine?" she says to him. "We'll eat something else later on. I made this just for Claire."

The man turns away to pour the drinks and the woman watches closely as the little girl swallows her first mouthful of stew.

"Eat it slowly, Claire," the woman says, smiling. "You don't want to choke on all those big words of yours."

The little girl stares at the woman and continues to chew.

When the man places the drinks on the table, he watches his daughter for a moment before speaking.

"She can't have that," he says. "It smells rancid. Claire, stop eating it."

"I want to eat it, Daddy," smiles the little girl, moving another spoonful towards her mouth. "It's delicious. It tastes sweet," she says, flicking her eyes towards her mother. "It tastes just like honey."

The woman stops smiling. And then the shouting starts.

"Where's my cat?" she screams, looking under the kitchen table. "Honey! Honey! Where are you? Stop eating that!" she hollers, hitting the child's hand, propelling the spoon across the room. "What have you done with my cat?" she screams. "Oh my God, she's put my cat in the stew. What did you do?" she shouts, shaking the child. "What did you do with my cat?"

"Calm down!" says the man, moving the woman away from the girl. "What are you talking about? Of course Claire hasn't put the cat in the stew. What's wrong with you? You sound mad."

"She's the mad one!" shouts the woman, pointing towards the little girl.

"She's evil. Pure evil. Just like your mother. Don't you see?" she pleads, desperate now. "She's got that darkness in her too. Don't you see it? Why can't you see it? Honey! Honey! Oh my God. She's killed my cat. I see it in her eyes."

"What are you talking about?" says the man again. "She's a child. An innocent six-year-old child. Our child."

"You ask her!" screams the woman. "Ask her what she's done with my cat!"

"This is insane," says the man. "Claire, did you put the cat in the stew?"

"No, Daddy. I didn't," says the little girl. "Can I have my cake now?"

"No, you can't!" shouts the woman. "Get up to your room. You evil little bitch. Honey! Honey! Where are you? I can't bear it," she cries, peering into the pot on the stove. "My poor baby."

"Honey is far more likely to be outside in the garden than in that pot," says the man. "And you shouldn't speak to Claire like that."

The woman races outside then, and the man turns towards his daughter. "Best go up to your room for a while, Claire," he says. "Just until Mummy calms down."

The little girl jumps down from the table and runs upstairs to her bedroom. From the window she looks down into the garden below. The woman is on her hands and knees peering under a bush, calling for the cat. Her short black nightdress has ridden up and the boys from next door are standing at the fence, laughing and jeering. The woman is crying and shouting the cat's name, over and over again. The boys from next door mimic her panicked, desperate voice and laugh even louder.

The woman wades into the stinging nettles at the end of the garden. The man tries to stop her, but the woman brushes him away.

The little girl smiles and moves away from the window. Sitting on her *bed, she snuggles up with her favorite toy, Bambi, gets a fresh sheet of paper and starts to write. This new story will be good. Maybe even better than the last one. A cat the color of honey emerges from its favorite sleeping place under the bed and jumps up next to her. The little girl strokes the cat's head and listens to it purr as she thinks about her new story. Maybe this one will have a happy ending. Maybe they do exist.*

15

There's a memory book in Kathleen's room that's always left on the coffee table but doesn't look out of place. Books out of bookcases can so often take on the appearance of clutter, like those novels and puzzle books stacked messily on the floor by the armchair—finished, discarded, forgotten by the reader. But this book is ornate, with a padded cover and tissue paper dividing each page, each photo and page of typed text inserted with precision and care. Black-and-white photographs depict the young Kathleen sitting on a horse, sparkly eyes, toothy grin and jodhpurs, not a care in the world. She's playing in a manicured garden in another photo and standing next to her parents in a room similar to this one in another. Her father epitomizes dignity, looking so proud of his glamorous wife and immaculate daughter. Everything in each image is styled to perfection—their hair, their clothes, even the Labrador. I turn the page and wonder how perfect their world really was.

The young Kathleen wore her long blonde curls in plaits, had it cut into a short bob as a teenager and woven with flowers as a bride. Her decision to marry a younger version of her father must have pleased her parents no end. I stare at photographs of her wedding day and imagine Kathleen's father and new husband retiring to a quiet room to drink port. I can see it so clearly in my mind—two handsome, knowledgeable ambassadors of decency, smoking cigars and discussing important matters of the day. They look like the kind of men who always wore suits, always held doors open for ladies and never, ever swore in front of one. Well, that's what they look like. The truth, of course, may have been very different. For all I know, Kathleen's father and husband may have been alcoholic, drug-addicted womanizers who beat their wives the moment the camera was put away. After all, ordinary people have always enjoyed projecting phony images of themselves into the world. It's one of the few quirks that makes them interesting.

I've always been fascinated by this particular aspect of human nature—the insatiable need to be envied and admired. Every day, millions of ordinary people become locked in a relentless battle to accumulate "likes" on social media, never stopping long enough to question whether they still like the person they're pretending to be. We have evolved to the point where the truth is no longer an inconvenience, it's irrelevant. Ever since the invention of the camera, people have rejected their authentic selves to project a false image, and that's why I can look through the photographs in Kathleen's memory book but still have no idea what her life was really like.

I stare at her now, sleeping soundly in her warm, comfortable bed. She looks so small and fragile. And sane. I wonder whether madness encroaches into her dreams or whether sleep remains her last refuge. I close the book, return it to the coffee table and hope that her husband and father were as gentlemanly as their photos suggest. I hope for Kathleen's sake that the life she can no longer remember was a happy one.

The door is pushed open and in walks authentic Ben. He checks on Kathleen first and then smiles at me. This is a man with his priorities in order and moral compass ever ready. How on earth does he survive living amongst all the fakes?

"Hello, Claire," he says. "How are you on this beautiful day?"

Is it beautiful? I can't say I'd noticed.

"I'm very well, thank you, Ben," I reply. "How are you?"

"I'm great, thanks," he says. "Well, emotionally speaking, I'm great. Top of the world as a matter of fact. Physically speaking, though? Not so good. I ran a half marathon yesterday. Got a load of sponsorship for the Alzheimer's Society, which is fantastic, and the atmosphere was absolutely electric. But my word, it was a beast of a course. I've never seen so many hills! I had an ice bath as soon as I got home, but my legs are so sore today and I think I've got more blisters on my feet than toes!"

I'm staring and listening and wondering how a three-word question can elicit such a lengthy response when I realize he's waiting for me to speak. The problem is I stopped listening as soon as he became boring, and I don't know what to say. Can't even think of a cliché. My eyes fall on the memory book, and I change the subject.

"I was just looking through Kathleen's photographs," I say. "It looks like she lived a very glamorous life."

"Yes," agrees Ben. "I think that's why her son was so keen on her moving here. He wanted her to live out her days in the style to which she was accustomed."

Ben's eyes cloud over for a moment, and I wonder why. The reference to Kathleen's missing, presumed dead son perhaps? Or simple recognition that style means nothing to those locked up behind the walls of insanity?

"Her son told me Kathleen spent time in a psychiatric ward before she came here," Ben continues. "He said he hated his mum being there and it was such a relief when she was able to leave."

Kathleen has started to stir, and Ben is at her side in an instant. I watch him pour out a glass of water from the jug and think about Lucas Kane. Who would have thought Lucas and I had anything in common? Now that I know about our mutual hatred of psychiatric wards, I can't help but warm to him a little. Beneath all the blackmailing, arrogance and inability to click on the correct email address, he probably wasn't a bad person. Just a loving son trying to do the best for his mum. I think about his dismembered body parts rotting in my garden. I might move them later and bury them somewhere else. Somewhere nicer. With a better view. Underneath a big tree perhaps? Or by a lake? I wonder which he'd prefer.

Kathleen is fully awake now and fretting about the doll. I tell Ben I'll wait in the sitting room while he gets her dressed. Vampire Smoker is in the corridor, accompanying an elderly lady— could be Janet but I think it's Edith. He's stifling a yawn. I'm not surprised he's tired because I'm tired too. I followed him home last night to find out where he lives and then stayed up until one thirty this morning watching him through a gap in the yellowing curtains of his living room window. Playing *Call of Duty* for hours and endlessly reaching for cigarettes, Vampire Smoker leads the most unbelievably dull life. Fortunately, his death will be anything but.

Miranda is stooped over in front of the TV in the sitting room when I walk in, furiously stabbing at buttons on the remote control. She jumps when she sees me and looks afraid. Then she smiles.

"Hi, Claire, thank goodness it's only you. I know I shouldn't be doing this . . . Deb has made it quite clear that the TV is for residents only but there's no one in here and I thought that a bit of *Peppa Pig* might calm Oscar down. Well, for a couple of minutes at least!"

I have no idea what this woman is talking about but, as it seems to involve a frenzied search through TV channels, I leave her to it and allow my attention to be drawn to the window. One of the thick red velvet curtains is moving. Something is behind it. Then I see him. Oscar the child is balancing on his toes on the windowsill. He appears to want to climb out of the open window and he seems quite determined. I remember reading somewhere that small children, unlike adults, can bounce after falling from a great height. Something to do with them being more relaxed when they're in the air. I wonder whether Oscar will bounce if he gets out that window. I don't think he will. This room is on the third floor. I don't think it matters how relaxed he is. I don't think there'll be any bouncing. I think he'll splatter all over the ground of the sun terrace below.

Miranda is still focused on the TV, still trying to find something interesting to watch. If Oscar gets out that window, I'll have something *really* interesting to watch. His fingers have reached the edge of the window now and he's pulling himself up. He's surprisingly strong for a small, chubby person. After he splatters on the ground, there will be sirens and wailing and question after question. With their skewed idea of justice, the ordinary people who investigate his death will investigate me. Even though none of this is my fault. I'm not forcing Oscar to climb out the window just as I'm not forcing his mother to be distracted by the TV. It's not fair but I don't need the aggravation of a child's death right now. I've got bigger plans. Oscar's flying lesson will have to wait.

"Miranda?"

"Yes?"

"I think Oscar might be doing something a bit dangerous."

"What? Oh my God! Oscar! What are you doing? How on earth did you get up there?"

Oscar is swept away from the window and cocooned in his mother's arms within a second. He doesn't look happy about it at all. His little arms reach out towards the window, and he screams like someone having their skin peeled off. Which is a very specific type of scream and one I haven't heard often, probably because I only like to peel the skin off queue-jumpers and not many people push in front of me. There *was* a woman in the post office a few years ago, though. Very impatient. Said she was too "busy busy busy" to wait in the queue and went right to the front. Very rude.

I hold my breath. Oscar smells. He smells really bad. Actually, he smells like Busy Busy Busy having her skin peeled off. Miranda sits on the sofa with her wriggling, stinking, screaming son and holds him close. How can she bear to be so close to that smell? Then she picks up the remote control again and after a few seconds a cartoon pig wearing a red dress appears on the screen. The pig is wearing yellow wellies and jumping in muddy puddles with another pig. Oscar forgets his devastation and points at the TV in delight. Then he hops off his mother's lap and starts jumping like the pigs. I watch the pigs who are now rolling around in the puddles. Then I watch Oscar who is now rolling around on the floor. Then I watch Miranda who is watching her son and smiling inanely. Then I look back to the open window. If only Oscar had been quicker and managed to climb out, this ridiculous scene could have been completely avoided.

Ben appears at the door of the sitting room with Frank at his side and Kathleen in a wheelchair.

"Here we all are," he declares happily. "Shall we get going?"

"I'm so sorry, Ben," says Miranda. "I need to change Oscar's nappy before we go. I'll meet you back here in five minutes."

With that she gets up from the sofa and tries to persuade her son to stop rolling around on the floor. From what I've seen of Oscar today, I don't think this is going to go well. Sure enough, he brushes his mother's hand away while keeping his eyes locked on the preposterous, pretend pigs.

Ben looks over his shoulder. "Miranda," he whispers, "why don't you change Oscar in here? The TV will keep him entertained."

"No, I better not," says Miranda, attempting to scoop Oscar off the floor. "Deb wouldn't be happy if she found out."

"Deb's in a meeting and no one here is going to tell her," he says, glancing towards me.

"My lips are sealed," I say with a smile, wondering whether ordinary people seriously care about things like this. Who cares where you change the stinking nappy? Just change the stinking nappy so we can all breathe through our noses again.

"Come on," says Ben, looking over his shoulder again, "there's no one around."

"No!" snaps Miranda. "I'll change my son in my father's bathroom." And with that she throws the changing bag over her shoulder, hauls the shrieking Oscar out of the room and disappears.

After a few moments, the screams disappear too. Sadly, the stench lingers. After that Frank takes a seat in the armchair facing the TV. The two pigs are now in a classroom, sitting at desks and being taught by a gazelle with a foreign accent. There's a sheep in the classroom too. And an elephant and a fox. Frank clears his throat and turns towards me.

"What the fuck is this shit on the television?" he asks.

I really like frank Frank.

Ben pushes Kathleen towards the sofa and then takes a seat. He grimaces slightly as he sits down. Those sore legs and blisters must be hurting.

"I wonder what's for lunch today," he says to no one in particular. Kathleen and Frank keep their eyes on the TV. I don't think they care about the lunch menu. Ben perseveres.

"It was chicken curry on Saturday. It smelled unbelievably good. That's the problem with having a dining room on this floor. The smell makes me permanently hungry!" He turns to me. "Did you know that the chef used to be the sous-chef at a Michelin-starred restaurant! So incredibly talented—it's unbelievable, the meals that come out of that kitchen. And such a perfectionist. Chef often comes up here to check everyone's enjoying the food, even though there's only one kitchen assistant to help."

There's a moment of silence before I realize Ben has stopped talking and is still facing me. The people with dementia are allowed to look bored and stare at the TV. I'm expected to respond.

"Too many cooks spoil the broth," I say.

"Yes!" He smiles. "You're so right."

Miranda appears in the doorway, and we all prepare to leave.

"Claire, would you mind pushing Kathleen?" asks Ben, as I move towards the door. "Miranda's got her hands full with Oscar and I need to keep an eye on Frank."

"Of course," I say, pushing the wheelchair out of the room.

Once in the corridor, I realize there's a problem. I'm not going to be able to push the wheelchair down the stairs. I'm going to have to take the lift. I hate lifts. I don't like anywhere without a window or a door that I can open at a moment of my choosing. In we all traipse—two old people, one tired-looking mum, one headstrong toddler, one achy half marathon runner and me. All trapped together in the same box in time. Ben presses a button, the doors close and Miranda clears her throat.

"I'm sorry if I sounded a bit snappy earlier," she says.

"When?" asks Ben. "I didn't notice you sounding snappy."

I'm beginning to lose a bit of respect for authentic Ben. Why is he lying? He knows she sounded snappy. Why isn't the lift moving? Is this normal? Maybe it has started moving. But why aren't the numbers on the display changing? It's still saying we're on the third floor. Ben pressed that button ages ago. Why hasn't it started to move? Does this lift actually work?

"It's just that Oscar isn't sleeping very well at the moment," says Miranda, "and sometimes I feel so tired, I get really irritable. I'm sorry."

The lift finally starts to move, and I watch the display. The number three morphs into the number two. Not long now.

"Have you been keeping your mummy up all night?" asks Ben in a ridiculously squeaky voice and Oscar starts to giggle.

"Yes, he has!" smiles Miranda. "He's such a cheeky little monkey!"

And with that she starts to tickle the writhing mass of child in her arms. Oscar's giggles accelerate into laughter, and he throws his arms above his head. Suddenly the lift stops. Too sudden. The number on the display flashes. The doors don't open.

"Oscar!" laughs Miranda. "I'm so sorry, everyone. I think Oscar accidentally hit the stop button. Oscar! What are you doing? People don't want to spend the day in this lift with you."

"More tickle, Mummy!" Oscar shouts, kicking his foot against the control panel as an alarm sounds. The lift still doesn't move. "More tickle, Mummy!" he shouts even louder. If we get stuck in here and people start using my oxygen, I am definitely killing that kid first.

"Hello? Is everything OK?" A voice speaks through the control panel.

"Hi, Irina," says Ben. "Frank's grandson is being a cheeky little monkey and has managed to stop the lift and set off the alarm. Would you be able to get it moving again? It's a bit cozy in here!"

"Oh, right," says Irina. "I think I know how to do that. If not, I'll have to get Deb. Please bear with me."

The voice disappears and we all stand in silence. I close my eyes and take a deep breath. I need to stay calm. The lift will start moving in a moment and the doors will open. Irina the receptionist knows about our plight and is working on the solution. A sharp blade of panic slices into my heart. Who am I kidding? Irina is probably in front of a mirror troweling yet more foundation onto her face, her conversation with Ben already forgotten. I'm trying to breathe deeply but I keep thinking about the limited amount of air in this box. It feels very warm and I notice beads of sweat on Kathleen's forehead. She's whispering to the doll, oblivious to everything else. That poor woman is arguably half dead already. Killing her would be an act of kindness. And it would free up oxygen for other people.

"I'm so sorry about this, everyone." Miranda smiles. She doesn't look sorry. Why is she smiling?

"Don't be silly," says Ben, returning the smile. "It's not your fault. Just one of those things."

One of what things? What a stupid expression. It's not even a proper fucking cliché.

"Besides, it's adding a bit of excitement to our day, isn't it?" he continues. "We thought we were just going out for a walk. Little did we know fate had something far more interesting in mind!"

"Why don't you ever shut the fuck up?" asks Frank, verbalizing my exact thought.

"Dad!" shouts Miranda. "Don't be so rude. Sorry, Ben."

"It's OK, Miranda," says Ben. "Your dad is quite right. I do talk too much and sometimes I should learn to be quiet."

In the silence that follows, I stare at the flashing number on the display. Then I look at the windowless walls and the door I can't open. Panic has sliced my heart into two and is now dissecting those two halves into quarters . . . eighths . . . The pieces of heart are trying to pump oxygen to my cells but it's not working. My chest feels constricted. My skin is clammy and I'm nauseous. There's a pain in my head. The air in this box is running out. Somebody needs to stop breathing. And soon.

"I wonder what Deb will say if her meeting is interrupted and she has to come and rescue us," asks Miranda.

"I shouldn't imagine she'll be too happy about it," answers Ben, the faintest smile on his lips. "I shouldn't imagine she'll be too happy at all," he adds. That last sentence was completely unnecessary. Why did he say it? Why did he say anything? Whatever happened to learning to be quiet?

"Oh, I don't know," says Miranda. "I bet Deb will relish saving the day. I bet she's slipping into her superhero cloak and mask as we speak!"

And with that there's laughter. Huge oxygen-quaffing bellows of laughter bouncing off the windowless walls and the door I can't open. And I'm looking from Ben to Miranda and back to

Ben again and I know that the laughter is coming from them, but the sound is different now. It doesn't sound like laughter anymore. This sound is ominous, threatening. This is the sound of a key turning slowly, terrifyingly slowly inside an old rusty lock. I close my eyes and register the arrival of a migraine wrapped in a panic attack. Every neuron is swamped in pain and then the images emerge from somewhere deep inside my mind. I see a Michelin-starred sous-chef working in the care home kitchen. The knife in his hand hits the chopping board with precision, over and over again. He's cutting into a pile of red, slimy meat. The meat smells rotten. It smells like death. Where are you, Dad? Where have you gone? He's lying alone in the darkness. Inside a small, cold box in the ground. There's not enough air in here. Is this what it feels like to drown?

The lift starts to move and when the doors open, I push Kathleen out as fast as I can. I need to get outside. I need to lie down in the middle of a field and stare at the never-ending expanse of sky. I head towards the door, but I'm blocked by another never-ending expanse. Pumpkin-Head Deb is looking down at me and talking about the visitors' book. About how I need to sign myself and Kathleen out. She's wearing . . . oh, I don't know what she's wearing. It's long and orange and flowery and looks like something ABBA might have worn to win Eurovision. She's talking about fire regulations and the importance of health and safety rules and now she's turned her attention to Ben and is reminding him to change his shoes before going outside.

Through the swirling vision of my migraine, I sign the visitors' book and suddenly Deb is at my shoulder, explaining how visitors and residents are free to wear whatever shoes they like inside Waterbridge Oak, but staff must wear outdoor shoes outdoors and indoor shoes indoors. I'm pushing Kathleen towards the door and Deb is still talking to me. She's pointing out a staff changing room and when I see Ben pulling a pair of wellies out of a locker and onto his tired, blistered feet, I'm suddenly consumed with hatred for ordinary people and their ridiculous ways.

Deb's voice melts into the background as I think about massacring every last person in this place. I picture myself marching along each corridor—outdoor shoes on my feet, hammer clutched in my hand. And not a moment too soon, I push through the door and allow a wave of fresh air to engulf me. The hatred recedes. But it doesn't go far.

16

The man buried next to Dad certainly packed a lot into his sixty-five years on this earth. From the tributes, floral and otherwise, left on his grave, I know he was a dad, a grandad, a brother, a son, an uncle, a friend, a football supporter, a darts player and a lover of Guinness. I think Dad would approve. There are worse people you could lie next to for eternity. Dad's grave isn't as decorated as Mr. Charisma's but, since developing an unlikely interest in plants and flowers, I ensure it always looks neat and stylish. Today I note that the pansies are enduring well but the daffodils are not surviving the elements at all. How disappointing. Tidying the grave, I make a mental note never to buy daffodils again.

"I only put these roses here on Thursday. Look what the frost has done to them."

I turn and see an old man standing at a recently dug grave. He's holding a bunch of roses and pointing to the frost-covered petals, and I think I'm expected to care.

"She shouldn't be in the ground," he continues. "She only went into hospital with a cough. Three days later she was dead."

"I'm sorry for your loss," I say before turning back to the job at hand: the removal of battered daffodils from Dad's grave. I hear a shuffling noise and look up. Old man with the roses has made his way over and is looking at me.

"Young people like you, you don't understand grief," he says. "Not properly anyway. Me and my wife, we were married for sixty-seven years. Sixty-seven years!" he repeats, staring at me through tiny, pink-rimmed eyes.

I notice for the first time that his skin is tinged an unhealthy blue. It's not that cold today. Is that his natural coloring, or is he beginning to look ghostly? Should I kill him?

"Can you imagine being with someone every single day for sixty-seven years?" he asks, and his face is so close to mine, I can smell his breath. His teeth are yellow, and he definitely doesn't floss. I'm not sure whether he even brushes.

"Can you imagine waking up next to the same person every morning for sixty-seven years and then suddenly that person is gone?" he asks.

With breath like that he should forget about the roses and hang a medal on his wife's grave.

"Young people like you, you'll never understand what this grief is like," he says. Again. Hasn't he already said that?

I turn my back and continue pulling dead daffodils out of the ground. I can't be bothered to kill him. I can't even be bothered to think of a cliché. This is a graveyard, and the rules of grave-yards are quite simple. Everyone is expected to come and re-member their dead in silence. There is no need for interaction and there is certainly no need for competitive grieving.

"Excuse me, young lady, I'm talking to you!"

His voice is raised now and when I fail to respond, he grabs hold of my arm. Shrugging him off, I stand up slowly and turn to face him. I'm taller, younger and stronger but I know that's not why he stumbles backwards or why his facial expression shifts. I know that's not why he's suddenly wishing he had never ventured from his wife's grave.

"I'm sorry," he says, his voice lowered again. "I just miss her so much. I don't know what to do without her. I wish I was dead."

I know no one else is in the graveyard. I know his wife's grave was only recently dug. I know he's already looking fairly ghostly, and I know he wants to be dead. I know I'm still annoyed about the daffodils, and I know a kill will probably cheer me up. I also know this man is terrified. Not about dying. He's probably already dying. I know he's terrified because when I turned around and stared down at him, he looked into my eyes and saw it. The same cold empty nothing all the others saw. The very last thing any of them ever saw. I know I'm going to enjoy this old man's terror. I know I'm never going to want his terror to end.

My phone rings and the spell is broken. My phone hasn't rung since before Dad's funeral and, as I stand here now amongst all the tombstones, dead flowers and murderous intent, the ringtone is as unexpected as it is unwanted.

"Hello?" I say into my phone as the old man turns and shuffles away.

"Hi, Claire, it's Helen."

The heron.

"Hi, Helen, how are you?"

"I'm good, thanks, Claire. What are you up to? Are you free to talk for a minute?"

"Sure. I'm just at the cemetery visiting my dad's grave."

"Oh, I'm sorry, Claire. I can call you back later. I don't want to disturb your time with your dad."

"No, it's fine. He's not going anywhere."

"Oh right! No, I suppose not." There's nervous laughter on the other end of the line now and I imagine the heron pacing, brow furrowed, free hand pushing through greasy, unwashed hair.

"I just wondered if we could meet up again," she asks. "I found out some interesting information from Lucas's colleagues. You know, the people he worked with."

"Really?" I ask, surprised that the heron felt the need to clarify the definition of colleagues.

"Yes," she says, sounding excited. "It turns out Lucas was in fairly serious debt. He had a gambling problem by all accounts and owed a lot of money to a lot of people."

"Really?" I repeat. A gambling problem would certainly explain all the extracurricular blackmailing. Poor Lucas. Such a lost soul.

"Yes, I'm beginning to realize that there's much more to the disappearance of Lucas Kane than meets the eye. Quite a number of people probably wanted him dead."

"Do we know for sure that Lucas is dead?" I ask innocently. "Have they found his body?" I add, thinking about his makeshift grave in my back garden. I never got around to moving his body parts somewhere nicer. Maybe I'll do it later.

"No, not yet," she replies. "But he must be dead. I mean, he's been missing for ages. From my investigations . . ."

Investigations? The heron really needs to get a job.

"From my investigations," she repeats, "I've discovered that Lucas spent all his time at work, at the care home visiting his mother, at the casino or at the bookmaker's. He hasn't been seen at any of those places for weeks now. If he isn't dead, where is he?"

Work, care home, casino, bookmaker's. What a miserable existence. I don't think I'll bother moving his body parts. I think he'll be happy staying where he is.

"It's a mystery," I say, watching the old man shuffling into the distance. He's still holding the frost-covered roses.

"You've got that group meeting tomorrow, haven't you?" she asks. "Could we meet up afterwards again? I'm just so confused about everything," she adds before waiting for my reply. "Apart from the care home, I can't find any connection between Jemma and Lucas. So why did she have his briefcase with her? If you know you're going to shoot yourself in the head, why leave a three-word note? Why didn't she explain her reasons, tell us what happened to Lucas?"

"Maybe she didn't feel like writing very much."

"Maybe. Or maybe she didn't shoot herself. Maybe somebody else killed Florence, shot Jemma and then arranged the scene to make it look as though Jemma was responsible."

"Why would anybody do that?" I ask, watching the old man get into his car and drive away.

"To cover up the murder of Lucas Kane. Like I said, Lucas owed money to lots of people. Any one of them could have killed him and then framed Jemma for his murder."

"Why would they kill him if he owed them money? I mean, he's never going to pay anyone back if he's dead."

"Good point," says the heron and I can almost hear her thinking. "Well, maybe Lucas got into a fight with someone he owed money to and was killed by accident. And then the killer framed Jemma to cover it up."

"I don't know, Helen. It sounds a little far-fetched."

"I know. But no more far-fetched than Jemma suddenly becoming a mass murderer. Why would she kill Florence and Lucas? It doesn't make any sense."

I think you have to kill more than two people to be considered a mass murderer, but I let this go.

"I think it will help me get everything straight in my mind if I talk it through with someone. Claire, I know it's a lot to ask but would you mind meeting up again? I'll buy you coffee and a slice of that chocolate cake I saw you eyeing up last week!"

"Sure," I say. "I'll see you after the meeting tomorrow."

"Perfect. Thank you so much. I'll leave you in peace now. Sorry to have disturbed you."

"Sometimes it's good to be disturbed," I say and after a little more nervous laughter at the end of the line, we say our goodbyes and she is gone.

I finish clearing dead daffodils from Dad's grave, water the pansies and then walk away. When I get to the most recently dug graves, I pause. The woman who went into hospital with a cough and never came home was called Alice. It's far too early for a headstone so her grave is marked with a simple silver plaque on a simple wooden cross. Alice was born in 1938, which by my calculation means she got married to her foul-smelling husband when she was only eighteen years old. Poor Alice. Bending down, I gently lay the daffodils at the foot of the cross. At least she's finally getting some peace.

After that I walk to my car and as I approach, I see them. The frost-covered roses strewn all over the ground. There are waste bins all over the cemetery, but the old man decided to throw the flowers onto the ground, making it someone else's problem. I scoop up each rose and that's when it arrives. Anger. Stupid old blue man. No consideration for anyone else. I'm marching back towards the graves now with the anger escalating into rage. I've arrived at Alice's grave and I'm tearing the stems and the petals from each flower. Thorns are cutting into my fingers as I throw bloodstained, frost-covered pieces of dead flower onto her grave. And then I run towards the simple wooden cross, and I lift my foot behind me, and I kick it. And I kick again and again until the wood splinters.

And even though I'm kicking the cross that marks her grave, I know I'm not angry at Alice. I'm not even angry at her horrible blue husband. I'm angry because my facial expression never gives anything away, but the heron noticed me looking at the cakes. I'm angry because I underestimated her. I'm angry because, whether she knows it or not, she's on my trail. And with that I kick the cross again and the last piece of wood flies out of the earth and ricochets across the headstones. If only everything could so easily disappear.

t's the penultimate meeting of the bereavement group. By this stage we should be discussing acceptance, the fifth stage of grief, but for some reason we seem to be back on anger. Welshman is alarmingly robust and becoming more so with each passing moment.

"If a train driver made a mistake doing his job," he rants, "he would be sacked. If a gas engineer made a mistake doing his job, he would be sacked. If a bricklayer made a mistake doing his job, he would be sacked."

I turn towards Star who is sitting with her eyes closed and nodding. Is she seriously going to let Welshman list every occupation he can think of?

"If an air traffic controller made a mistake doing his job, he would be sacked."

Apparently so.

"If a forklift driver made a mistake doing his job, he would be sacked."

Is there a point to this?

"But if a doctor makes a mistake? Well, that's a different story."

Ah, we're back to this. Back to . . .

"My wife's tumor was the size of a grapefruit!" he shouts.

I'm sure it was the size of a walnut in week one.

"How the hell did they miss that? Bloody doctors," he says, sitting back in his chair and shaking his head. "They think they're so much better than the rest of us. Strutting around in their white coats with their clipboards. Who the hell do they think they are?"

We all recognize the question as rhetorical so continue to sit in silence.

"My wife is rotting in the ground and not one of those posh idiots in a white coat has been held accountable. Not one of them has even said sorry. It's an absolute disgrace."

Star continues to nod while opening her eyes and I think she's preparing to speak but Welshman isn't finished.

"They should all be shot," he declares determinedly. "They should all be rounded up in their white coats and shot."

Star opens her mouth to speak but Will forms his words faster. "I don't think it's fair to tar all doctors with the same brush," he says in his peculiar little voice, taking a break from writing everything down. "And I certainly don't think they should all be shot."

"Maybe not shot dead," concedes Welshman, "but they should all be wounded. At least then there would be some accountability for their actions, and they'd properly understand the meaning of pain."

I'm not sure about this plan. If all the doctors are shot and wounded, who will patch up all the gunshot wounds? I don't think Welshman has thought this through and, now that I think about it, he definitely seems more agitated than usual. He doesn't look good either. Glazed eyes, shallow complexion, shaking hands . . . I wonder whether he's hungover. Or drunk. Either way, he looks even worse now than he did in week one. Not a great endorsement for Star and her magical mindfulness.

"This is all really rich, really rewarding," says Star. "I thank you for your thoughts and your opinions," she directs at Welshman, "they are all very valid, very worthy of discussion and debate."

What? Even the mass maiming of medics?

"One's journey through grief is seldom smooth," she adds, mindful eyes boring into a hungover/drunk Welshman while the rest of us sit and wait. Eventually she sits back in her chair, closes her eyes and takes a deep breath. What a weirdo.

"So, does anyone else have anything they would like to share with the group?" she asks finally.

There are a few moments of silence before Will puts his head down and starts scribbling in his notebook. If he's hoping to deflect attention, his curious behavior is having the opposite effect. Everyone stares at the top of Will's head, particularly Christiana with the name badge.

"Will? Wasn't there something you wanted to say?" she asks.

The top of Will's head starts to turn red under his few wispy strands of hair and I'm genuinely interested. Maybe he's going to challenge Star on her alleged qualifications. Or ask Welshman whether he's been drinking. Or maybe, just maybe, he's got something he needs to say to me. My heart beats slightly faster and I hold my breath as Will slowly raises his bright red face, clears his throat, looks around the group, opens his mouth and speaks.

"Today is my sixtieth birthday."

I let go of the breath and any last hope that Will may be remotely interesting. As predictable birthday platitude after predictable birthday platitude is directed his way, I wonder what it is about ordinary people and their need to declare birthdays. Who cares? Who honestly cares that on this day sixty years ago Will squirmed into the world? It's of no consequence to me, it's of no consequence to anyone in this room, but look at them all. Smiling and wishing him many happy returns, pretending they care. It's repulsive. If any of them genuinely cared, they'd stop wishing him happy birthday and tell him what needs to be said. At sixty years old, the time has definitely arrived to get rid of that earring and goatee.

"Will mentioned it to me a couple of weeks ago," gushes Christiana. "And I said to him, 'You'll have to tell the group. Everyone will want to do something to mark your sixtieth.' And Will said, 'No, Chrissy,' because that's what he calls me now, 'People won't be interested in my sixtieth.' And I said, 'Of course they will! People will want to celebrate with you.'"

I stare at this disgusting exhibit of ordinariness and wonder what pleases her more. The fact that she and Will are friends? Her new nickname? Or maybe the knowledge that she has manipulated her friend into doing something he clearly didn't want to do. I stare at him. Red-faced, fidgety, uncomfortable with the attention.

"So," says Christiana, brimming with self-satisfied importance, "Will would like to know whether you will all join him after group for a birthday coffee."

Will lowers his head again. His discomfort is so palpable, if it were a person, it would be more robust than the Welshman. It would probably march across the room and headbutt the Welshman, and probably Christiana too—for bringing about its existence in the first place. The atmosphere in the room is suddenly charged—we've left awkward far, far behind. Will can't bring himself to look up. He's terrified that nobody will want to celebrate with him.

"Will was thinking that we could all go to a coffee shop in town," continues Christiana. "It is his sixtieth after all."

In the silence that follows I stare at this woman who gets excited about nicknames and name badges and suddenly Will's sense of failure takes center stage. I stare at his lowered, red head and his hand nervously fidgeting with the pencil and I know that he knows. He knows that if you get to the age of sixty and have to use someone like Christiana as a mouthpiece, you are monumentally failing at life.

"So, what does everyone think?" persists Christiana.

"Do we have to go to a coffee shop?" asks Welshman. "Can't we go to a pub?"

"I don't know," says Christiana, glancing at her watch. "It's still rather early."

"Nonsense!" declares Welshman. "It's one o'clock. Pubs have been open for hours."

"I think Will has his heart set on a coffee, don't you, Will?"

says Christiana, directing possibly the most pitiful sentence in the history of pitiful conversations to possibly the most pitiful participant. Will's sense of failure is putting on one hell of a show.

"I really don't mind where we go," mutters Will, still staring at the floor.

"Right, well, that decides it then," declares Welshman robustly. "Let's go to the pub."

"When was that decided?" asks Christiana. "I must have missed that discussion."

"Will said he doesn't mind where we go," answers Welshman, "and I want to go to a pub because I don't like coffee."

Ah, so that's why he wants to go to a pub. Makes perfect sense now. I imagine most pubs are filled to the brim with coffee haters. All sitting on bar stools, getting drunk and discussing the evils of caffeine.

"I think we should take a vote," says Christiana. "We do live in a democracy after all."

"Actually, I think Will should decide," says Star. Poor redfaced, mortified Will. Even flower-power Star is jumping to his defense. That sense of failure is working the crowd and lapping up the applause.

"I don't mind having a vote," he stammers. "That seems like the fair thing to do."

"Raise your hand if you would like to go to a warm, cozy coffee shop," says democracy-loving Christiana. "Now raise your hand if you'd like to go to a noisy, smoky pub."

"Smoky?" laughs the Welshman. "When was the last time you were inside a pub, Chrissy?"

"Right, that's three votes each," she says, ignoring the Welshman's unauthorized use of her nickname, "which means Will has the deciding vote."

"I noticed Claire didn't vote," says Will somewhat remarkably. How the hell did he notice that? He hasn't raised his red head since his birthday was mentioned.

"Is that true, Claire?" asks Christiana. "Did you vote?"

Two direct questions. Which one should I answer first?

"Yes," I say.

"Yes, that's true or yes, you voted?" asks Christiana, looking confused, which in itself is confusing seeing as any confusion is entirely of her own making.

"Yes, that's true and no, I didn't vote," I reply.

I think Christiana actually gasps. How the hell has she survived in this world for so long?

"Why, Claire?" she asks. "Why didn't you vote?"

"Because I can't meet up after the meeting," I reply. "I already have plans."

"What plans?" she demands. "What is more important than Will's sixtieth?"

"I've arranged to meet up with someone else," I say, wondering whether cuckoo Chrissy needs a lie-down, psych evaluation and some medication. "And I don't feel I can let her down."

"Bring your friend to the pub," says Welshman.

"We're still in the middle of voting," snaps Christiana. "No final decision about venue has been made."

"Claire, I don't mind if your friend wants to come along too," says Will quietly.

"Thanks, Will," I smile. "But I'm not sure whether that's a good idea. You see, I'm meeting up with Helen, Jemma's sister."

"Jemma?" bellows Welshman. "Killer Jemma? Suffocate-you-with-a-pillow-and-then-blow-her-own-brains-out Jemma?"

Now that's what I call a nickname.

"Yes, I'm meeting up with her sister, Helen."

"Why?" asks half the group in unison.

"Because she still has many unanswered questions and I think she needs someone to talk to," I reply.

"That's kind of you, Claire," says Star. "Very kind indeed. But just remember that you're grieving too. It's important to take care of yourself before you try to take care of others. It's like when you're on an airplane. You have to put your oxygen mask on first before you can put oxygen masks on anybody else."

I look at her and nod. What the bloody hell is she talking about?

"Well, I don't think it's a good idea to go for a coffee with Jemma's sister," sniffs Christiana.

"Me neither," agrees Welshman. "Although I'll happily go for a pint with anyone. Claire, why don't you ask whether Helen wants to join us in the pub?"

"We're not going to the pub!" shouts Christiana. "Will was just about to vote for the coffee shop."

"Were you, Will?" asks Welshman. "Don't be bullied by Chrissy, it's *your* birthday."

All eyes are back on the top of Will's head. Slowly he sits back in his chair, takes a deep breath, avoids eye contact with Christiana and says, "I think I would like to go to the pub."

The Welshman actually cheers. No standing ovation as Will's sense of failure takes a final bow and leaves the stage.

"That's sorted then," says the Welshman triumphantly. "Claire, bring Helen along. We're all in this together."

In what together? What is he talking about?

"I'll see what she says," I say although I've already decided that I'm going to persuade her to go to the pub. With the others there, my exposure to the heron and her inquisition will be diluted. Plus, I'd quite like to witness the festering friction between former best friends Chrissy and Will.

"Thank you, everyone, for that very illuminating, very honest discussion," says Star. "I'm afraid it won't be appropriate for me to join you, but I hope you have a good time celebrating Will's special day."

Nobody tries to persuade Star to change her mind but if she has any sense of rejection, its presence is barely perceptible. As she invites us to close our eyes and concentrate on our breathing, I take one last look around the group. The Welshman's hands are still shaking, Christiana's face is molded into an angry scowl and Will looks broken—slouched forward in his chair. Then I look at Star, who appears more peaceful than any person I have ever known. I close my eyes and give her words my full attention. It's never too late to start believing in magic.

18

The red Mercedes is parked in exactly the same place as last week. As I approach, the heron leans across, opens the passenger door and smiles up at me. She looks marginally better than last week. Her hair is washed and her makeup is applied a little more sparingly so there's less caked into the wrinkles around each eye.

"Hi, Claire, thanks so much for agreeing to meet me," she says. "It's really kind of you."

That's the second time today I've been called kind. You wait your whole life for a compliment and suddenly two show up at once. I guess it's not just thoughts that are like buses. I wonder why I noticed the compliments. I wonder why I'm still thinking about them. I let this bus go.

I get into the car and strap myself in.

"Same place as last week?" asks the heron, starting the engine.

"Actually there's been a change of plan," I say. "One of the group is sixty today, so everyone's going to the pub. I told him I was meeting you, but I think he'll be a little offended if I don't show up. So, I wondered if we could go there instead? We don't need to stay long."

The heron keeps her hands on the steering wheel and stares straight ahead. She's biting her bottom lip and seems lost in deep thought. This matter is clearly important enough to warrant serious consideration.

"I don't know, Claire," she says eventually. "I wasn't that keen on the others when I met them."

"I can't imagine why," I say, mirroring her serious tone.

She looks at me for a moment then throws her head back and laughs.

"They are a bit odd, aren't they?" she asks, giggling.

"A bit?" I say, smiling. "Christiana's been wearing the same name badge for over a month now and as for Will? You can't sneeze in that room without him making a note of it!"

"Oh, Claire, you are funny," she says, laughing.

Am I?

"Joking aside," she says, looking serious again, "are you sure they won't mind me turning up? I mean, I didn't leave on the best terms. I seem to recall storming out in the middle of a meditation."

"Everyone wants to storm out in the middle of a meditation." I smile.

"Oh, Claire, you do make me laugh."

Do I?

"The only thing is," she says, looking worried, "I'm not really dressed for the pub."

"I don't think there's a dress code."

"Oh, Claire, you kill me." And she's laughing again and I'm thinking about what it would feel like to actually kill her when I realize I don't want to. I'm not sure why but I quite like the heron today. Is it possible I like making her laugh? What's wrong with me? I need to snap out of this.

I direct Helen to the Red Lion, and we park behind the pub. Just before we get out of the car, she reaches behind and pulls her bag onto her lap. As she retrieves a compact mirror and starts applying lipstick, I notice the back seat of her car is covered in boxes.

"That's Jemma's stuff from her locker at work," she explains, applying an astonishing amount of blusher to miniscule cheekbones. "I've just come from there. The police have finally finished going through everything, so I'm allowed to take it home. It's heartbreaking actually," she says, reaching behind and opening up one of the boxes. She retrieves a brown soft-soled shoe. Must be one of Jemma's indoor shoes. Heaven forbid any of the staff take one step on that luscious carpet in an outdoor shoe. Stupid, shallow Pumpkin-Head Deb and her ridiculous rules. I can't wait to kill her. Good, I'm beginning to feel normal again.

"Most of those boxes are filled with old newspapers," says the heron, applying mascara to the lashes of each beady eye. "You wouldn't believe the number of old newspapers I found crammed in her locker. I had no idea she was such a hoarder. I'm not looking forward to sorting through her house."

The heron reaches into her bag and retrieves a bottle of perfume. I watch her dab it onto her long neck and then silently observe as she runs a comb through her hair. She returns the comb, perfume bottle, makeup and compact mirror to her bag and we finally get out of the car. Poor heron. Burdened by a heavy bag and a ton of insecurity. No wonder she looks so exhausted.

On our way into the pub, we see the Welshman.

"Thank God you've arrived," he bellows, stubbing his cigarette out on the ground and ushering us inside. "These two," he says, gesturing towards Christiana and Will, "are a right pair of miseries."

It's quiet inside and, even without the Welshman's guidance, Christiana and Will are easy to spot, seated at a large table. I register the empty chairs and awkward silence. This might actually be fun.

"Where's everyone else?" I ask.

Will is staring at the table and fidgeting with a beer mat.

"No one else has turned up," snaps Christiana, "I think they all wanted to go to a coffee shop."

"Well, Will didn't," slurs the Welshman, tipping the remainder of his pint down his throat, "and it's Will's birthday so his decision is the only decision that actually counts. Right, stick a tenner in the kitty, girls, and I'll go and get the drinks in."

With the Welshman at the bar, Helen and I take our seats at the table. Helen looks nervous. Her eyes dart around the pub before eventually settling on Will.

"Happy birthday, Will," she says politely. "Are you having a good day?"

"No, he isn't having a good day." Is Christiana sounding even posher than usual? "He hasn't had a good day ever since his partner dropped dead of a heart attack three months ago."

The silence returns, more awkward than ever. What is wrong with the woman? She appears to have removed the name badge, which I guess is a positive, but what's with all the nastiness? I've never understood why ordinary people feel the need to be so incredibly unkind.

The Welshman returns with a tray that he places, rather unsteadily, onto the table. There's a pint, two bottles of Pinot Grigio and five glasses.

"Come on, Helen," he says. "Pour out the wine."

Helen does as she's told and as soon as a wineglass is placed in front of him, Will takes a far heftier swig than I expected. I expect Christiana to be more reserved, but she pounces on her glass and drinks steadily, pausing only to wipe something from her eye. Naturally, the Welshman has already finished his pint and is downing his wine but perhaps the biggest surprise is Helen. Her lipstick-stained glass is already empty and she's eagerly pouring out another. Has she forgotten about the red Mercedes in the car park? I pretend to take a sip from my glass and watch as alcohol loosens the shackles of ordinariness. I guess I can't blame them for wanting to get drunk.

The Welshman has pulled a newspaper out of his rucksack and is talking loudly about something on the front page and looking angry. Halfway through the rant, he forgets what he's talking about and starts to smile. Christiana continues to drink, dab at her eye, drink, dab at her eye. Will is still fixated with the beer mat, keeps turning it over and over in his hand. Helen is sitting back in her chair, strumming her fingers gently against her glass and now the Welshman is getting up and walking away. This is one hell of a celebration.

The eye-dabbing starts to intensify. Everyone takes another mouthful of wine and stares at Christiana who is crying. Huge, uncontrolled tears slide down her face. The eye-dabbing isn't working. I don't think the drinking is either. The heron is out of her chair and by Christiana's side in a moment. She puts her arm around the other woman and starts talking, saying, "It's OK. Just let it out."

Christiana obliges and takes the crying up a gear. Will stands but is so eager to comfort his sobbing Chrissy, he stumbles over his briefcase and ends up on the floor. The crying stops for a moment, Will pulls himself up and hurries to Christiana. The crying begins again, more urgent than ever. The heron places her bag on the table and retrieves a box of tissues. Of course there's a box of tissues in there. She's got everything in that bag. She'll probably find Will's lost pride if she roots around for long enough.

I sit back and wait for this ridiculous pantomime to end. Why is Christiana crying? Why is the heron comforting her? Why is Will so embarrassing? And where is the Welshman? He returns a few moments later, stinking of cigarette smoke, and places another bottle of wine and five shots of tequila on the table. I glance out of the window and imagine a spaceship landing in the car park outside. Invading aliens could burst into this pub at any moment and what would they see? A grown woman crying like a baby, drinking more and more of a drug known to make people cry. Alien laughter fills my head as the Welshman places a shot glass in front of me. Glancing out of the window again, I'm not imagining a spaceship anymore. I'm willing one to appear.

Everyone drinks their shots and then more glasses of wine are poured. No one notices that I'm tipping my drinks into the plant pot on the windowsill. Drunks aren't known for their observational skills. Now that Christiana has stopped crying and is able to speak, she seems to be making up for lost time. I'm not sure what she's talking about, repetition isn't providing any clarity. She's going on and on about her fears for the world, talking about the evil everywhere and how everything seems so scary since her husband died. She feels so lost without him, that's what she's saying over and over again, so lost and so unsure of what to do.

Will is holding her hand and murmuring words of agreement. The Welshman is sitting back in his chair with his eyes closed. I'm wondering whether he's asleep when suddenly he sits forward and talks about evil ruining everything that is good in the world. Will takes a large swig of wine and says that evil is everywhere, hidden in the most unexpected of places. Listening to all this drunken drivel, it occurs to me that maybe the evil they're talking about is Jemma. She did kill Florence after all. Maybe not literally but they don't know that.

I look towards the heron. If they are talking about her sister, she doesn't seem to have noticed. Her beady little eyes are vacant and fixed upon a spot on the table. Suddenly she blinks and appears to reboot. Her eyes flicker and rest upon her bag sitting on the table. She pulls the bag towards her and places it on the floor. Two wineglasses are knocked over in this maneuver. This is the point to call it a night. Instead, the Welshman throws a twenty-pound note in my direction and tells me to get another bottle of wine.

It takes a while to get served. The pub is getting busy with the after-work crowd. I glance at my watch. Five thirty. We've been here for hours and, apart from Will falling over, nobody's done or said anything remotely entertaining. Returning to the table, Christiana and Will are helping each other to stand.

"We think it's time we got home, Claire," says Will. "This has been such a wonderful birthday. Thank you all so much."

"Yes, I agree," slurs Christiana, clutching her handbag as support. Her handbag is red. Matches her jacket. And her eyes. "It's been lovely. Although I think I might have had a little too much to drink! I fancy getting home and having a nice cup of cocoa."

Giggling, they stumble towards the door of the pub. I feel certain that one or both of them will fall but, somehow, they manage to rejoin the outside world on their feet. Shortly after that, the Welshman disappears too. I'm not sure where he's gone but I shouldn't imagine he's gone home to drink cocoa. Now I'm left with a drunk heron. Everything is working out perfectly.

"So, Helen," I say, refilling her glass. "Tell me what you found out from Lucas's colleagues."

"Oh yes, I must get my notebook out," she says, listlessly reaching towards her bag. "I wrote everything down. Basically, Lucas had gambled all his money away. He'd borrowed money from several colleagues. Hadn't paid any of them back. Oh, Claire, why did she do it?" she says now, changing topic as abruptly as posture. Slumped over the table, she lifts her glass once again towards her mouth. "And why didn't I reach out to her, Claire?" she asks. "In all that time? Four years!" she shouts. Why is she shouting?

She's staring at me and her bag is still on the floor. I think she's forgotten about getting her notebook out. She takes another large mouthful of wine.

"Four years and I never called her. Not once. All because of a stupid argument. Stupid. I need to find out what happened to her, Claire. I need to find out what happened to my baby sister," she slurs, taking another large gulp of wine. Too large. She's coughing now. Then she puts her hand to her mouth and gags.

My alarm is mirrored in her eyes. Is she going to throw up in the middle of the pub? There's panic in her voice as she says she needs to get to a toilet. She knocks over her chair as she stumbles to her feet. I pick up her bag and guide her through the pub towards the ladies. When the door of the toilet cubicle closes behind her, she starts to cry.

"I'm such a mess, Claire," she says, sobbing. "Nothing makes sense anymore."

I stand on the other side of the door and reassure her. Tell her I'm here for her and I'm not going anywhere. She thanks me and starts to vomit, which seems like the perfect moment to rummage through her bag. My hand finds the perfume bottle, makeup, comb and tissues before locating the notebook. I open it as the door to the ladies swings open. Two young women in business suits appear and ask whether I'm waiting to use the toilet. I shake my head as the heron groans loudly. Now she's shouting at me through the cubicle door.

"Claire, are you still there?"

As I reassure her, and she continues to vomit, the two women disappear into vacant cubicles, and I flick through the notebook.

Helen has listed Lucas's colleagues by name. Simon, Nicola, Adrian, Hannah, Kristian. None of these names are important. What did they tell the heron? Were any of them in the bar that night? Did any of them see Lucas with me? I turn the page. The writing is still neat and well-spaced but looks slightly rushed, as if the heron made these notes as people spoke.

Lucas was friendly . . . just someone I worked with. I wasn't that close to him.

Lucas was a nice guy . . . I didn't have anything in common with him. He was always talking about horse racing.

Lucas was nice enough, but I stopped going for drinks with him . . . he never bought a round.

A toilet flushes and one of the women emerges from a cubicle. A moment later, the other one joins her at the sink. I read through the rest of the page.

Lucas seemed to get on well with everyone at work . . . no close friends.

Lucas came out once for my birthday and I ended up paying for all his drinks.

Lucas once told me about all the money he'd lost gambling. I felt sorry for him, so I lent him £200. He never paid it back.

The two women are at the hand dryer now, talking about the disgusting stench of vomit. Their voices are loud over the noise of the dryer. Too loud. Maybe they want the heron to hear what they're saying. Maybe they're hoping she'll be hurt by their words. Maybe I should smash their heads together—that will probably be the quickest way to shut them up. Instead, I wonder why I care about the heron's feelings, and turn the page of her notebook.

I don't know if Lucas had a girlfriend . . . he never mentioned one.

I don't think Lucas had a girlfriend. He was quite flirty at the Christmas party.

I don't know and I don't care whether Lucas had a girlfriend. I stopped talking to him when it became clear he wasn't going to pay me back my £200.

I flick through the rest of the notebook. Blank pages. Is that the full extent of the heron's investigation? The two women are staring into the mirror, applying lipstick as I register my relief. She doesn't know anything—poor drunk, vomiting heron. I knock on the cubicle door and ask how she's feeling. She groans and I tell her I'll go to the bar and get her a glass of water. She thanks me and then starts gabbling, sounding panicked. She left her bag on the floor by the table. Someone may have stolen her bag. I reassure that I've got her bag; all her belongings are safe. As I leave the toilets, the women at the mirror are talking about someone called Annie. How she's so bloody full of herself. I drop the notebook into Helen's bag and push it back down to the bottom. She may be no closer to understanding the mystery surrounding her sister's death but at least the heron's makeup is safe. And her perfume and her comb and her purse and her notebook and her . . .

My hand brushes against something unfamiliar. Amidst all the clutter, I didn't notice it at first. I pull it out. It's a brown hardback envelope with *"Please do not bend"* printed in red letters. On the front someone has written in capitals, "HELEN." I turn the envelope over. It's still sealed.

I go to the bar and wait to be served. A woman is standing in front of me, asking the barman to list all the white wines. Now she's asking for a wine that isn't on the list. I glance back towards the ladies' toilets. The heron left her bag unattended. If I hadn't looked after it for her, it could have been stolen and she would have lost everything. Including the sealed envelope. Of course I'm going to open it. I break the seal and study the contents.

The woman in front of me is talking to the barman but I can't hear her voice anymore. The world is silent. Until suddenly there's noise everywhere. I look towards the barman pouring wine into a glass. He's passing it to the woman to taste. They're speaking to each other, which means they can't hear it. The sound is inside my head. The sound gets louder, the creaking more intense. The rusty key has started to turn. I force myself to stay calm and focus on my breathing. I glance down at my hands still clutching the contents of the envelope. I need to stop shaking.

I look up and the barman is staring at me. His mouth is moving but I still can't make out any words. Movement is difficult to coordinate but I manage to return the contents to the envelope and turn slowly, away from the bar. As I walk past a group of office workers sitting at a large table, two young women in business suits look familiar. They're staring towards the bar and laughing. Look at Up-Her-Own-Arse Annie the Wine Connoisseur. Who the bloody hell does she think she is?

Back in the ladies', the heron is at a sink splashing water onto her face. I ram the envelope down the back of my jeans before she turns and stumbles towards me. She throws her arms around my shoulders and starts to cry. I tell her the queue at the bar is massive, but I'll buy her a bottle of water from a shop while we wait for a cab. The smell of vomit intensifies as she thanks me. I move my head away from hers and start leading her out of the pub. When she steps into the fresh air she stumbles and leans heavily against me and that's when I think about the cab drivers parked up around the corner. Will any of them agree to drive someone so drunk? And where will they drive her anyway? Is she sober enough to remember her address? Then I think about the purse in her bag amongst all that junk. Is there enough money in there for her cab fare home? And how will she collect the red Mercedes tomorrow? Will it be safe in the pub car park overnight? I try to stay with these thoughts but it's impossible— the contents of that envelope keep calling my mind away.

The enormity hits me for a moment, and I'm forced to stand still and catch my breath. My mind rewinds a few moments. I'm standing behind that woman at the bar. The barman is pointing out bottles in the wine fridge and I break the seal on the envelope, remove the contents. There are photographs inside and I stare at the first one. It's me, standing on the doorstep of a gray semi-detached house. I'm holding Lucas Kane's briefcase in one hand and reaching for the doorbell with the other. My hand is brushing against a solitary hanging basket. I know those flowers are fake.

Just as I know this fear is real.

THEN

here's no need to be frightened, Claire," says the teacher to the little girl. "You're not in any trouble. Quite the opposite," she adds, smiling.

"Is this going to take long?" asks the woman wearing the short tight dress and skyscraper heels. "It's just I've got quite a lot of things I need to do. We just moved into a new house and we're having a stone staircase put in. I need to get back and make sure the builders are on schedule."

"No, it won't take long," smiles the teacher. "Please sit down," she adds, pointing to two chairs in front of her desk in the empty classroom. "Will your husband be joining us?"

"No," says the woman, inspecting her pointed, red, manicured nails. "He works extremely long hours. He won't be home until late."

"I see," says the teacher. "That's a shame. I was hoping to speak to both of you but no matter. Perhaps you could let your husband know how pleased I am with Claire."

There's silence now as the teacher looks at the woman. The nail-inspecting continues. So does the silence.

"I know Claire has got herself into a little trouble at school in the past," says the teacher.

"That's an undercurrent," laughs the woman, interrupting.

"Statement," says the little girl. "It's an understatement, not an undercurrent."

"Ssshh, Claire," says the woman, glancing towards the teacher. "It's rude to interrupt grown-ups when they're talking. Sorry about that," she directs at the teacher. "She just can't help herself sometimes. Always trying to be clever."

"But she is clever," says the teacher, quickly. "That's what I wanted to talk to you about. Her artwork is extraordinarily good and the stories she writes, as you undoubtedly know, are really quite remarkable. Since Claire started in my class, she's hardly been in any trouble at all. I'm extremely proud of her," the teacher adds.

The woman inspects her nails, and the silence persists until the teacher speaks again. "Claire tells me she'd like to be a teacher one day. Apparently she likes to play school with her toys at home. You know what, Claire?" The teacher leans towards the little girl. "If you carry on working hard, I know you can achieve anything you set your mind to."

"I'm terribly sorry but I'm really going to have to go now," says the woman, glancing at her watch. "I've got so many things I need to do."

"Of course," smiles the teacher. "It's Claire's birthday, isn't it? Seven years old today. How will you be celebrating?"

"We've got plans," says the woman, getting to her feet.

As they approach the classroom door, the teacher calls out to the child. "Claire!"

"Yes?" says the little girl.

The teacher searches through a pile of books on her desk, chooses one and then hurries over. Opening the book, she flicks to the middle and then pulls several pages from the spine.

"Here, Claire," she says, handing the pages to the child. "Blank pages from the register. Now you can use proper register paper when you're playing school with your toys. Happy birthday."

"Thank you," says the little girl.

They drive home and when the car pulls up outside the house, he's there, waiting outside. The man with the angry tattoos.

He smiles at the woman as she gets out of the car. Her short tight dress has ridden high up her thighs, and she doesn't pull it down. He whispers something to her as she opens the front door, and she laughs. They all walk into the house.

"Don't be annoyed," the man says to the woman, as the door closes behind them. "But I've sent the other blokes home early."

"What? Why?" she demands, marching up the sweeping stone staircase. "Have they finished the banister? Oh, for fuck's sake!" she screams as she reaches the top. "They've left their tools all over the bloody floor and look at the gaping great hole in the banister! I could trip over and fall down the bloody stairs."

The man has followed her up the staircase. He stands behind her and encircles her in his arms. "If you fall, I'll be there to catch you," he whispers quietly, running his tongue along the side of her ear. She smiles and strokes her hands gently over his arms. Over the wolves, snakes and panther—so many teeth bared. So much skin covered in angry tattoos.

"Seriously, though," she says, turning towards him. "You know I wanted the banister finished today. Why did you send the other men home?"

"The job was taking longer than expected and I wanted to make sure we got our time together," he says, running his hands down her back. "You mentioned your husband might try to get home a bit earlier because it's the kid's birthday."

At the mention of the kid, the woman looks down at the little girl still at the foot of the stairs.

"Claire," she says, walking down the stairs, "the builder and I need to talk about the building work. Grown-up talk. Run up to your room, shut the door and don't come out. We need to talk in private."

"I'll stay in my room with the door closed," says the little girl. "But don't lock me in. It's so hot in that room and the window doesn't open. It's hard to breathe in there when the door's locked."

"OK, OK, I won't lock the door," says the woman, reaching the bottom of the staircase, shrieking with laughter as the man with the angry tattoos whispers something into her ear. "Yes! You are a wonderful builder," she says, turning towards him, "very good with your hands." She moves closer to the man and then flicks her eyes back towards the little girl. "What are you still doing here?" she shouts. "Fuck off and leave us alone."

The little girl runs up the stairs to the smallest room in the house and closes her bedroom door behind her. Sitting on the floor, she arranges her toys into two neat lines. Bambi, her favorite, sits at the front. Then she smooths out the register paper and, with a pencil, lists all her toys' names down the left side. Then she quietly calls the register and puts a line or a circle in the box next to each name. This is how proper teachers call the register. She can pretend to be a proper teacher now. And then she becomes lost. Lost in her game. Lost in the lesson planning and the teaching of her toys. So lost that when she hears the laughing and the loud, excited voices outside the door, it barely registers. Maybe nothing will ever matter again.

'm running on the treadmill, struggling to breathe. Nothing wrong with my fitness level. Something very wrong with the air in this room. There seems to be less of it. Have the walls of my living room moved closer together? Is the ceiling lower? The floor higher? I jump off the treadmill and fight through the suffocating lack of air. I need to get outside. I slam the front door behind me and continue to run. This is better. Loads of air. Loads of space. Now I can think.

Somebody was there the night I killed Florence and Jemma, watching Florence's house. How did anyone know I was going to be there? *I* didn't even know I was going to be there. Not until that afternoon. Not until my visit from Jemma. Not until I decided I didn't like her job offer. I speed up to run across the road and think back to that night. Standing outside Florence's house, reaching up towards the doorbell. If only I'd turned around. Who would I have seen?

Who knew where Florence lived? I think back to the day she told Jemma her address. It was the day everyone went to the Old Bengal. The meeting had ended but the Welshman, Christiana and Will stayed behind talking. I remember I was just about to put my chair away when Jemma called me over. Florence said her address out loud, and Jemma wrote it down in her phone. I heard it; Jemma heard it. Those three people standing by the stacks of chairs could have heard it. But even if someone heard the address, why go there? Why wait outside and take photographs? Nobody could have known what I planned to do. At that point, even I didn't know what I planned to do. None of this makes any sense.

I put my head down and sprint. I'm going to run past three lampposts before I slow back down to a jog. The air builds up around my eardrums, squeezing all thoughts out of my head. My chest burns, my legs ache but my mind is free. I sprint past the third lamppost, then the fourth and the fifth. I wish I could sprint away from my thoughts forever.

I slow to a jog and think about the five photographs in that envelope. The first shows me reaching for the doorbell. Florence is in the second, standing in the doorway, smiling and inviting me in. I'm taking Lucas Kane's briefcase into Florence's house in the third. The fourth shows the door closing behind me, and in the fifth Jemma is pushing the front door open and walking inside.

I speed up to cross another road and run towards the park. Somebody was there while I was killing Florence and counting seventeen doilies and fifty-three ornaments. Somebody took those photographs and printed those photographs with the time and date on each. Somebody then turned each photograph over and wrote in capital letters on the back: "WHY WAS CLAIRE

THERE ON THE NIGHT THEY DIED?" Somebody put those photographs in an envelope, sealed that envelope and then waited for an opportunity to slip it into Helen's bag. And here, at last we can narrow the field of suspects.

It must have happened while I was waiting to be served at the bar. The heron's bag was on the floor, and she was drunk. She wouldn't have noticed anything. Will had his briefcase with him. He tripped over it when Christiana started to cry. The envelope could have been in that briefcase. Christiana had her red handbag with her. It matched her jacket and her red-rimmed eyes. The envelope could have been in that handbag. The Welshman had his tatty rucksack with him. He pulled a newspaper out of it before starting to rant. The envelope could have been in that rucksack. Any one of them could have heard Florence's address and any one of them could have put the photographs into Helen's bag. But that doesn't *mean* it was any one of them. It could have been two of them. It might even have been all three.

I'm in the park now and start to run slightly faster on the soft grass. My thoughts race ahead of me. Is that what they were talking about? The Welshman, Christiana and Will. All those drunken ramblings in the pub about evil. Were they talking about me? My thoughts are spinning out of control but suddenly it's there. Wild strands of thought knotted into one tiny word.

Why?

Why put the photographs into the heron's bag? Why not send them to the police? My chest hurts, my legs ache, my mind starts to clear but suddenly I stop. I can't run any further. He's blocking my path. I recognize him straightaway, and he knows exactly who I am. He sees me. The real me. And he's been waiting for this moment for a long, long time.

I hold my breath as the ugly black dog circles me. He's growling, baring his teeth. I'm vaguely aware of Mrs. Davis in the distance. She's running towards us and shouting the dog's name, but she's too far away. She's not going to get here in time. The dog stops circling me, fixes me with his eyes and prepares to pounce. I close my eyes and wait for the attack. I wonder if I look like a ghost. To the dog, I mean, or is it just me who sees that? Maybe this is how it was always supposed to end and maybe it's for the best. Death is preferable to a prison cell and that ugly black dog has earned this kill. He's waited patiently, bided his time and chosen the perfect moment. Every dog has his day.

But not today. I open my eyes. The dog is still looking at me and snarling. Why hasn't he attacked? What's he waiting for? I look over towards Mrs. Davis. She's close now. I can see her red, panicked face. That dog doesn't have long before she gets here. I stare at him. I see the hair standing on end, the sharp pointed teeth and saliva drooling in lines from his mouth. He looks so vicious, so determined. But it's all just an act. Yet another phony in the kingdom of fakes, pretending to be something he's not.

Mrs. Davis reaches us and grabs hold of the dog's lead.

"I'm so sorry, Claire," she stammers, trying to catch her breath. "He caught sight of you running and that was it. He was off like a bat out of hell. I'm so sorry but please know, his bark is much worse than his bite."

"It's OK, Mrs. Davis," I smile. "All's well that ends well."

"It's not OK, Claire," she says, eyeing me with concern. "You look as white as a sheet. You must have been frightened to death. Be quiet!" she shouts at the dog who has started to bark. "Honestly, this dog is all talk and no trousers. Are you sure you're OK?"

"Right as rain."

"Really? I'd be up in arms if I was you. Sends a shiver down my spine thinking about how scared you must have been. Right, well, if you're sure you're OK, we'll leave you to enjoy the rest of your run. This one will be in the doghouse for quite some time, I can assure you of that."

I watch them walk away and then jog towards a bench near the play area in the middle of the park. With no children there today, the swings, slide and seesaw stand silent. I sit on the bench. All talk and no trousers. That's how Mrs. Davis described her loud, underwhelming dog but it could just as easily describe the Welshman. Week after week he sits in that group and gets angry. But what does he do about those doctors who misdiagnosed his wife? Nothing. And then there's Will. A pathetic pen-pusher—endlessly making notes, living out each day as a spectator. As for Christiana, she said it herself. She's lost without her husband, doesn't know what to do. I think about all three of them. Gutless. Each and every one.

While I was in Florence's house being proactive, one of those gutless individuals was hiding outside. Too gutless to intervene, too gutless to even send the photographs to the police. All talk and no trousers. They must have thought they were so clever, slipping them into Helen's bag. Making it her problem before scuttling away to hide. But fate intervened in the form of a vomiting heron. Mrs. Davis would call that fortune favoring the brave. I call it having Dad in my corner. He's here, I know it. Watching in that quiet, knowing way—doing whatever he can to keep me safe. Thanks to you, Dad, none of those gutless individuals were there when Helen left her bag unattended and rushed to the toilet. None of them know she hasn't seen the photographs. None of them know that I have.

I stand up and take one last look at the empty play area. I see the swings, slide and seesaw, patient and still—waiting for something to happen. I could do that. I could wait patiently for the knock on the door, the handcuffs, the questions and the life imprisonment.

I'm not going to do that. But I could.

I turn to run towards home, thinking about the person or persons who took those photographs—try to picture the faceless entities in my mind. Who are they? Why were they there? Where did they hide? How long did they stay? Why the gutless inaction?

Gutless inaction. The perfect epitaph.

20

Even though drunk heron thanked me repeatedly for looking after her and making sure she got home safe, and hungover heron phoned me yesterday to thank me again, it seems normal heron also has a need to express gratitude. I'm on my way to Waterbridge Oak when she calls.

"Hi, Claire, it's Helen. I just wanted to thank you again for looking after me the other night. And also, thank you so much for looking after my bag. It would have been a nightmare if I'd lost that. I'd have had to cancel all my bank cards and as for my phone . . . It could have been an absolute nightmare, seriously—I'm so grateful."

"It's fine." I think about her use of words, the ease with which an inconvenience is magnified into a nightmare. I wonder how she'd describe losing something really important. Her mind perhaps? Or her freedom?

"I'm so ashamed about how drunk I was," she says. Again. "I'm so embarrassed."

"It's fine," I say. Again. "You were fine. You have nothing to feel embarrassed about."

"You're so kind. I just feel so bad that you had to look after me."

"It's fine," I say. Again. "No big deal."

"It is a big deal. A really big deal. When I think about what could have happened if you'd left me in that state. If I'd lost my bag, how would I have got home? I'm so grateful. Honestly, I really am. My car keys were in my bag, and I don't have a spare set. If I'd lost those keys, it would have been a complete and utter nightmare."

"It's fine," I say, for the last time. "Now if you can excuse me, I'm just about to go into a . . ."

Where? Where am I going to say I'm going? A shop, perhaps? A doctor's appointment? A car wash? A church? A library? The possibilities are endless.

"A meeting," I decide to say. "I'm just about to go into a meeting," I repeat. "Can I call you back later?"

"Of course! I'm so sorry, I didn't mean to hold you up. The reason I'm phoning is to see whether I can treat you to dinner some time. My way of saying thank you."

"That's not necessary," I say as her words pile up in my ear.

"It is necessary. When I think about the aggravation if I'd lost that bag. It would have been—"

"Dinner would be lovely." I can't listen to another definition of Helen's idea of a nightmare. "Now, if it's OK, I really must go."

"Of course, I'll speak to you soon, goodbye."

"Goodbye."

"Oh, and Claire? Thank you again. It honestly means so much—"

I end the call. It's not rude. It's necessary. I drive towards the care home and think about two sisters. I think about Jemma the blackmailer, tormenting innocent people in her care. Then I think about the heron, bursting at the seams with a constant need to please. I wonder whether the siblings were always so different or whether something happened to make them so. I think about their mother living in Bognor Regis by the sea. Is it her fault Jemma turned out the way she did? Is it true that she favored Helen? Does she blame herself for Jemma's death? Is she tormented with grief? Does she even care?

The care home car park is unusually busy. Just like my mind. Why am I thinking about Jemma's mother? How is that helpful to me? I eventually find a space and make my way into the building. Irina on reception looks weird. The heavy makeup is in place, maybe even more red lipstick than usual, but what's happened to her hair? It appears to have been styled into tight curls which have been pinned into a pattern on the top of her head. How odd. I sign the visitors' book and walk up the stairs to the third floor. I peer into Kathleen's empty room and follow the sound of music into the sitting room.

"Good afternoon, Claire!" bellows Deb as I walk through the door. "Welcome to our 1940s tea party!"

Good grief. Now I know exactly how invading aliens feel when they land on a strange planet. What the hell is going on? First of all, there's the music. Something about the white cliffs of Dover is being belted out by a shriveled-up old lady. Could be Janet but I think it's Edith. Whoever she is, she has an astonishingly powerful voice, albeit slightly shrill. Then there's the dancing. Ben is shuffling backwards and forwards in the center of the room with another old lady. Could be Edith but I think it's Janet. He's smiling and she's looking angry; she's dancing but her heart isn't in it. Then there's the clothes. Pumpkin-Head Deb who literally never sits down is sitting in an armchair and smiling at me and I'm trying to decide what to focus on first. Her greasy hair has been scraped back into a severe-looking bun, accentuating the enormity of that head. And why has she come to a 1940s tea party dressed as a Victorian governess? Why are her outfits always decades out of date? The whole thing is just too weird. She's sitting there, smiling at me—waving a plastic Union Jack, wearing a long black dress with a fussy white lace collar. It's horrible.

"Wow!" I say, which is always a good word to throw in when all other words are missing in action.

"Please help yourself to tea and cake," she says. "The chef has followed a 1940s recipe. Bit bland but worth a taste. Anything created by someone who worked in a Michelin-starred restaurant is worth a taste!"

I grab a cup of tea from the trolley and look around the room. Kathleen is sitting on the sofa next to Frank. An ashen-faced Miranda and a bored-looking man are sitting on dining room chairs next to the sofa, against the wall. Oscar the child is jumping in the middle of the room. He keeps sitting on the floor and laughing.

"Oscar!" says the bored-looking man. "This isn't musical bumps. Either dance or sit down. Don't keep doing both."

I don't know anything about toddlers but from what I've seen of Oscar, I don't think he will stop doing both. As the jumping and the sitting down and the laughing continue, bored-looking man sighs and starts to stand up but Miranda stops him.

"Leave him, Nicholas, he's not doing any harm. He'll have a tantrum if you try and stop him."

"Fine, fine," says Nicholas, sitting back down. "Just remember what the book says. One can't spend one's life living in fear of the next tantrum."

"The book also says we need to pick our battles," snaps Miranda.

"While remembering that we are the ones calling the shots," says Nicholas. "Do you remember the chapter about maintaining control of a situation at all times?"

"I do," says Miranda. "I also remember the chapter about encouraging freedom of expression and free will."

"While maintaining control at all times," says Nicholas.

What the hell are they talking about? Is this how ordinary people communicate now? Quoting chapters from a book?

"Hello," says Miranda, catching my eye. "Claire, this is my husband, Nicholas. Nicholas, this is Claire."

Nicholas stands up and shakes my hand.

"Nice to meet you, Claire," he says, studying me with dark, intense eyes. "So," he adds, running his hand through his mop of thick black hair before gesturing around the room at the elderly residents, "which one of these is yours?"

"I've come to visit Kathleen," I reply, deciding that I don't much like Nicholas. The Welshman would call him a prick. And I would agree. Poor Miranda. No wonder she looks so miserable.

"Hello, Kathleen," I say, crouching down and gently kissing

the side of her face. Lavender invades my senses and when her dark blue eyes lock onto mine there's a moment when I think she's going to speak. I stare into her eyes. Is she still in there some-where? Fighting the invisible force? Is she aware that madness has stolen her past and is robbing her of her future, trampling every last trace of identity into the ground? Can she overcome that invisible force long enough to utter one word of sense? Her gaze drops to the doll in her arms, and she starts to mumble. She's gone. I'm not sure she was ever there.

"Terrible disease, isn't it?" says Nicholas as I sit down on one of the dining room chairs.

"Yes," I agree. "Truly awful."

"I take my hat off to the people who work here," he says. "They must have the patience of saints, all of them."

Sniffing out the compliment, Pumpkin-Head Deb who liter-ally never sits down is at his side in an instant, sitting down on a dining room chair.

"That's so kind of you, Nicholas!" she exclaims. "But it's me who should be taking my hat off to you. You're a doctor, you save lives! Claire, Nicholas is a doctor! He saves the lives of tiny premature babies."

"Sadly, one can't save them all," Nicholas says with a humil-ity I don't quite believe, "but one does one's best."

"Of course one does," says Deb. "You doctors deserve med-als. You're superheroes, every single one of you."

"Well, one doesn't know about that." Nicholas smiles. "I'm just part of a good team. Neonatal Nick and his army of angels, that's what we're called!"

I glance towards Kathleen, still staring without blinking at the doll, and experience a perverse moment of envy. At least that invisible force means she doesn't have to listen to this.

"Nicholas is right," I say, deciding to turn this sycophantic fest to my advantage. "You work so hard, Deb. How much time off do you get during the week?"

"Not enough!" she laughs. I smile but do not respond. I want her to elaborate.

"I have two days off each week," she says. "Well, I'm supposed to have two days off each week, but the truth is I'm always on call."

No rest for the wicked, I think but do not say.

"I always have Tuesdays off," she says, filling the silence. "And the other day varies."

"And what do you like doing in your free time?" I ask, thinking about Tuesday. As good a day as any for a kill.

"I clean my house, go for a walk, do some gardening, buy my groceries—my life is so busy," she sighs. "I literally never have time to sit down."

"What about your family, Deb?" I ask, thinking about the Tuesday I will break into her house and kill her. "Do you get enough time to spend with them?"

"My career is so important to me," she says, her voice tinged with defensiveness. "It never left any time for children. I was engaged to be married a few years ago but it didn't go ahead because I . . ."

Revolted him?

"I realized I was settling for less than I deserve. I have extremely high standards in everything I do. Including men." At that she laughs and places her hand on Nicholas's shoulder to steady herself. "Oh my! That sounded rude. I didn't mean it like that!"

My smile is genuine. With no husband, boyfriend or offspring turning up unannounced, there will be no need to rush. I can take my time when I kill her, and I like taking my time. I stare at that huge head now, wobbling with laughter on such a long, elegant neck, and allow myself a moment of excitement. Carving into pumpkins—always such good fun. And this year I don't have to wait until Halloween.

"The truth is, I love my career," she's saying now. "I take an enormous amount of pride in my work. Do you know, we've been nominated in this year's Care to Join Us Awards? As you can imagine, winning one of those awards would be quite the achievement."

"I've had enough of this nonsense!" Frank says, standing abruptly. "I would like to go home now, please."

Miranda hurries towards her father. "You *are* home, Dad. This is where you live now, remember?"

"No, I don't live here with all these people," he says, looking around the room in horror. With that he marches over towards the window, shouting at Edith as he walks past. "Stop singing that bloody song!"

When he gets to the window, he stares at the outside world and the horror on his face transforms into fear. "Where's the sea?" he shouts, panic splintering his voice. He rushes towards another window. "Where's the sea?" he repeats. "What have you done with the sea?"

Vampire Smoker has appeared from somewhere and is slowly approaching Frank, followed by Deb. Miranda is at her father's side, trying to calm him down.

"You don't live by the sea anymore, Dad, you live here, remember? This is your home now."

Frank stares at her for a minute, clears his throat and smiles politely. "Young lady," he says. "If I could trouble you for a moment of your time, could you please help me find my way home? I seem to be lost."

He looks out of the window again, furrows his brow and studies the view before turning back to Miranda. "I need to get to Eastbury Avenue," he explains calmly. "If you drop me at Bournemouth train station, I'll be able to find my way."

"Dad," says Miranda softly. "Dad, it's me. Miranda. Dad, you don't live in Eastbury Avenue anymore. You live here."

The room is quiet and in that moment of stillness I'm unsure what's going to happen next. There's something in Frank's eyes that I can't read. Is it understanding? Recognition? There's a chance he will remember his daughter, remember where he is and calm down. There's also a chance . . .

"Young lady!" he shouts. "I demand you take me home. This instant!"

"Dad!" pleads Miranda. "Dad, it's me, Miranda. Your daughter. Dad, you are home. I visit you here every day with Oscar, your grandson. Dad, please calm down—"

"You're not my daughter!" he screams. "My daughter is young and pretty and she would never take me away from my home. I don't know who you are or what you're talking about. I live in Eastbury Avenue in a house overlooking the sea. I live there with my wife, Sophie. Where is she? Where's my phone? I need to make some phone calls. Give me my phone now! How long have I been here? Who's running the business? I've got three hundred people relying on me for their livelihoods. Get me my phone!"

"Dad," says Miranda, her voice breaking, "Mum died six years ago. Dad, you don't run the business anymore. You live here. You've still got me and Oscar—"

"I don't know you and I don't know Oscar!" he screams before looking around the room. He stares at everyone and then straightens his tie. "Look," he says, maintaining eye contact with Vampire Smoker, "I don't want to cause any trouble, but I think there's been a dreadful misunderstanding. I think it's best that I speak to the person in charge."

"Frank," says Deb, softly, "my name is Deb and I'm the manager here. Why don't we go to my office and have a little chat?"

"Yes, that would be good," says Frank, clearing his throat. "I'm sure we can get all this sorted out. Probably best if you give my wife a call. She's probably worrying about me."

"Yes, let's go and get this all sorted out," says Deb. "My colleague will show you to my office. I'll join you there in a moment."

As Vampire Smoker accompanies Frank from the room, Deb guides Miranda back to her chair.

"It might be best if you leave it to us to calm your dad down," she says. "You being there is likely to cause even more upset, for him and for you." Turning towards Nicholas, she adds, "We've been trained to deal with these situations."

With that she leaves the room, ducking slightly—it's a tight squeeze, cramming all that self-importance through the door.

The music has stopped but the old lady is still singing about the white cliffs of Dover. I'm sure there must be verses in this song but maybe she doesn't know the words; the chorus seems to be stuck on an irritating loop. Ben keeps glancing towards Miranda. He looks concerned. The person who *should* be concerned is scrolling through his phone, eyes locked onto the screen. Perhaps Nicholas is searching the internet for clues as to how one should comfort one's wife when one's father-in-law no longer remembers one's wife.

"He doesn't know who I am." Miranda's eyes are blank, unseeing and all-seeing in that same moment. "He doesn't know who I am," she repeats and her eyes flicker as she registers the years ahead, the stoicism, the fear, the frustration and the tears.

Nicholas is still looking at his phone. Ben keeps glancing at Miranda. I know he wants to reassure her. I even know what he wants to say because I've heard it all before. Back in Dad's psychiatric ward I sat in countless meetings with doctors who explained the nature of dementia to me. One even drew a diagram to demonstrate how dementia doesn't follow a straight path, how it winds back on itself—how Dad may forget my name one day and remember it the next. I didn't need the diagram; I understood the words. I just never understood why they were supposed to provide comfort. There's no cure for dementia and when the only destination is death, would you choose a long, meandering path through indignity and confusion or a more direct one? I know Dad would have preferred the more direct route. I think Frank would too. I think anyone in their right mind would.

I notice the intensity in Ben's eyes and wonder whether I'm wrong. Maybe he doesn't want to reassure Miranda about her father. Maybe he wants to tell her that she still looks pretty and young. But he can't. Ordinary person convention is quite clear on this point. A man cannot comfort an upset woman if the upset woman's husband is in close proximity to the aforementioned upset woman. Even in this messed-up version of real life where half the people in the room don't know what planet they're on, ordinary person convention prevails.

Miranda's eyes are fixed unblinking on the carpet when the tears start to fall. She doesn't brush them away; I respect her for that. She slumps forward in the chair and places her head in her hands. She's making a sound now—each raspy breath louder than the last. "The White Cliffs of Dover" will soon be drowned out and still Nicholas stares at his phone.

Without thinking I'm out of my chair and by Miranda's side. I place my arms around her and feel the warmth of her tears. Ordinary person convention dictates that a woman can comfort an upset woman when the upset woman's husband is in close proximity of the aforementioned upset woman, but I'm not governed by ordinary person convention. So why am I holding her close and telling her everything will be OK? I wonder whether it's because I understand how she's feeling. I wonder whether it's because I had to watch Dad stumble along that long, meandering path. I wonder whether I'm experiencing empathy. And if so, I wonder why it's chosen this moment to arrive.

Eventually the sobbing subsides. Slowly she raises her head from my shoulder and stares at something behind me. Pumpkin-Head Deb who literally never sits down has reentered the room and is sitting down on the sofa, in the seat recently vacated by Frank. Reveling in her position of power, she takes a deep breath. The bearer of news.

"Your father is much calmer now," she says, addressing Miranda. "He's back in his room, having a rest."

"Thanks so much, Deb," says Nicholas. "Thank goodness that's all sorted out."

"All sorted out?" snaps Miranda, whipping her head around to glare at her husband. "What exactly is all sorted out? Didn't you see how upset he is? How disoriented and confused? This is just the beginning, Nicholas. Nothing is sorted out."

"Well, if this is just the beginning," says her husband, returning the glare, "maybe you need to toughen up. What's the point of crying every time your dad gets upset? This could go on for years."

I glance towards Ben and see the flinch. It's got to be hard for someone as nice as him to breathe the same air as Nicholas.

"Nicholas has a point," says Deb. "Dementia is so cruel, and I understand why you're upset, but you have to stay strong. Your dad is perfectly safe and well looked after. You visit him every day, you're doing everything you can."

"Am I?" asks Miranda. "You heard how much he wants to

go home. We took him away from Bournemouth, away from everything he knows."

"For his own good," snaps Nicholas. "You know the trouble he was getting into—wandering the streets, forgetting where he was. He nearly burnt his house down. Do you remember that?"

"Yes, I do," hisses Miranda. "I just wonder whether we should have got him home care. Or put him somewhere in Bournemouth."

"That's what I suggested!" shouts Nicholas. "But you said that you wanted to visit him every day. You insisted that when we moved, your dad came too. These were all your decisions. I went along with everything you wanted."

"Well, maybe I made the wrong decisions," she says softly.

I return to my chair and close my eyes. With so much raw emotion zipping through the air, it's just like being in a group meeting. I half expect Star to poke her head around the door and invite us all to picture our thoughts as buses. When ordinary people unplug themselves from the grid of inauthenticity and speak honestly, they almost become endearing. Even Nicholas.

"He's beautiful, your little boy. What's his name?"

I snap my eyes open and try not to look alarmed. One of the old ladies has silently crept into my personal space and is speaking. Her face is so close to my own, I can feel the warmth of her breath on my cheek.

"He's beautiful," she repeats, glancing away. "What's his name?" I follow her eyes to Oscar. The little boy is sitting on the floor surrounded by building blocks. He's piling them up, one on top of the other; patiently starting over each time the tower falls. His lips are pursed in concentration and every so often he brushes a golden curl away from his blue, saucer-like eyes. The old lady standing too close to my face is right about one thing. He is beautiful.

"He's not my son," I say.

"Not your son?" she says, flicking her eyes back to mine. It's hard to focus with her face so close but I'm aware of hairs growing on her chin and more broken blood vessels than skin covering her sunken face. "Not your son?" she repeats. "So where are your children?"

"I don't have any children," I reply.

"No children?" she gasps. "No, that's no good. A nice-looking girl like you should be a mother. You don't know the true meaning of love until you give birth."

Her breath is on my face again and there's a mustiness I hadn't noticed before. The room feels hot, uncomfortably so. Why doesn't anyone open a window? I'm aware of sobbing from somewhere and muffled conversation I can't quite hear and now Ben is by my side and guiding the old lady away. Everyone else in the room is looking at Miranda. She's crying again.

"Come on, Miri," says Nicholas, "I understand you're upset but, as Deb said, your dad is well looked after here. Think about Oscar, Miri. Our gorgeous little boy needs his mum to be happy. I know it's terribly sad but your dad has had a really good innings. The Frank I know would tell you to dry your eyes and turn that frown upside down."

He sits back in his chair and looks around the room, expecting perhaps a round of applause. As motivational speeches go, it's not the worst I've ever heard but I object to the irritating overuse of the word "Miri" and the inappropriate inclusion of the innings cliché. Frank isn't dead yet, which renders such a sentiment crass and premature.

"Nicholas's right, Miri," says Deb. "You have a fantastic future ahead of you. And you know, not everyone is so lucky." Heaving herself forward, she grabs a tissue from the coffee table and dabs at her eyes before continuing to speak. "I can't stop thinking about Jemma," she sniffs. "Jemma who used to work here," she adds by way of explanation, looking at each of us in turn. "It breaks my heart when I think about it, it really does." With that she blows her nose into the tissue and studies the contents. She really is the most repulsive specimen of ordinariness it has ever been my misfortune to observe.

"Jemma was my colleague," she continues. "But she was also my friend. I still can't believe she's gone." Another heave forward, another tissue, another dab of the eyes. "You know, she wasn't much older than you, Miri. And do you know the really scary part? I didn't have a clue about what was going on inside her mind."

Why is that the really scary part?

"I mean, I knew she was eccentric," Deb says. "You only had to look at the way she dressed to know that. But suicidal? No. I didn't have a clue. And how do you think that makes me feel, Miri? How do you think it makes me feel knowing that my friend kept something like that from me?" Deb shakes her head sadly, a sign I optimistically assume indicates the end of the story.

"If only I'd known what was going on in Jemma's mind," she

adds, shattering my optimism, "I could have done or said something. Instead, I have to live the rest of my life with the knowledge of what she did." More shaking of that enormous head now followed by a deep intake of breath.

"I know you're upset about your father's illness, Miri," she sighs, "but at least you've still got your future ahead of you. Think about Jemma. She threw her future away. And think about the impact that's had on me."

As Deb sits back in the chair and closes her eyes, I silently acknowledge the shift in atmosphere. At some point during the last few moments, the 1940s tea party has transformed into a masterclass of narcissism.

The room is so silent I can hear Kathleen's barely audible murmurings to the doll. If listening to Deb is like rolling in a field of nettles, this silence is being cocooned in a soft, velvet rug.

"I'll never forget the last time I saw Jemma."

Ouch. The nettles hurt more after the velvet. Why doesn't anyone tell her to shut up? Where's Frank when we need him?

"I think I'll remember it until the day I die," which means she won't have to remember it for long. "I'd just come out of my office when I saw Jemma going up the stairs. She was wearing one of her outrageous outfits. A kilt, I think. And wellies. I called out to her, and she turned and smiled. She looked so happy, Miri. So happy and carefree."

An extended pause follows but I know Deb will start talking again. I glance at my watch and try to calculate how long I've been here. Fifteen minutes? Twenty, maybe? I think about ordinary person convention and wonder what it says about the appropriate length of a care home visit. Fifteen minutes would probably be considered too short, but I reckon twenty-five is perfectly acceptable. I start a mental countdown. Five more minutes and I'll leave.

"I was on my way to a lunch meeting, so I didn't have time to talk to Jemma," Deb says. "I told her I'd meet up with her later, but do you know what happened later, Miri? Miri?"

Slowly Miranda raises her head. Considering she's been crying for the best part of ten minutes, she doesn't look too bad. Her dark eyes look tired, but her olive complexion is unblemished as she asks, "What happened?"

"What happened, Miri," says Deb, taking another deep breath, "is that I never saw Jemma again. She killed herself later that day."

Deb looks slowly around the room before settling back in the sofa and closing her eyes. In the silence that follows, I'm reminded of a film I watched once. Or maybe it's an amalgamation of films I've watched. It could even have been a book I've read. Wherever it came from, the image I have in my mind is of a group of people sitting around a campfire telling ghost stories. We've gone from a 1940s tea party to a masterclass in narcissism to a camping trip. Maybe this is where Deb's story has been heading all along. Maybe she's been building up to the big reveal that the ghostly form of Jemma has been spotted floating up and down the stairs of Waterbridge Oak. Maybe she patrols the corridors, forever doomed to wear those wellies and that kilt.

"So, as you can imagine, Miri," says Deb, opening her eyes, "this has all been very upsetting for me. Very upsetting indeed."

Someone stamp out the campfire, we're heading back to the narcissist's classroom.

"That is so tragic, Deb," says Nicholas. "Such a waste of a young life and devastating for you." Turning to his wife, he adds, "We're so lucky, Miri. Your father has had a wonderful life. A fantastic innings."

Wow. A repeat of the innings cliché and yet another use of the word "Miri." Nicholas is fast becoming my new least favorite.

Standing, I return my teacup to the trolley and go over to Kathleen to say goodbye. Her eyes are closed, and I think she may be asleep. Kissing the top of her head, I imagine the invisible force as a relentless army taking the opportunity to regroup, plotting new attacks on what's left of her mind. I wish it would leave her alone—doesn't it see the white flag? I head for the door.

Walking along the corridor, my feet sink into the velvet carpet as a door opens ahead of me and Vampire Smoker steps out. Approaching, he has the gait of an underachiever, the presence of a nobody and the sneer of a man who enjoys pissing on old people and needs to be stopped. My plans for his death are coming along nicely. Just need to collect a little more urine for the waterboarding and then I'll be good to go. Note to self—drink more Evian. As our paths cross, his eyes meet mine and I smile. He looks better as a ghost—almost interesting. Not long now.

21

rriving early at the final meeting, I help Star place chairs in a circle and sit in the one that gives me the best view of the door. Star chooses the chair nearest to the window and, when I glance in her direction, her eyes are closed. I wonder if she's meditating. I wonder if she meditates before every group meeting. Before eating every meal. Before making every decision. Maybe she fitted in a brief meditation before choosing that chair. I wonder whether anyone has ever overdosed on meditation. Is it like red wine? A little every day is healthy but too much and you might just hit rock bottom. Star doesn't look like she's heading towards rock bottom but then Star doesn't look like she's heading anywhere. Star looks perfectly happy being exactly where she is.

A car pulls up outside and I return my attention to the door. I want to see their faces when they walk into the room. In particular I want to see their eyes when they lock onto mine. Whoever put those photographs in Helen's bag will expect me to be under arrest by now. Who will be the most surprised to see me?

The most afraid? One of those gutless individuals is bound to give away something. And when they do, I'll be watching.

Will is the first to enter the room. He glances in my direction and then scampers towards a chair next to Star. He sits down and places his briefcase on his lap, clicks it open and starts rummaging inside. I wonder what he's looking for. Maybe he's not looking for anything. Maybe all the rummaging is a ruse. Maybe he's trying to keep busy so that he can avoid my gaze.

Christiana is the next to arrive and her eyes widen for a split second when she sees me. The ridiculous name label may suggest otherwise but Christiana is no fool. She knows I noticed.

"Hello, Claire," she stammers, settling into the chair next to Will. "You're not usually here this early."

Will is still rummaging in his briefcase and doesn't even lift his head to acknowledge Chrissy. He definitely seems nervous and shifty today but then he always seems nervous and shifty.

More people enter the room, and the Welshman is the last to arrive. He looks truly awful. And he stinks of cigarettes. Slumping into the last available chair, he glances around the room and when his eyes reach mine, they stop. Abruptly. Too abruptly? I glance at Will. Still rummaging in the case. My eyes flick towards Christiana and she immediately looks away. When I look back at the Welshman, he's staring at something above my head. Glazed, broken and staring—what is it he sees? What's going on inside his head? The shell of a person is impossible to read.

Star is inviting us all to focus on our breathing. I close my eyes and think. It could be any of them. Any of them could have hidden outside Florence's house, taken the photographs and slipped them into the heron's bag. Star is asking us to imagine our thoughts as buses and I wonder what bus Christiana is jumping aboard. Is she thinking about life after the bereavement group? Wondering what she'll do with that crumpled name badge? Or is she thinking about me? Does she know what I did? Is she planning to go to the police? And what about Will? Is he going to creep back into a life of obscurity or is it possible that someone as insignificant as Will could bring an end to someone like me? And then there's the Welshman. He looks like a man who needs to get back to oblivion, but will he pop into a police station on the way?

Star's voice is the perfect blend of comforting calm but it's no good. My mind is too busy, the buses are backing up and it's taking every inch of self-control to stay seated. This must be how a caged animal feels. Watched, waiting, powerless. But I'm not caged yet and I'm far from powerless. I'm stronger than everyone else in this room. Stronger than all of them put together. I could get my hammer out of my bag right now and send them on their way. A group of ghosts bound together forever. If I'm going to get caught, I might as well go out on a high. One last killing frenzy to bring the killing to an end.

Star is speaking again, urging us to gently collect our thoughts and guide them back to our next breath. A bus pulls away from the traffic and I hop on board. Frenzy is not my style. I don't even like the word "frenzy" and I don't *want* the killing to end. At least not yet. I think about the plans I've made for Vampire

Smoker and Deb—their deaths will be meticulous and decidedly unfrenzied. My breath deepens and my mind becomes calm. I'm on the right bus. All I need to do is eliminate this obstacle. All I need to do is find out who took those photographs and stop that person from going to the police. There must be a way . . .

I snap my eyes open and they're there. I knew they would be. Those two eyes are always there. Always lingering, always looking with something I can't quite read. Those eyes have always viewed me differently, ever since Florence and Jemma died. Those eyes see me, the real me. I meet the stare. The eyes flick away but now I know.

Star brings the meditation to an end and then smiles inanely at every person in the room.

"As you know," she says eventually, "this is the last meeting of our little group and what I'd like to do is to move around the circle and ask everyone to share one thing they have learned from the course. One thing they will take away with them. So, is anyone brave enough to start?"

There follows the inevitable awkward silence sandwich: awkward silence followed by the awkward clash of voices as two or more people start to speak at the same time followed by more awkward silence. I observe Star throughout. She's sitting with her eyes closed, the gentle caress of serenity adding an almost illuminous glow to her face. More awkward silence followed by another clash of voices, but this time Christiana raises her voice and takes control. She seems keen to sink her teeth into the awkward silence sandwich.

"I think the biggest eye-opener for me," she says, "has been the introduction to mindfulness. It's brought me such tranquility and calm; I honestly don't know how I coped without it!" She pauses and looks at Star but if she's seeking encouragement, she'll have to search elsewhere. Star remains perfectly still—eyes closed, expression neutral. Christiana closes her eyes too and the room is plunged into silence once again. I wonder why Christiana's biggest eye-opener involves her sitting there with her eyes closed. I wonder if I'm the only one to pick up on the irony.

"I've learned that grief is the loneliest place on earth," says the Welshman.

"Excuse me! I hadn't finished speaking," says Christiana, her eyes suddenly open.

"So, speak," says the Welshman.

"You've made me lose my train of thought now," she says angrily.

"Well, I'm sure if you close your eyes for long enough," says the Welshman, "all the trains and buses and submarines and juggernauts of thought will come hurtling straight back towards you."

"Have you ever considered that the reason you find grief such a lonely place is because you are such a thoroughly unpleasant man?" asks Christiana.

"Where's all that tranquility and calm now, Chrissy?" asks the Welshman.

"All this emotion is good," says Star, sitting forward in her chair, suddenly serious. "As is diversity of thought. After all, no two journeys through grief are the same. However, we have to remember to be respectful of each other's journeys."

"I'm extremely respectful of other people and their journeys!" exclaims Christiana. "He, on the other hand," she says, pointing towards the Welshman, "is always trying to undermine mindfulness and its importance to me."

"Don't make me laugh, Chrissy!" says the Welshman. "You only learned about mindfulness a couple of weeks ago. How important can it be?"

"How dare you!" shouts Christiana. "You really are the most odious—"

"Will," says Star, with unexpected force. "I'd like to come to you. What do you think you will take away from the course?"

"I hadn't finished explaining what *I* will take away from the course," says Christiana.

"I'd like to move on to Will now," says Star firmly.

"I don't mind waiting until Chrissy has finished," says Will.

"Will!" shouts Star. "Please tell us what you have learned from the course."

Will fidgets nervously with his pencil. Star's eyes are closed again and the mask of serenity is back in place, but we all saw the slip. Even the guru of all that is Zen loses her rag now and then.

"I've learned that even though our journeys are different," says Will, "there are some common features of grief. For example, we all seem to experience denial and anger."

"And how does that make you feel?" asks Star.

"I find it comforting," answers Will. "It makes me feel less alone."

"But we are alone," says the Welshman. "We came into this world on our own and we will leave on our own. Grief is the ultimate reminder of that."

"I really don't think it's fair that he gets the chance to elaborate on his chosen topic," sniffs Christiana, "but I am denied the opportunity to speak about mine."

"And how about you, Claire?" asks Star, sweeping Christiana's comment aside so effectively I'm not sure whether the whiny posh voice was real. "What have you learned?"

I sit in silence for a moment and think. What have I learned? I've learned that grief is brutal and uncompromising—that it messes with my mind, causing me to doubt myself and make mistakes. I've learned that grief affects everyone, even people like me. I've learned that I will always feel the presence of Dad, he will always be in my corner, forever by my side. Most importantly I've learned that even though I don't belong in this world, I will do anything to survive. Someone somewhere coughs and I'm reminded that the group is waiting for me to speak.

"I've learned that every ending is a new beginning," I decide to say. "Grief allows a new chapter to start."

The rest of the meeting passes without incident. Christiana is given her opportunity to talk about mindfulness, Will sharpens a couple of pencils, the Welshman stares at the ceiling and Star leads us through a final meditation. Stacking my chair away at the end, I wonder about the next chapter in my life. How will it start? Will the police be waiting for me when I get home? Will

Mrs. Davis be interviewed after my arrest? Will she become the first person to actually choke on an overdose of clichés?

I hear my name as I walk towards the door, and I know this is it. This is how the next chapter starts. Turning, I stare into eyes that always seem to be focused on mine.

"Claire," the voice says. "I think we need to talk."

"Yes," I say simply. "I think we do."

22

My hammer is a thing of great beauty. To the rest of the world, it's just a hammer. To me, it's a bridge, linking my desires to my reality. Always reliable, always there, allowing me to excel at what I do. The best kind of friend, my hammer has been with me during all the important moments of my life. Naturally it will be with me now.

I'd assumed that the confrontation would be immediate. As soon as I heard my name, I'd assumed the accusations would fly. I expected shouting and panicked phone calls to the police but there was none of that. Instead, quiet arrangements were made to meet at seven o'clock this evening in town. We're meeting in a public place on the understanding that we need to talk. I can't help thinking it's a trap. Will the police be there, hiding in a parked van, pretending to be British Gas or Virgin Media? That's what they do in films. Maybe they're watching my house. I glance out my living room window. Huge raindrops are falling. The street is empty and quiet. I check my watch. It's time to go.

I pause before opening the front door and remove Dad's umbrella from the coat stand. I never use an umbrella; I've never seen the point. In a world where ordinary people expose their whole lives to every predator on the internet, it amuses me that they shield themselves from rain. Dad's umbrella is classic, smart—very much like him. I wrap my fingers around the wooden handle and wonder when this umbrella was last used. When was the last time Dad shook it dry, closed it up and hung it on the coat stand? Did he know it was the last time? Does anyone, ever? Will this be the last time I walk out of my front door? I think about looking over my shoulder, taking one last look at everything I've ever known. I open the front door and step into the rain.

It's quiet outside, eerily so. I walk past houses and imagine the people inside. Cooking meals, watching television, talking about the rain—all so certain about what tomorrow will bring. So certain they're probably not even thinking about tomorrow. The complacency sickens me. I tighten my grip on the wooden handle of Dad's umbrella and continue on towards the high street. There are more cars on the road now. One slows down and swerves around a puddle to avoid splashing me. I think about the driver and wonder whether that decency is a constant. Was swerving around that puddle the one good deed of the day or does the driver always strive to make the next right decision? A jogger runs past me, breathing heavily, moving fast. The rain must be blinding him. His top has a logo on the back and the words, "Just Do It." Is that what he thought when he laced up his running shoes and looked outside at the weather? Is that what he thinks before doing anything? He must be irritating to live with.

I've reached the shops and the restaurants. A gust of wind blows Dad's umbrella inside out and I stand still to fix it. A couple are having a conversation by the war memorial. A little girl is holding the woman's hand and climbing up the steps. The man wants to eat in the tapas restaurant, but the woman isn't so keen. She wants to go somewhere where there will be a children's menu for Jessica. The man says that Jessica can have some bread or something, but the woman says she wants Jessica to have a proper meal. Jessica is wearing yellow wellies and keeps jumping from the third step of the memorial into a puddle before marching up the steps again. She's laughing loudly with each splash and doesn't look like she cares where she eats. The man tells the woman to make a decision so they can get out of the rain. I tighten my grip on Dad's umbrella and walk on.

I'm almost at the meeting point and thinking about Dad again. I wonder when he last held this umbrella. Was he thinking about me? Worrying? Is he still worrying about me? Will I ever do anything to make him proud? I'm twenty yards from my destination and wondering what Dad would say if he was here. I close my eyes for a moment and try to channel Dad's calm, soothing presence. A few more minutes of walking and I'll be there.

I stop walking. Something is wrong. Something I've seen or something I've heard; something isn't right. I mentally retrace my steps since I shut my front door. What was it? I think about the car slowing down to swerve around the puddle. Was it slowing down to swerve around the puddle or was it slowing down so the driver could see me? What about that jogger's logo? Was that random or a sign? And then there was that couple arguing about the tapas restaurant. I think about their daughter, wearing yellow wellies, splashing in the puddle.

Suddenly there's a connection. My mind is back in Waterbridge Oak and I'm watching those pigs on the television. Those ridiculous cartoon pigs wearing yellow wellies and splashing about in muddy puddles. Is that it? Is that what I'm reminded of? Why is that important? I start walking again and within moments I've arrived at the Red Lion. I need to stop spooking myself and stick to the plan. I walk past the front door of the pub and into the car park at the back. Once there, I stand behind a parked car in the corner, lower Dad's umbrella and drop it into my bag. The hood of my black raincoat obscures my face and on such a dark, rainy evening, no one will see me here. I check my watch. Ten minutes to seven. I'm in position at the correct time. Now I just need to wait.

As the minutes pass by, I wonder whether Dad ever wished I was different. I wonder whether he ever dreamt of having other children. Ordinary children. He never said so if he did. He said it was OK to be me, that he liked my quirky sense of humor, so similar to his own. I wonder whether he'd find this situation funny. Me, standing in a pub car park in the pouring rain waiting for the most important meeting of my life. And the name of the person I'm meeting? Well, that's the best part. I have absolutely no idea.

The back door of the pub opens and someone steps outside. It's him. He's alone. I see the spark as he lights a cigarette. This is it. My only chance. I move out of the shadows and silently approach. He has his back to me. The rain is slapping into my face, making it difficult to see so I follow the stench of cigarette smoke. Blinking rain out of my eyes, I remove my hammer from my bag and then I stop. The smoke isn't moving through him; he doesn't look like a ghost.

Then I remember. The thing that told me something isn't right. Nothing to do with those cartoon pigs. And suddenly I'm not sure of anything anymore. But this is my only chance. It's now or never.

I drop the hammer back into my bag. He turns around.

"Claire!" says the Welshman. "You're soaking! I thought we were going to meet inside. Come on, let's go."

I let him usher me into the pub and find me a seat next to the fire. When he returns to the table with a bottle of red wine and two glasses, I notice him stumble and wonder how much he's already had to drink. I knew he'd get here early. I knew he'd go outside for a cigarette before I arrived. I didn't know I'd be sitting here sharing a bottle of wine with him. I thought he'd be dead by now.

"Claire," he says, "thank you so much for agreeing to meet me." He drains his glass before pouring another. "Dutch courage," he smiles, and I smile back. "I've been so nervous," he says. "It's been many, many years since I went on a date with anyone other than my wife."

Suddenly, it all starts to fall into place. All those times I caught him staring at me when he was supposed to be meditating. I'd mistaken that look in his eyes for knowledge. I thought he knew something about me. I was wrong.

"I've been so lonely, since my wife died," he says, "and I never believed that someone as pretty as you could be interested in me. But the way you looked at me today, Claire," he says, leaning towards me, "well, as you yourself said, every ending is a new beginning. Grief allows a new chapter to start."

I pick up my glass, take a sip and think. When I put the glass down, I'll let this sad, lonely drunk cry about his dead wife for a while, rant about the doctors and, by the time my glass is empty, I'll let him down gently, get up and leave. No hard feelings. A simple misreading of signs.

Misreading of signs. So easily done.

THEN

can't make myself any clearer," says the man with the angry tattoos. "I want to be with you. All of the time. Not just when your husband is at work. I want you all to myself."

"But you do have me all to yourself," says the woman. "Well, as good as. He's always away working. His boss works him like a dog," she adds with a smile, placing both arms around the man's neck. "He works like a dog so I can live like a queen."

"My beautiful, sexy queen," says the man, pulling her towards him. "So beautiful, you should be a model. Talking of which, are we going to have this fashion show or what?"

"On one condition," says the woman, suddenly serious. "You make sure my banister is finished tomorrow."

"It's a deal," smiles the man.

They both run up the stairs, shrieking and laughing, before pausing outside a bedroom door. "Hang on a minute," says the woman, turning a key in the lock. "Don't want that little bitch coming out and disturbing us. Tried to make me look stupid in front of that teacher. She thinks she's so clever."

"Sshhh," says the man. "Don't waste your time even thinking about her. You've got a fashion show to get ready for!"

The woman laughs as the banging starts.

"Let me out!" calls the little girl from behind the locked door. "It's too hot in here and the window doesn't open. Let me out!"

"Shut up, Claire!" shouts the woman. "The more noise you make, the longer I'll keep you in there. And darling Daddy won't be home for hours," she adds, laughing again, "so I'd keep quiet if I was you. Sorry about that," she says to the man, before disappearing into her bedroom. After a while she emerges wearing a short black business suit with another pair of sky-scraper heels.

"Very nice," says the man, "the sexy secretary look. Give me a twirl. Now, walk down the stairs." The woman smiles as she walks past before slowly making her way down the steps. "Beautiful," shouts the man. "Go slower. Now stop," he says as she reaches the middle of the stone staircase. "Look at me and take off the jacket slowly. Now walk back up. Slower. Keep looking at me. It's nice but I know you can do better. The heels could be higher, and the skirt could be shorter. I'll give it six out of ten."

"If you want the heels higher, you'd better clear these tools away," says the woman. "I could trip and break my neck."

"OK, OK," says the man, rounding up the tools with his foot. Kicking hammers, chisels and screwdrivers into a messy pile at the top of the stairs. "Can't wait to see the next one," he calls as the woman once again disappears behind a closed door. "And remember the rule. Outfits have to get smaller each time."

"I think you're going to love this one," calls the woman after a while. "Are you keeping a note of the scores?"

"I don't have any paper on me," he says, tapping his pockets. "Give me a minute. Oi, kid," he says, turning the key in the lock and barging into the little girl's room. "I need some paper, give me that paper."

"No, that's my register!" the child shouts. "I'm using it."

"Well, now I'm using it," says the man, smiling, snatching the register from the little girl's hand. "Christ, this room is tiny!" he says, laughing. "Your mummy's wardrobe is bigger than this. And it's boiling hot in here. Why don't you open a window? Oh, yes. I forgot. The window doesn't open, does it. Let go!" he shouts as the little girl grabs hold of the paper. "Christ, you're freakily strong for such a tiny thing." He pulls the paper free with one hand and pushes her away with the other.

"Give it back," shouts the little girl, running towards him.

Laughing, he turns away and shuts the door.

"Are you ready for outfit number two?" shouts the woman.

"Hell, yes!" replies the man. "Now, this is more like it," he says as the woman emerges. "Shorter, tighter. And are those heels higher? This is all adding up to extra points. Yes, that one is a definite eight out of ten."

The woman walks slowly past him and pauses when he tells her to stop at the middle of the staircase. "What's that by your foot?" he shouts from above.

"Where?" she asks, sounding confused. "I can't see anything."

"There's something there," he shouts. "I can see it. On the middle stair. By your foot. Bend over and have a look."

"There's nothing there," says the woman, bending down. "I can't see anything."

"Are you sure?" shouts the man. "Turn around and bend over. Have a good look."

"I seriously can't see anything," says the woman, turning around and bending over, revealing her underwear.

"My mistake," shouts the man, laughing. "Come back up here, my beautiful, sexy queen."

When the woman climbs to the top of the staircase, he pulls her towards him. "I declare this outfit the definite winner," he says, running his hands over her body.

"The show isn't over yet," she says, smiling. "You're going to love the next one. It's tiny. I think I'm going to get a ten for sure."

"In that case, I think we'll have some music," he says as she disappears once again into her bedroom. "I fancy seeing you dance in number three." And with that he picks up the workman's radio, which sits discarded by the gap in the banister next to the messy pile of tools. He tunes it for a moment before music starts to play, then increases the volume until it blares.

"Oh my God, you made me jump," he says, sounding startled. "Freaky little kid. Did I forget to lock you back in? How long have you been standing there?"

"I need my register," says the little girl calmly. "Give me my register. I need it for my game."

"Well, I need it for my game," says the man, sneering. "So, fuck off."

"How do you do that?" asks the child, taking a step towards him.

"What?" he says, confused.

"Make your tattoos disappear. How do you do that?"

"You're so weird," he laughs, glancing at the tattoos on his arm. "No wonder you haven't got any mates. Fuck off back to your room."

"I can see straight through your tattoos," she says, quietly. "I can see straight through all of you."

"What the fuck are you saying?"

"You look like you've already gone."

"Right, get back in your—" And suddenly there's movement. Freakily fast movement accompanied by a freakily strong shove. He stumbles backwards in shock. For a second it looks like he may retain his balance. But then the next shove is just as freakily strong. The sound when it comes is *perfection. In time with the music and at the perfect pitch. It's the sound of emptiness escaping. From a head still reverberating on stone.*

"Close your eyes and don't open them until I tell you," calls the woman over the blare of music. "I think this is going to be a ten for sure. Keep those eyes closed—Claire, what are you doing out here?" she asks as she emerges from behind the closed door. "Oh my God," she says, sounding panicked. "Has Daddy come home early?"

"No," replies the little girl. "Why are you wearing a bikini, Mummy? Are you going swimming? And why are you wearing it with those long boots?"

"None of your bloody business, nosy little bitch," snaps the woman. "You shouldn't even be out here. Did you see where the builder went?"

"That thing that he said, he was right, Mummy," says the little girl.

"What? Who?" asks the woman, confused.

"The builder. What he said was right."

"What do you mean? What are you talking about?"

"There is something on the middle stair."

"Christ, Claire. Can you ever not be weird?" asks the woman, teetering on high heels towards the unfinished banister. "What's down there?"

And then she screams. And under the screams and the music, there's a silence. Uncluttered. Inviting stillness to invade a busy mind.

"Oh my God!" screams the woman. "Why isn't he moving? Is that blood? Claire, what happened to him?" She pushes past the little girl and hurries down the stone staircase, then crouches beside the man. "Claire, did you see him fall?"

"Mummy!" calls the little girl from above.

"Claire, he's not breathing. Oh my God, what happened?"

"Mummy!" calls the little girl again, from four steps above.

"*I think he's cracked his head on the stone.*"

"*Mummy!*" *calls the child, three steps above.*

"*I need to get an ambulance,*" *says the woman, crying now.* "*I need to get him some help.*"

"*Mummy!*" *calls the child, two steps above.*

"*Not now, Claire!*" *screams the woman.*

"*But I need to tell you something. It's important.*"

"*What, Claire?*" *screams the woman, turning to face the little girl standing one step above.*

"*You look so much more beautiful as a ghost.*" *And the hammer, when it hits, is perfection. Greeting a skull and bidding farewell to a life of disdain. The woman slumps over the man, her eyes fixed open. Staring, unblinking, towards the top of the stairs.*

The little girl drops the hammer and runs to her room to retrieve Bambi, then runs back and forth a few times to get the rest of her toys. She positions some along the man's back. Others lean against the arms covered in angry tattoos. The register is still clasped in the man's hand. The little girl pulls it free, then turns her attention to Bambi. She places him on her mother's naked stomach at the front of the class. And now everything is ready. Finally, she can return to her game. The focus of unblinking attention, she smooths out the register. Smiles as she adds two new names.

've laid everything out on my living room floor but I'm still no closer to seeing the truth. It must be here. She said it herself. I plonk myself into my armchair and think back to the day she died. Jemma was sitting right here, in this chair, when she said it. I've been so distracted by the bereavement group; I missed all the signs. But the truth has always been here. Right under my nose. Why can't I see it?

It was the comment by Pumpkin-Head Deb. That's what was wrong. I saw the child wearing wellies, climbing up the steps of the war memorial, and it triggered a memory. Not of those cartoon pigs but that comment by Deb. She said that the last time she saw Jemma she was marching up the stairs wearing wellies and a kilt. It didn't occur to me at the time but that's what was wrong. The wellies. On the stairs. Deb is fairly draconian when it comes to this rule, she even mentioned it to me. What were her exact words? Visitors and residents are free to wear whatever shoes they like inside Waterbridge Oak, but staff must wear outdoor shoes outdoors and indoor shoes indoors. Wellies are the most outdoor of outdoor shoes so why was Jemma wearing them to march up the stairs? Why didn't she change into her indoor shoes?

Getting up, I head into the kitchen, flick the kettle on, drop a teabag into a mug, then change my mind and pour myself a glass of water instead. I'm restless all of a sudden, irritatingly so. Switching the radio on, I listen to a song I vaguely recognize, close my eyes and think. If Star were here, she'd tell me to concentrate on my breathing. I focus on my next in-breath, try to slow it right down. If Star asked me today what she asked me yesterday, I'd have a very different answer for her. The one thing I've learned about grief is that it blinds me to the truth, rendering me stupid. Because I have been stupid, there's no doubt about that.

I take a sip of water and think back to what Deb said. She was on her way to a lunch meeting, she said, the last time she saw Jemma alive. Jemma was walking up the stairs of Waterbridge Oak wearing wellies and a kilt. She killed herself later that day. Why didn't I pick up on it at the time? On the morning she died, Jemma was at the bereavement group, crying fake tears into Florence's navy-blue cardigan. Then at four o'clock that same day, she came to my home. According to Deb, at lunchtime Jemma was at the care home. Why? She wasn't working. If she was working, she would have been wearing her uniform and indoor shoes. What was she doing there? There were only a couple of hours in between the group ending and her meeting with me. It was an important day for Jemma, the day she was going to blackmail a murderer. Why waste time going to her place of work if she didn't need to be there?

Unless she did *need* to be there. Unless she needed to get something. But what? I think back to when she arrived at my house that afternoon. She was carrying a bag; I remember her pulling her phone out of it to speak to Florence. She didn't appear to have anything else of great importance with her. And if she did go to the care home that day to retrieve something, wouldn't it be stored in her locker? The lockers are all in the staff changing room on the ground floor. Jemma was marching up the stairs. Where was she going? There's nothing up those stairs apart from residents' bedrooms, plus the sitting and dining rooms. There's nowhere up there to store anything. Upstairs, there's just . . . people.

Another song has started playing on the radio and I turn up the volume. If I'm trying to drown out what my gut is saying, it doesn't work. It's screaming at me; has been ever since I stood in the pub car park last night and didn't use my hammer. Is it possible that Jemma was marching up those stairs that day because she was going to see someone? Did Jemma have an accomplice? Does somebody else know about Lucas? About me? I close my eyes again and take another deep breath as a hundred thoughts gate-crash my mind. I wish I could recognize which buses are important and which ones I should let pass me by but I'm not sure of anything anymore. In this tangled web of blackmail and murder, I no longer know whether I'm the spider or the fly.

Returning to the living room, I sink back into the armchair and think about my most dangerous of foes. Assumption. When Jemma sat in this chair on the day she died, she led me to believe the blackmailing partnership involved only Lucas and herself and I assumed she was telling me the truth. Weeks later, when I found the sealed envelope of photographs in the heron's bag, I assumed they had been put there by somebody in the pub. When am I going to appreciate the power of assumption? Bringing as it does a premature end to all rational thought. That envelope of photographs, for example; I should have given that envelope much more thought. Assuming it had been slipped into the heron's bag while I was queuing at the bar, I failed to consider the possibility that the envelope was placed into her bag before she even got to the pub. The heron could have been carrying it around for hours. I cringe now as I realize she even told me where she'd been earlier. She couldn't have given me a bigger clue but, such is the power of assumption, I failed to appreciate the significance of her words.

The song on the radio has finished and a newsreader begins giving the headlines. She sounds brisk and authoritarian. As she starts talking about a Westminster scandal, I think back to that day. I'm sitting in the red Mercedes in the pub car park and the heron has started highlighting her insecurities with lipstick, blusher and mascara. There are boxes of old newspapers and junk on the back seat of her car, and she explains that she's just emptied Jemma's locker at the care home. She tells me she's come straight from there. Why didn't it occur to me before? Somebody at the care home could have slipped that envelope into her bag. Maybe the same somebody Jemma was marching up the stairs that day to meet.

I can't help thinking this has something to do with the job Jemma spoke about. She was sitting right here when she said it. Told me she and Lucas had just started working on something big. She said she'd given Lucas the details the day before and that's what she was calling to talk to him about on the night he died. I'm fairly certain Lucas would keep the details of this new job in his blackmailing briefcase along with all his other blackmailing paraphernalia. But I have the contents of Lucas's brief-case laid out over my living room floor and I don't see anything. I see the newspaper Lucas used to conceal the incriminating images and I see the images themselves. I see the envelope of cash and that's it. There's nothing else. The only other items in Lucas's briefcase were some work files and his wallet. I looked through them at the time and didn't see anything of any interest.

Is there a chance I missed something? I don't think so. But I can't deny that I've been making mistakes lately, have been ever since Dad died. Was it a mistake to leave the wallet and work files in Lucas's briefcase at Florence's house? Was it a mistake to leave that briefcase next to Jemma's dead body? I'm not used to doubting myself, but nothing seems to be making sense anymore. The only thing I know for certain is that the police have the brief-case and the wallet and the work files so, if I did miss anything, it's too late now.

The newsreader is talking about the missing nurse, Sebastian Sinclair. Apparently it's been almost two months since he disap-peared, and the police are issuing a fresh appeal for information. Why is this still news? People go missing every day. I wonder why some capture the media's attention while for others, it's almost as though they were never here.

A fascinating question to ponder but I have to stay focused. If Jemma was marching up the stairs that day to see somebody, who was it? I've always been suspicious of Irina. Anyone who wears that much foundation must have something to hide. But Irina is always at the reception desk on the ground floor. What about the Michelin-starred sous-chef I've heard so much about but never seen? Who often goes up to the dining room on the third floor to check everyone's enjoying the food—could Jemma have been going to meet him? Or her? Why has it only just occurred to me that the Michelin-starred sous-chef might be a woman? Another fascinating question to add to my list of fascinating questions to ponder. And what about Ben? Honest, authentic, half-marathon-running, nice-guy Ben? Is it all an act? Is Ben involved in the blackmailing? Was he working with Jemma and Lucas on the mysterious big job she spoke about?

Restless again, I stand up and walk to the window. It's a beautiful day outside. Such a contrast to the rain of yesterday. Blue sky and sunshine jar with my mood so I pull the curtains shut. None of it makes any sense. Even if somebody else is involved, even if Jemma was walking up the stairs to see somebody, none of it makes any sense. First of all, if Jemma had an accomplice at the care home, why did she risk arousing suspicion by going to see them? What did she need to tell them that was so important? She'd been at the group that morning where she'd made plans to meet me at four o'clock and Florence at eight. Was this the information she needed to pass on? If so, why didn't she just speak to the accomplice on the phone? Why did she need to see them in person?

Despite all her bravado, she must have felt scared. Jemma wasn't an inconsequential character like Florence or Mrs. Davis. To be inconsequential, you have to be nice, and you have to be stupid. Jemma was neither. She knew that at four o'clock, she was going to walk willingly into the home of a killer. She *must* have felt scared. Is that why she was at the care home that day? Did she want to tell somebody her plans? Let somebody know where she was going, what she was doing? Did she give her accomplice my address? And Florence's? Was it her accomplice who stood outside Florence's house and took photographs? If so, this is the part that makes no sense whatsoever. If Jemma's accomplice watched me walk into Florence's house, why on earth didn't he or she warn Jemma that I was inside? Whoever took the photographs of me hung around long enough to take a photograph of Jemma walking into Florence's house too. And then what? Why didn't they warn Jemma? Or call the police? Or barge into the house or get help? Apart from slipping the photographs into the heron's bag, the accomplice, if one exists, has taken no action whatsoever. None of it makes any sense.

I suddenly realize I'm pacing back and forth between the window and the running machine. I've become a person who paces. I list unanswerable questions in my mind, and I pace. What is happening to me?

The newsreader has moved on from Sebastian and is now talking about the latest household name who put his hand up young girls' skirts forty years ago and probably still can't fathom why anyone cares. Apparently, he lost his appeal today against his six-year prison sentence. Six years. I wonder whether he'll spend one moment of that time feeling anything other than self-pity and indignation. I wonder how his victims feel today. As their sentences enter year forty. I pick up Lucas's newspaper from the living room floor. I remember seeing a photograph of the latest household name on the front page. I stare at him now, study his face. Interesting how men like him always seem to have the same look. I wonder what molds such an unattractive sneer. The pious combination of entitlement and arrogance, perhaps? In the newspaper article, the latest household name is quoted as saying he will contest these ridiculous accusations and clear his name. He describes himself as an honest, God-fearing family man. Sebastian was described as God-fearing too. Didn't stop him abusing vulnerable patients in his care. I'm not sure whether a fear of God can ever be used as a reliable judge of character.

I drop the newspaper back onto the floor, walk over to the window, turn around to face the running machine and then stop. What was it the latest household name said? He would fight the accusations and clear his name. Accusations? Aren't we a long way past the stage of accusations? Hasn't he just lost his appeal? I pick the newspaper back up and turn it over to look at the front page. It's right there. Has been all this time. I just never noticed. I stare at the front page of the newspaper. Look at the date. This newspaper is almost three years old. Why did Lucas have such an old newspaper with him on the day he died? And then I think about something else. All those boxes on the back seat of the red Mercedes. What did the heron say about Jemma? Her locker was filled with old newspapers. She never threw anything away. I look at the newspaper in my hand. Is this it? Is this what Jemma gave to Lucas the day before he died? Are the details of the big job hidden somewhere within the pages of this newspaper?

My eyes skim over the articles on the front page. I read about the indignation of the latest household name. The horror of the drug-addicted young mother who awoke to find her baby gone. The tragedy of the teenage girl killed in a hit-and-run; a girl described as being "everyone's friend." My mouth feels dry as I open the newspaper and read the detail of each story. Then I close the newspaper, walk back towards the window and open the curtains. The sun doesn't irritate me anymore. I want it to shine on what I am beginning to see.

Within an hour I'm on a train to the coast.

24

After it happened, we came to a place like this. It was July and didn't stop raining. Everywhere we went, people raised their eyes and spoke about "the great British summer." I didn't care about the rain, barely noticed it. I was on holiday with my dad and my mother was dead. It was the happiest time of my life. Even his sadness didn't ruin anything. He drank a lot of whisky and he cried a lot of tears, but I guess that was the shock. I wonder what's worse? Coming home after a long day at work to find your wife dead? Or finding her draped semi-naked over another man? I'm not sure which part upset Dad so much. I don't suppose it matters. Whatever the cause, his pain was real. I know that now. Now that I know about grief.

On my seventh birthday, he came home and found me playing with their bodies. He collapsed on the stairs and took her dead head in his arms. He brushed her hair away from her staring eyes and he cried. He howled. He loved her. He really loved her. That's one of the two things I'll never understand about my dad. His love for my mother, and why he never said that he knew about me.

After the howling finally finished, he looked up into my eyes.

Really looked as he asked me what had happened. But before I could answer, he changed his mind. He decided he'd rather not hear my reply. Instead, he laid her dead head gently down and picked up Bambi. He said we had to return all the toys to my room and, once that was done, I should wait for him up there. I stood at the top of the stairs and watched him. He took a handkerchief from his pocket, carefully picked up the hammer and wiped away any evidence that I might have touched it. Then he wrapped the builder's dead hand around the handle of the hammer—I guess it would have been suspicious if nobody's prints were on it—before dropping it back onto the floor next to my mother's head.

After that he came upstairs, knelt down in front of me and put his hands on my shoulders. He looked so serious. He said there had been an accident, a terrible accident, and Mummy was dead. He said we had to tell everyone it was an accident. A terrible accident. It was really important everyone know it was an accident. A terrible accident. He kept saying those words over and over. Like an echo, amassing credibility each time. There had been an accident. A terrible accident.

"Claire," he said, "do you understand what I'm saying? This was an accident. A terrible accident. Claire, do you understand?"

"Yes, Daddy," I said. "I understand." Which was true. I did understand. Understood I was going to get away with it.

And then there was a phone call to the police and blue flashing lights and lots of people traipsing around the house. I stayed upstairs with Dad, but occasionally peered down. When someone started taking photographs of the bodies, I squeezed his hand.

"Daddy," I whispered, "can we keep those photos?"

"No," he said quietly. "No, Claire, we can't."

"OK," I said. "Daddy?"

"Yes?"

"Can I have my cake now?"

He crouched down then and wrapped me up in his arms. Moved his face close to mine, before whispering, "Claire, can you pretend to be sad? Just while these people are here."

"OK," I said. "But why?"

"Because Mummy has just died," he whispered.

"OK," I said, almost silently. "But when these people have gone, then can I have my cake?"

"Yes, Claire," he whispered.

For a while he was under suspicion. They thought he'd killed them both in a jealous rage. Dad told me to wait in my bedroom while he talked to the policeman in charge, a man in a horrible brown suit. I stood behind the closed door and listened as they talked about time of death and alibis. The broken banister got mentioned next and the stone steps. My mother's high heels and the tools scattered all over the floor. And I kept waiting for my bedroom door to open. For someone to come in and expose the real me. But instead, they talked about the hammer. How it had fallen from a great height to strike with such force. And by the time that echo returned, I felt cheated. Was that it? Was I not even worthy of a moment of their consideration?

The man in the horrible brown suit opened my door then. He crouched in front of me, his yellow teeth bunched together in a crooked smile. He told me there had been an accident, a terrible accident, and my mother had died. He said he could see I was devastated and frightened. But he could also see I was so brave and so strong. He said he'd been in the police force for many years now and, in that time, he'd seen many scary and upsetting things. But he'd also seen the best of human nature. He'd seen the resilience, the hope and the love. I stood there and listened and wondered whether he would still sound so incredibly sure of himself if he knew all the things he couldn't see. He ruffled my hair then and smiled. Told me everything was going to be OK. I focused on looking sad to distract myself from flinching, offended by the touch of such inconsequential ordinariness.

After her funeral, Dad suggested we get away for a while and we came to a place like this. A place where seagulls wake you every morning, buckets and spades welcome you into every shop and everyone feels compelled to eat ice cream, regardless of the weather. And during that holiday, we found our place, my dad and me. The inspiration for so much of my artwork—the space between my happiness and his grief. A place where his memories sustained him. And my life could blossom and grow.

THE SEAGULLS IN THIS SEASIDE town are calling to each other somewhere above my head as I give the address to the driver and settle into the back of the cab. The driver says the journey should take twenty minutes or so. Give or take. I look out the window and think. That second thing I've never understood about Dad. I think about it a lot. Why did he never talk about what I really am?

The driver's going on about a new traffic system, and I'm murmuring words of interest but I'm not giving his chat any space in my mind. I'm not even thinking about appropriate clichés. I'm thinking about a time when I thought Dad was finally going to confront me with how much he knew. It was about ten years ago, and we were sitting at the kitchen table. I'd been teaching at the local infant school for a while. I must have been about twenty-four years old. Dad asked me about my day, and I told him. About how I'd been called to the headmaster's office because a complaint had been made about me. I told Dad about the ridiculous parents, always bleating on about their wonderful offspring. Always seeing brilliance that just wasn't there.

One woman was particularly heinous; she complained about me because I'd cast her child as a camel in the nativity play. She had a real problem with camels, this woman. A camel wasn't good enough for her son, she wanted him to be Joseph or one of the wise men. A solo singing shepherd at the very least. I remember standing in the headmaster's office watching her mouth move, daydreaming about silence. The uncluttered silence beneath her screams.

And somehow, I think Dad knew what I was planning. Because as we sat at the kitchen table talking, he became quiet. And then he told me there were always going to be ludicrous parents. There were always going to be people out there to despise. He suggested I give up work for a while and let him support me. Focus on my painting and keep away from all the ridiculous people outside. And that's when I knew, because it was obvious. He knew I was going to kill her. He knew the camel-hating bitch had to die.

But he never actually said so, and out of respect for my dad, I gave up teaching. But he knew I could never give up being me. So, he bought a secluded house for us to live in. And on the eve of each of his frequent business trips, we developed a ritual. He would tell me how much he loved me. How he'd love me until the end of all time.

"Have fun while I'm gone, Claire," he would say then, "and please be careful. I would hate it if anything happened to you."

And I would hug him and silently acknowledge the coded meaning. *Do whatever you have to do while I'm gone, Claire. But be careful. Whatever you do, Claire, don't get caught.*

The cab turns inland, and the seagulls quiet. We're moving away from the panoramic views and the tourists and their money. Leaving the world of sandy beaches, kitesurfing and optimism far behind. Arriving at my destination, I pay the cab driver and look around. It's exactly what I expected. A gang of youths is hanging around on the street corner. Hoods up and smoking, they look up from their phones and eye me with suspicion as I approach.

I show them the picture in the newspaper and ask if they can give me an address. More staring. More smoking. I offer them money. They give me the address. As I remove a tenner from my purse, there is a communal shuffle towards me and surreptitious glances towards a youth with blue eyes and bad skin. The Leader. Stillness and silence for a moment as he stares at my purse and then raises his face to look at me. He sees it straightaway. As soon as he looks into my eyes. Cold, black, nothing. I can tell he wants to step backwards but his gang is watching; he can't lose face. Snatching the tenner from my hand, he forces a smirk and says, "Nice . . ."

Nice what? Nice arse? Nice tits? What is this acne-covered baby thug going to say to me? How brave does he feel? ". . . doing business with you," he says, and I smile at him before dropping my purse back into my bag and turning away. They're probably not bad kids, this gang of hooded youths. Sure, they're too young to be smoking and hanging around on street corners but what else are they supposed to do? Study for exams? Learn to play the clarinet? These hooded youths don't live in a world of clarinets and revision. They live here, in this world—playing the hand they've been dealt. Isn't that what we all do?

I walk into the dilapidated tower block and climb the stairs up to the seventh floor. As I stand outside flat number eleven, I wonder about the person living inside. She opens the door after several minutes of knocking, and even though she's only young—early twenties at the very most—as soon as I see her, I can tell. She hasn't been dealt a good hand.

"Lauren?" I say as I put my hand out. "I'm—"

She doesn't wait to hear who I am, just turns and walks back into her flat. I follow and close the door behind me. It stinks in here. Cigarettes, rotting food, filth. If I had to market this aroma, I would call it Desolate. I follow her into the living room and stand by the door as she sits on the sofa in the center of the room and starts to roll a cigarette. Empty cider cans cover most of the floor. She lights the cigarette, inhales deeply, picks up one of the cans and flicks ash into it. Then she retrieves another can from somewhere behind her, opens it, takes a swig and places it on the floor. She sits forward on the sofa and rocks slightly as she sucks deeply on the cigarette. Then she picks up a can and takes another swig. She grimaces and moves the cigarette back towards her mouth. I think she may have picked up the wrong can. She raises her eyes and blinks when she sees me. Is that surprise? Did she forget I was here? It's impossible to read any emotion on such a blank canvas.

"Are you from the social?" she asks, taking another swig. "Have you come about the mold?"

"Yes, Lauren," I decide to say, "I've come about the mold."

She nods and takes another drag on the cigarette. Her arm reaches out towards the can. It's so thin, her arm. Like a twig. She's tiny. Must weigh about six stone. I could easily snap her in half. If she wasn't already broken.

"How are you, Lauren?" I ask. "How are you feeling?"

"Good, good," she says, running her free hand through her hair, "I'm feeling good." Her blonde hair is lank and unwashed. "It will be good to get the mold sorted," she says, "before . . ."

"Before what, Lauren?"

"Before he comes home," she says, flicking her enormous blue eyes towards me before reaching again for the can.

"Before who comes home, Lauren?"

"My Alfie. My baby. I don't want him playing near mold."

"Of course you don't. We can get the mold sorted." I smile.

"Thank you," she says, flicking the cigarette into the first can, draining the second and opening a third. "I want to have everything ready for him when he comes back. His toys are here waiting."

She reaches towards the other seat of the sofa and picks up two small stuffed animals. One of them looks like a blue elephant. The other a yellow polar bear. Aren't polar bears supposed to be white? This one probably once was.

"He loved these toys," she says, dropping them and moving the can towards her lips. "We'll all wait here for him. We've been waiting for nearly three years; we can keep waiting."

"I'm sure he'll be home soon, Lauren."

"Do you think so?"

"Yes, I'm sure of it."

"He was lying over there, near where you're standing now when he disappeared. I only closed my eyes for a moment. And when I woke up, he was gone. I searched everywhere. All round the flat and all over the estate. But he was gone. Disappeared into thin air. Do you really think he'll be home soon?"

"Yes, I do."

"Where do you think people go when they disappear into thin air?"

"I don't know."

She takes a final drag on the cigarette, drops the butt into one of the cans at her feet and blows a perfect smoke ring into the middle of the room. "One minute he was there," she says, mesmerized by the smoke, "and the next he was gone." The smoke ring disappears but still she stares at where it was. "Do you need to see the mold?" she asks suddenly, turning her head to look at me.

"Yes, that would be helpful," I reply.

She remains seated on the sofa and lifts the can towards her lips. "I wish he'd stayed in the hospital," she says, before tipping the remainder of the cider into her mouth.

"Who?" I ask.

"Alfie," she replies. "I visited him every day. Couldn't wait for him to come home. But now I wish he'd stayed in the hospital. He was safe in there. I knew where he was."

"Why was he in the hospital?" I ask.

"He was poorly when he was born," she replies, staring at something on the floor. "I thought it was because of the thing on his leg, I thought that's why he had to stay in the hospital, in one of those incubator things, but they said it was nothing to do with that."

"What thing on his leg, Lauren?" I ask.

"There was a red mark on his leg. Right here," she says, placing a trembling hand on her bony right thigh. "It was there when he was born."

"A birthmark?"

"Yes, if you like," she says, distracted. Her eyes have started to dart, and I wonder what she's looking for. Another can? Another cigarette? Another chance? "They said he was poorly because he was so small when he was born," she says, reaching behind for another can. "His lungs needed help. And it wasn't my fault," she says, her eyes suddenly locked onto mine. "I was healthy when I was pregnant. I swear to you. I ate fruit and vegetables, and I didn't do any . . ." Her voice disappears as she lifts the can towards her mouth. "I didn't do anything wrong. I hope his lungs are OK now," she says, reaching for her tobacco tin.

"That's why it's so important to get the mold sorted. I don't want him to become poorly again."

"Of course," I say. "Where is the mold?"

"Over there," she says, pointing vaguely in the direction of the window before rolling another cigarette. I cross the room and pause as I pass her. Transfixed by the tobacco and rolling paper, she has no idea I'm standing right behind her; completely oblivious to the danger she is in. I study the back of her neck. She's tiny. So easy to destroy. I imagine placing my hands on her shoulders and then squeezing that neck. Nothing could be simpler. Or more kind. In less than a minute I could end all her anguish, bring a halt to all those days stretching out ahead. Day after day, waiting and hoping for something that is never going to happen. My fingers twitch. I could do it right now. I would be doing her a favor. I would be doing society a favor. Think of all the money I'd save the taxpayer in benefits and healthcare costs. I could put this parasite out of her misery and then find others and do the same for them. Dignitas for the masses. No need for airfares to Switzerland and deep pockets. I'd do it for free.

She lights the cigarette and inhales deeply. Then she lifts the can to her mouth, drinks and stares at whatever it is on the floor she keeps looking at. I think again about putting my hands on her neck but it's no good, it feels wrong to claim this kill. Addiction has done all the groundwork. Addiction has stripped her of pride and joy and any chance of a future. Addiction should have the win.

She's blowing smoke rings as I let myself out. Walking down seven flights of stairs, I have plenty of time to think about what will happen afterwards; after addiction claims its prize. Lauren is a drug-addicted alcoholic who probably thought that eating a few grapes and carrots during pregnancy was adequate preparation for motherhood. She allowed her baby to be stolen from under her nose and, instead of spending every day searching for him, chooses to languish in the self-imposed exile of addiction. There's got to be a special place for the mothers like that. The ones who put their own needs and desires before those of their children. As I descend the final staircase, I find myself thinking about Lauren's enormous blue eyes when she finally comprehends her fate. I see them flickering with terror as she realizes there are no drugs to numb the pain, just the heavy burden of regret to share with all those other useless mothers. Surrounded by their mistakes and burning forever.

Right at the center of hell.

25

wonder why she feels the need to wear a mask. Every morning she must look at her face in the mirror and start the laborious task of transforming herself into someone else. Her fake smile is directed at me now as I sign my name in the visitors' book. Maybe the smile isn't fake. Maybe that's her real smile. Maybe, despite all the makeup, Irina the receptionist is the most transparent of us all. At least her mask is an obvious one.

I climb the stairs to the third floor and push open the door of room twenty. Kathleen is sitting in a wheelchair by the window. She looks tiny and pale. Even more frail than usual. Ben and an efficient-looking nurse are standing on either side of the wheelchair. The nurse is holding Kathleen's slim wrist, checking her pulse.

"What do you think it is?" Ben asks.

"Not sure," answers the nurse, writing notes in Kathleen's file. "Her temperature's raised but everything else seems to be OK. It's probably just this bug that's doing the rounds. Even so, I'm going to get the doctor to come and check her later. Just to be safe."

The nurse leaves the room as Ben tucks a blanket over Kathleen's legs and settles the doll into her arms. "Try not to worry, Claire," he says, catching my eye. "Like the nurse said, it's probably just this bug. Half the residents and staff here have caught it and poor Miranda doesn't look well at all. She looks as though she hasn't slept for—" Ben is interrupted by sudden shouting from outside and hurries from the room.

The male voice in the corridor is loud, forceful and uncompromising. "I've got my coat and my hat on, and I would like to go outside, please," it says with unwavering authority.

"OK, Frank," says Ben soothingly, "let's get ready for our walk." I picture Ben gently guiding Frank back towards the sitting room. Frank is still shouting. He sounds remarkably robust today, almost as robust as the Welshman mid-rant.

"Yes, we know you want to go outside, Frank," says a different male voice. "You've mentioned it at least fifty times already." This speaker sounds bored and haughty. Nicholas. I picture him sitting in an armchair staring at his phone.

Then there's a female voice, frazzled and tired, just on the right side of tears. Miranda. "Stay still, Oscar!" she's shouting. "Stay still for one moment so I can button up your coat." There's silence for a few moments, broken by a child's laughter. "Right, Oscar," says Miranda weakly, "where are your mittens? Oh, you know what? It's not that cold outside, you don't need mittens. Come on then, Dad, let's go for a walk."

"Miranda," says a male voice gently, too gentle to be anyone other than Ben. "Why don't you let me and Nicholas take your dad and Oscar out for a walk? You look like you could do with a rest."

"She'll be all right," says Nicholas briskly. "A bit of fresh air will do her good."

"Normally I'd agree," says Ben. "But if she has this bug, then she should keep warm."

"Don't worry, Ben. I'll be fine," says Miranda and I imagine her smiling bravely. "I had some paracetamol just before we came out and I think I'm starting to feel a little better . . . Oh, Oscar!" she exclaims, suddenly. "What have you done with your shoes?"

"I'd like to go outside now, please," shouts Frank, above the child's laughter. "I've got my coat on and I'd like to have a cup of coffee outside, please. I'd like to go outside in the—"

"OK, Dad!" screams Miranda. "Nicholas, can you get up and find Oscar's shoes, please?"

"What do they look like?" he asks, and I can picture the sulky expression.

"They're small and blue with a picture of a dinosaur on each side," she snaps.

"Where did he last have them?" asks Nicholas, as I sense Miranda's frustration. I can imagine it snaking around the sitting room, grabbing Nicholas by the throat.

"I don't know where he last had them!" she spits. "Why don't you ask him?"

"Oscar, buddy," says Nicholas, against a backdrop of giggles and scampering sounds. "Where did you put your shoes, Oscar? Do you remember where you last had them?"

"No, I don't!" shouts a child's voice before the giggling and the scampering start up again.

"Miri, I don't think Oscar can remember where he last had his shoes," says Nicholas. "Oh, hang on. Are these them? Miri, these little blue shoes with the dinosaurs on them, are these Oscar's shoes?"

"Yes," she answers wearily as I wonder who else he thinks might be wearing tiny dinosaur shoes in a care home. Frank, maybe? The efficient nurse? Mr. or Mrs. sous Michelin Star, perhaps? "Oscar!" shouts Miranda. "Please, Oscar. Look! Mummy has your T-Rex shoes. Please stop running around so Mummy can put your shoes on." From the sound of intensified scampering, it doesn't sound as though Oscar has any intention of stopping. Nor does he seem keen to have his feet encased in footwear, T-Rex or otherwise.

"This is a complete and utter nightmare," sighs Nicholas, and I imagine him sinking back into the armchair.

"Why are you sitting down again?" spits Miranda, proving that my imagination is spot on. "Why don't you help me get his shoes on?"

"I've already got my shoes on," says Frank before Nicholas can answer. "And my hat and my coat."

"Yes, I know, Dad," says Miranda. "Oscar! Come here right now!" More frenzied scampering before a burst of happy squealing.

"Superhero Oscar to the rescue!" says Ben, in one of those irritating voices ordinary people always adopt when entertaining smaller ordinary people. I picture Ben whooshing the little boy Superman-style through the air so that he doesn't notice when Ben slips the shoes onto his feet.

"Thank you, Ben," sniffs Miranda, and I wonder when she ventured over to the wrong side of tears. "Right then, shall we go?"

"Miranda," says Ben, suddenly serious. "I really must insist that you let Nicholas and me take them out. You look as though you might keel over at any moment."

If she protests, it's practically inaudible, although Nicholas has no trouble projecting his voice. "What? We have to take both of them out? At the same time? On our own? Can't we leave Oscar here?"

"No!" says Ben cheerfully. "Superheroes don't get left behind. Do they, Superhero Oscar?" More whooshing and squealing followed by footsteps moving along the corridor towards the lift. Frank declares that he has his hat and coat on, Oscar laughs so hard he starts to hiccup, Ben whooshes, Miranda calls goodbye from the sitting room and Nicholas's silence is perhaps the most deafening sound of all. As the lift door closes behind them, the voices gradually disappear and by the time I watch them from the window of room twenty, crossing the road and walking towards town, the third floor is silent.

Kathleen is still sleeping, despite that racket. Maybe sound has no meaning in her world, that uncharted territory between the living and the dead. I remove a blanket from the bed and tuck it over the one already across her tiny legs. I imagine it's cold in her world. Then I leave and close the door behind me. Privacy is important and should always be respected. Whatever the world.

Miranda is huddled in an armchair in the corner of the sitting room. Her eyes are closed, and I can see what Ben meant. She doesn't look well. I take a seat on the sofa opposite and wait for her to open her eyes. When she does, there's a moment of confusion followed by fear.

"I'm sorry," I say kindly, "I didn't mean to scare you."

"No, no," she stammers, "you didn't scare me. It was just a shock, that's all. I didn't hear you come in."

"Do you know what's funny?" I ask.

"No," she replies. "What's funny?"

"Every time I see you, you look scared."

"Do I?" she asks, glancing towards the ceiling. "I don't mean to."

"Do you remember the first time I met you?" I ask. "It was in this room, during that ridiculous quiz. You looked scared when we first spoke. Very ill at ease."

"I was probably just stressed," she says, fleetingly meeting my eye. "It can be difficult, keeping Oscar under control, especially in a place like this. It was very busy in here that day. I was probably preoccupied, didn't want Oscar running riot, tripping anyone up."

"Of course," I say. "I understand. But what about the second time we met? When there weren't any elderly residents around."

"I'm sorry, I don't recall—"

"You were by the television. When I walked in and you turned round, you looked scared."

"Ah, well, that was because I was nervous about Deb walking in and seeing me," she says, pulling her phone from her bag.

"You know what Deb can be like about nonresidents using the TV."

"I see," I say. "And what about the last time?"

"I'm sorry, when was that?"

"The tea party. I walked into the room, you looked at me and I remember thinking that you looked . . . ashen-faced."

"Ashen-faced?" she says with a smile, placing her phone on her lap. "I don't even know what that means. I wouldn't know how to look ashen-faced if I tried!"

"Crestfallen," I say by way of explanation. "You looked crestfallen."

"Oh," she says, circling the phone in her hand. "Was that the day my father forgot who I am and demanded to speak to my dead mother? I can't imagine why I wasn't beaming with joy."

"You were looking crestfallen before your dad forgot who you are and started shouting."

"Look, Claire," she says, sitting forward. The phone is hidden in her hand. I can't see what her fingers are doing, whether she's unlocking the keypad. "Is there a point to any of this? Because I'm not feeling well and was hoping to get a bit of peace and quiet before Oscar and my dad come back."

"I met Lauren Blake yesterday." And that's it. That's all it takes to shift the atmosphere. To change the course of fate. Five unremarkable words. No going back. The phone drops back into her lap.

"I got the train down to Poole," I continue. "You know Lauren, don't you, Miranda? Lauren Blake? She's a blonde lady. With huge blue eyes. Exactly the same eyes as Oscar." And as she stares at me, a thought occurs, and I can't resist. "See!" I say, marveling at the depth of emotion she isn't blinking away. "You do know how to do ashen-faced, Miranda. You're doing it right now."

ow was she?" Miranda asks eventually, wiping a tear from her eye.

"She's a drug addict who lost her baby three years ago. How do you think she is?"

"I don't know," she says. "I guess I always hoped that she'd have more children. That she'd be OK."

"Well, I don't know how she is today, but she certainly didn't look OK yesterday. Yesterday she looked like a junkie alcoholic, living in a filthy mold-covered flat, drinking cheap cider, smoking roll-ups and waiting for her baby boy to magically reappear."

"My God," she says, dropping her head into her hands. "What have I done?"

"You've given Oscar a chance at a decent life," I reply. "You should be given a medal, you and that hideous husband of yours. I assume it was his idea?" The newspaper rustles as I take it from my bag. "I got most of the information I needed from this," I say, turning to the relevant page. "The photograph of Lauren shows a clear resemblance to Oscar and the article names the estate she lives on and the fact that she gave birth in Poole hospital. Poole's near to Bournemouth, isn't it? Where you used to live." No response. If she's crying, the tears are silent. "Then when I met Lauren and she mentioned her baby being in an incubator, that's when I knew Neonatal Nick had to be involved."

"Don't mock him, Claire," she says, raising her face to look at me. "Who the hell do you think you are? You, of all people, are in no position to judge anyone."

"True," I say, placing the newspaper back into my bag, wondering how much Miranda knows or thinks she knows about me. "And I'm not judging anyone. As I just said, I think you and your husband deserve a medal. I'm just curious, that's all. Stealing a baby is highly risky behavior and you don't strike me as the kind of person who likes to take risks. I'm just interested to know why you did it."

"No great mystery," she says after a few moments' silence. "We couldn't have a baby of our own." More silence as her eyes dart towards the ceiling. She's remembering. "I can get pregnant easy enough," she says eventually. "I've got eight positive pregnancy tests at home to prove it. Could never bring myself to throw those tests away. The only link, I guess, to the babies I'll never hold. Never know."

She reaches into her bag. Takes out a tissue and something else. Something blue. "Despite what you may think of him, Claire, Nicholas is a good man. He held my hand after each miscarriage and told me we'd never give up, that one day we'd have our baby. And then one day I visited him at work, and I saw Oscar," she says, clasping the blue object in her hand. "He was so tiny. Tubes everywhere, struggling to breathe. And I looked at him and he opened his eyes and I know it sounds stupid, but I felt it. Straightaway. This was our baby."

She opens her hand and stares at the object. It's a child's mitten. "Nicholas told me about Lauren, about the drugs and the alcohol, and I don't know what it was, but something took control of me. Something took control of my mind. Maybe it was grief. I'd lost eight babies, maybe grief turned my mind inside out, allowed a darkness to take over, because I started to think that it was unfair. Why should a drug addict like Lauren have a baby when I couldn't? I'd see her smoking outside the hospital, and she'd go and visit that beautiful little boy. Stinking of smoke. I started to hate her. I didn't even know her, but I hated her. And every time I looked in that little boy's eyes, I'd feel this connection. Like we were supposed to be together. And when he left the hospital, it was as though I'd lost those eight babies all over again. I couldn't sleep, couldn't eat. Walked around like a zombie. Couldn't think of anything but that little boy."

She's silent now, looking at me. I think she wants me to say something, but I can't think of a single cliché. "But you're married to a doctor," I say. "Couldn't he have recommended a therapist or something?" When she doesn't respond, I do something I hardly ever do. I tell her the truth. "I've been going to a bereavement group for the last month or so," I say. "And I've actually found it quite useful. Sometimes talking about problems can help," I add. "There's no shame in it."

She laughs then. "I'm sorry, Claire," she says. "No disrespect to you and your group but I don't think the counseling is working. I watched you walk into that poor woman's house. I heard the gunshot. I know what you did."

"So, it was you," I say. "Standing outside Florence's house that night. Taking photographs of Jemma and me. Why?"

"She found out about Oscar," she says simply, staring again at the mitten in her hand. "Told me she'd go to the police unless I did what she said. She gave me an address and told me that if I went and took photographs, she'd keep quiet about Oscar."

"So, she blackmailed you," I say, understanding that part. "But how did she find out about Oscar? And how did she know I was going to be at Florence's house?"

"She was blackmailing me," she says. "We weren't friends. We didn't have cozy chats."

"Fair enough," I say. "Now I understand why you went there and took the photographs. But what I don't understand is what you did next." She's still staring silently at the mitten and doesn't seem keen to volunteer any further information so I continue. "Once you knew Jemma was dead," I say, "why did you put the photographs into the heron's bag? What was the point of that?"

"The heron?" she says, looking confused.

"Helen," I say, correcting myself. "Jemma's sister."

"You found the pictures?" she asks, twirling the mitten in her hand. "That's unfortunate. Explains why you haven't been arrested."

"Why did you do it?" I ask again. "If I was you, as soon as I found out Jemma was dead, I would have destroyed those photographs and never thought about them again."

"But you're not me, Claire, and you don't understand," she says. "I still have a conscience. I'm not sure the same can be said about you."

I think she wants me to respond but I can't think of anything to say.

"I met Jemma's sister here," she continues. "She'd come to empty Jemma's locker. The poor woman was going out of her mind, trying to understand what had happened. She just couldn't believe that her sister was capable of killing someone. So desperate for answers, she was tormented with not knowing. And I did know. I knew exactly what had happened to her sister. I put those photos in her bag because I wanted to ease her suffering. And because I needed to convince myself that underneath it all, I'm still a good person. That I still know the difference between right and wrong."

"You are a good person," I say, keen to get to the point.

"Am I?" she asks. "Would a good person steal another woman's baby?"

"Everyone makes mistakes."

"A mistake is driving in a bus lane. This was more than a mistake, Claire. I let darkness take control of my mind."

Why does she keep mentioning the darkness?

"Actually, forget what I said earlier. I don't think talking about this is going to help you," I say, wondering why I don't like hearing about the darkness. "Talking about it will drive you mad."

"No!" she says, suddenly direct. "Not talking about it, that's what's driving me mad. I've never talked about it to anyone other than Nicholas. I need to tell someone what I did."

"OK," I say, glancing at my watch and hoping she'll stick to the highlights. "Tell me."

"Once I let the darkness take control of my mind," she says as I shift uncomfortably in my seat, "I allowed myself to become a completely different person. Bitter. Jealous. I couldn't understand why someone like Lauren could have a baby but not me. I convinced myself that it wasn't fair but more than that, I convinced myself that that baby boy should be with me." She sits back in the chair now and looks towards the ceiling again. More investigations of memory. I wonder how that conscience is bearing up.

"Nicholas told me that social services were involved, and that Lauren would probably lose the baby anyway," she says. "It broke my heart thinking about that little boy going into care, being looked after by strangers. We belonged together. Before I knew it, the idea had become a plan. Nicholas started looking for another job and we moved house. Then one night, he went to Lauren's flat and took him. It was easy, he said. She'd left the door unlocked and didn't even stir. And we took Oscar to our new home, and I kept thinking that we'd get caught but we didn't. Nobody suspected us. I'd been hidden away for months and what with all the miscarriages, our family and friends understood why we'd kept my 'pregnancy' secret. Nobody asked any difficult questions and I set about becoming the best mother I could be. I felt alive," she says, the slightest smile settling onto her lips. "For the first time in my life, I felt properly alive. We were a family, and we were so happy." She drops the mitten onto her lap and looks at me. The smile gone. "Until one day we weren't."

I'm not sure whether she's finished talking but I've definitely heard enough. We've reached the point where we need to get to the point.

"There's no reason why you can't go back to being a happy family," I say. "I'm the only person who knows your secret and you're the only person who knows mine. If we both keep quiet, life can go back to normal."

"You don't understand," she says, still looking at me, but I have a feeling her focus is elsewhere. "We've committed awful crimes, you and me. Normal doesn't exist for people like us, I see that now." She's blinking rapidly, and I wonder what's going on in her mind. "How could I have been so stupid to think I could steal another woman's baby and live happily ever after?" she asks. "Life doesn't work like that. There's always a price to pay."

Her foot starts tapping in time with the blinking. "Shortly after we stole Oscar," she says, "that's when Dad's mental health deteriorated. Early onset Alzheimer's, they called it. I couldn't help thinking that he was being punished for my crime. And my marriage . . . Suddenly the man who would do anything for me—who stole a baby for me—suddenly he didn't look at me the same way anymore. He pretended everything was OK, but I knew. We irritated each other, he worked even longer hours. Became secretive. Always looking at his phone. I know he sees other women. The sad thing is, I don't even care. So, how can my life ever go back to normal, Claire?" She picks up the mitten again and passes it from one shaky hand to another. "I destroyed a woman's life. And because of that, I destroyed my own."

I watch the blinking and the foot tapping and the trembling. She needs to calm down.

"Miranda," I say kindly, "I think you're being a bit melodramatic. You've had a run of bad luck, that's all. You can't blame yourself for your dad's dementia and as for Nicholas, you can leave the cheating scumbag and start a new life with Oscar. No one ever needs to know what you did. Nicholas is never going to implicate himself by talking and I'm not going to tell anyone."

Her eyes are locked onto mine, but I can tell her focus is still elsewhere. I try something else.

"I think you're a really good mother," I say. "I see the way you look at Oscar. If everyone had a mother like you, this world would be a very different place. I don't want to hurt you, Miranda," I say truthfully. "I really don't want to hurt you. I want you and Oscar to live full, happy lives. But I need to know that you're not going to tell anyone about me."

The blinking, the tapping and the trembling stop. Her eyes refocus on me. She's back. And still. Too still. Is it possible to be too still?

"I broke the bond between mother and child," she says. "That most precious of bonds. Like the old lady said, you never know true love until you give birth."

"What old lady?" I ask, confused. "What, Janet or Edith? Miranda, those old ladies are both bonkers. You can't listen to a word they say."

"But it's true," she says. "Lauren loved her baby; she understood the meaning of true love. And I took all of that away."

I wish she'd start tapping her foot again. Why am I so unnerved by her stillness?

"When you're feeling better," I say, "I think you'll realize that you've given Oscar the best possible gift a person can give to anyone. You've given him a chance."

"I'm going to lose him one day," she says. "The universe will make sure of that. A crime like this won't go unpunished."

"You won't lose him," I say. "No one ever needs to know."

"And the worst part of all of it will be seeing my beautiful Oscar's face," she says, blinking away tears. "When he realizes what I did. That's what I can't bear," she says, letting the tears fall. "Knowing that moment is somewhere in the future. The moment when he sees the real me."

"Oscar never needs to know, Miranda," I say. "No one's ever going to tell him. Listen, it's probably just this bug, making you feel a bit down. You'll feel better about everything in a day or two, I'm sure of it. I just need to know," I add, sitting forward, emphasizing the importance of my next words, "are you going to tell anyone about me?"

She thinks for a moment and then smiles. She looks younger all of a sudden. At peace. "Don't worry, Claire," she says quietly. "I'll take your secret to the grave."

And after all the stillness, now there's movement. A flash of color and then the splintering of glass. My hand reaches up to stop her and I hear the word "No" and it must be coming from my mouth because the word is inside my head. I see her leap and for a moment she seems to be frozen in time, suspended in the air, still clutching that blue mitten . . . and then she's gone. The cold air rushes towards me and I'm left alone with my scream.

I run to the window. She's lying on the ground of the sun terrace. She's not moving but there's a chance she's still alive. This is the third floor. There's still a chance. I run out of the sitting room, head towards the stairs. I pass Kathleen in the corridor. She's wheeling herself towards the sitting room, shouting about her baby. I didn't know she could wheel herself. The glass smashing and my screaming must have woken her. Maybe sound does have meaning in her world after all. I'm almost at the stairs when I pause. Kathleen has reached the sitting room door, and I picture her heading towards the smashed window. I turn back.

"Hello!" I shout. "Is anybody here? I need someone to keep an eye on Kathleen." Has the bug rendered everyone mute? Invisible? I go to Kathleen and push her back down the corridor. I can't leave her up here. She could cut herself on the glass or fall from the window.

"Hello!" I shout again. No answer. I'm going to have to take her down in the lift. I press the button and wait for the doors of the lift to open. She's still shouting about her baby. I think about running back to her room and getting the doll but then the doors of the lift open and I wheel her inside. I press the button for the ground floor and wait. The doors of the lift close as panic arrives but I force myself to stay calm.

"Where's my baby? What have you done with my baby?"

"It's OK, Kathleen. We'll get your baby soon, I promise." I close my eyes. I'll be out of this box in less than a minute. I just need to stay calm. My mind goes back to the moment just before Miranda did what she did. She looked so peaceful. There must have been some comfort in the finality of her decision. It's good that she felt peace at the end. I snap my eyes open. I don't know that it is the end. She might still be alive.

"What have you done with my baby? Where's my baby?"

"It's OK, Kathleen," I say again, staring at the number display. We're on the second floor. Not long now. I close my eyes again. I keep seeing her body lying on the ground. I've seen enough dead bodies to recognize one, but I don't know for sure. There's still a chance.

The lift stops. Have we reached the ground floor already? I open my eyes as an alarm sounds, chasing all other thought away. The number one is flashing on the display and Kathleen's hand is on the stop button.

"Kathleen, Kathleen, did you press this?" I say, brushing her hand away and slamming every button on the control panel.

"Where's my baby? What have you done with my baby?"

"Kathleen!" I shout, frantically pressing at the buttons. "What did you do?"

"No, Claire. What did *you* do?"

And terror grips me by the throat as those six unremarkable words pierce through the deafening alarm and I turn to face the tiny woman in the wheelchair. I stumble back against the wall because what I see in her eyes in that moment is far more terrifying than the blackness I know she sees in mine.

"Looks like we have plenty of time, Claire," she says. "So, tell me. What exactly did you do to my baby?"

'm slumped on the floor of a box and I can't get out. I'm trapped inside my nightmare but wide awake. Kathleen's talking about the frightful alarm; she's well-spoken, with a refined voice. Saying she wishes it would stop for a moment, to give her a chance to think. She seems to be thinking just fine. Doesn't seem anything wrong with her thinking. Very structured and coherent. Far more so than my own. She's saying that if you press the stop button then the alarm, the lift stalls and has to be restarted externally. She's smiling now and talking about how it took the "airhead receptionist" ages to get the lift moving last time. And that was when someone hadn't just thrown themselves through a third-floor window. She thinks we will probably be stuck in here for quite some time which is nice, she says. Gives us a chance to become properly acquainted.

Why is she talking like this? What happened to the dementia? Where did she come from?

"Who are you?" I ask.

"Kathleen," she says, extending her ancient hand towards me. "Kathleen Kane. Pleased to meet you."

I shake her hand. Her skin is cool and thin, like paper. Her hand drops back into her lap, and I see the network of veins under that cool, paper skin. I think about her heart pumping blood through those veins, up to her brain. Her brain that still works. I close my eyes to stop the box spinning. I need to stop thinking about her veins.

"Are you feeling OK?" she asks, looking concerned. "You don't look very comfortable. I noticed that about you last time we were trapped in here."

"And I've noticed something about you, Kathleen," I say, forcing a smile. "I've noticed you don't appear to be raving mad anymore."

"You youngsters," she says, shaking her head. "No respect for the older generations. Not all elderly people have dementia, Claire."

"The ones that live on dementia wards do!" I shout. "Why are you living here? Why are you pretending to be mad?"

"For the same reason most people do most things, I should imagine," she says, calmly smoothing the blankets over her legs.

She *must* be mad. There's no other explanation.

"Well?" she says, fixing me with an icy stare.

"Well, what?" I say, confused.

"What do you think is the reason most people do most of the things they do?" she asks. Slowly and patronizingly. Like a teacher addressing the most stupid student in the class.

"I don't know," I say, pushing my hair away from my face. I'm sweating. It's so warm in here.

"Perhaps you'd prefer to talk about something else, Claire?" she asks, smiling. "Like the air inside this small, broken lift. The air that is a lot stuffier now than it was two minutes ago. I wonder what it will be like in another two minutes. Or another ten minutes—"

"Love," I say, forcing the word—any word—out of my mouth. The walls of the lift have started to spin again. "I think love is the reason most people do what they do."

"Wrong!" she says, tapping the fingertips of her hands together. "Why do you youngsters always have to romanticize everything? There's something far more important than love, Claire. Come on, have another guess."

"I don't know what you're talking about, Kathleen. I'm sorry but—"

"Come on, Claire," she says again. "Have another guess. We haven't got all day—"

"Family," I say.

"Wrong again," she says, shaking her head. "I have to be honest; I'm finding this most disappointing. This is the first intelligent conversation I've had in ages, and I was hoping you'd be rather better at it. No matter. The answer, of course, is money."

"Money?" I say, controlling my breathing. In through the nose. Out through the mouth. "I don't understand."

"Money is the reason most people do most of the things they do," she says. "Especially when they don't have any."

"I still don't understand—"

"Lucas gambled all my money away," she says. "I gave it to him to invest and he lost it. All of it."

"And?" I say, before the next controlled in-breath.

"Have you seen the care homes for people who don't have

any money? My physical health was failing and I couldn't stay at home, so Lucas took me to see some of the care homes within my budget. I was appalled. Absolutely appalled. Wallpaper peeling off the walls, chipped woodwork. Filthy curtains, stench of urine. And the food! No. None of those places would do for me. I like nice things, Claire. I've always been surrounded by nice things. Do you know, I was the only child in my school to have a horse? I wasn't going to end my life in a miserable fleapit with a shared bathroom and cheap lino on the floor."

"But if you don't have any money, how can you afford to live here?"

"I may not have any money, but I have this," she says tapping the right side of her temple. "I've always been a smart woman. Always streets ahead of my peers. There was no comparison between me and the other legal secretaries. They would come and go, tapping at typewriters with their perfectly manicured nails. But I worked at that firm for years and I did more than just type. I read. Files and articles and correspondence. I read as much as I could and taught myself about the law. Are you aware of the Mental Health Act?"

"Yes."

"Good. So, you know that a person can be detained for treatment in hospital under Section 3?"

"Yes," I say, staring at her face. Each ancient feature blurring into the next.

"But did you know that a person who has been detained under Section 3 can be entitled to free aftercare?"

"No," I say. It feels like my eyes are glazing over. "I did not know that."

"Yes," she says excitedly, "Section 117 of the Mental Health Act sets it all out. It was incredibly easy. All I had to do was get myself sectioned in a psychiatric ward for a while and then help Lucas guide the medical professionals towards this place. You see, Section 117 allows for aftercare services that reduce the risk of a mental condition getting worse. Every time they tried to move me somewhere I didn't like, my 'mental condition' got worse. But once they moved me here, I calmed down." She's quiet now and I can no longer decipher the expression of her facial features. Blended as they are into a mold of self-satisfaction and pride.

"But you have to pretend to be mad," I say, injecting a shot of reality into air congested with crazy.

"True," she says. "And the time I spent on the psychiatric ward was undeniably difficult. But I knew it was a means to an end and I learned a lot while I was there." She leans forward, closes her eyes and when she opens them, she stares at me. Vacant. Unseeing. Gone. "Where's my baby, what have you done with my baby?" she says, before blinking again. She's back. "Perfected that while I was there," she says with a smile. "Insanity can be a good teacher."

"I don't understand how you can do it," I say. There are waves of pain behind both my eyes. "How you can pretend to be mad all the time."

"I don't have to do it all the time," she says. "How often do you think people here look at me? The caregivers do their jobs but, for the most part, I'm left to my own devices. I listen to the radio, read, do puzzles, watch TV and wait for the next meal. And the meals here are incredible. Do you know the chef worked in a Michelin-starred restaurant? My favorite day is Monday. We have shepherd's pie and sticky toffee pudding on a Monday. It's unbelievably good."

"But how do you cope?" I ask. "You must get so bored being cooped up all day. Pretending to be mad."

"That was a big concern of mine when I first moved in. But thanks to the most extraordinary sequence of events, I haven't been bored. In fact, since I moved in here, life has been more interesting than ever before!"

"Really?"

"Well, first of all there was the abuse. Though it wasn't proper abuse, not really. Just that hideous Deb woman and Jemma throwing the doll around. Ridiculous, immature behavior. Anyway, I told Lucas about it, and he set up a secret camera to catch them in the act. That was exciting. When he confronted Jemma she tried to deny it of course. Even when he showed her the footage, she said Deb forced her into it. You should have seen her face when I spoke, Claire. When I said I'd *seen* her throw that stupid doll around. The look on her face was priceless. I honestly thought she was going to faint."

"Jemma knew about you?"

"Oh yes. We became quite close, Jemma and me. I liked her. She was smart. A quick thinker, good at talking her way out of trouble. When Lucas threatened to report her to the police unless she paid him, Jemma looked him straight in the eye, as calm as you like, and told him to go ahead! Such a plucky little soul. She pulled a paycheck from her pocket and showed us what she was earning, and I'll admit it, Claire—I was shocked. I don't know how people survive on such a pitiful wage. It's an absolute travesty. I mean, for the most part the caregivers here work very hard, and when you think about the daily nonsense they have to contend with, they deserve to be paid a lot more. Anyway, Jemma told Lucas he was never going to get rich by blackmailing individual caregivers, but if he wanted to make some decent money, she might be able to help. That's when she told us about other abuse in the home, worse abuse. She said she'd be able to get more footage and, with enough evidence, Lucas would be able to blackmail Care to Join Us, the parent company. A big organization like that would pay anything to keep those videos away from the *Daily Mail*. He wouldn't send them any showing her of course. She was very clear on that."

"But why would the parent company pay up?" I ask, squinting. The pain behind my eyes was growing more intense. "Surely, they'd just fire the abusive caregivers. And Lucas *did* blackmail an individual caregiver," I add quietly. My claustrophobia has never been tested for this long before, is that why my voice sounds strange? "That's what he was doing when I met him."

"Was he? Well, I can't say I'm surprised," she says with a smile. "Typical Lucas, always going off script. He probably wanted a quick payout, just to tide him over. He was absolutely atrocious with money, poor boy. And you're quite right, there was a good chance CJU—"

"CJU?"

"Care to Join Us, Claire. Do try to keep up. Obviously, there was a good chance they wouldn't pay, but Lucas and Jemma thought it was worth taking a punt. So, the plan was, Lucas wouldn't blackmail Jemma and in return she would provide him with footage of other members of staff misbehaving and also make sure I was always treated well. Life ticked along quite nicely for a while and just when everything was beginning to get a bit dull, something really astonishing happened."

I have a full-on migraine now and my eyes are no longer able to focus. My vision is blurred, and my legs are weak. I don't think I can stand but that's no longer a priority. The next breath, that's all that matters. Just need to remain focused on the next breath. And the one after that.

"I was sitting in the living room watching *Pointless*," Kathleen says, "when that awful couple and their horrible child came in. He immediately started running around making noise. So uncontrolled. In my day, children were seen and not heard. Lucas had beautiful manners as a child. I made sure of it. Young people do it all differently these days. They think they know best but all they're doing is making a rod for their own backs, mark my words."

I think about the beautifully behaved young Lucas and the blackmailing, gambling reprobate he became. But I say nothing, focusing instead on the next in-breath.

"The woman immediately changed the channel," Kathleen

says with disgust. "Put some childish nonsense on to try to entertain the boy. No regard for me, of course. No consideration for what I was watching. People like me are invisible to anyone under the age of fifty." My mind darts back to Florence. She said the same thing. About feeling invisible. I wonder what Florence would say if she was here. I wonder if she'd give me a hug and tell me everything's going to be OK. That I'm not going to die of suffocation inside a box I can't open.

"And then they started arguing," says Kathleen and I wonder who she's talking about. I'm finding it difficult to follow this story. "I wasn't interested at first," she says. "That couple were always arguing about something or other. But then they mentioned a birthmark and the woman became emotional and my interest was piqued. She was angry at the man for changing the boy's nappy on the floor of her father's bedroom. She said someone could have walked in at any moment, could have seen the birthmark. He told her to calm down, to stop being so dramatic. He said the story hadn't been in the papers for years and everyone had forgotten. Nobody was looking for a little boy with a birthmark on his leg anymore. Then someone else came in and they stopped talking. Do you know something, Claire?" she asks, leaning towards me. "They never even lowered their voices when they were talking in front of me. That's how invisible I am."

I look at the disgust chiseled deeply into each wrinkle on her face and can't help wishing she was invisible now. The only thing worse than dying inside a small box is dying inside a small box with someone who won't stop talking.

"Well, obviously, I couldn't wait to tell Jemma what I'd heard," she says, "and it didn't take her long to fill in the gaps. She found a newspaper from the time. Do you know, she kept years and years of newspapers in her house? She was a bit of a hoarder, was Jemma. Strange character. Odd dress sense. Anyway, this was when everything became really exciting. At last, Lucas had the chance of getting his hands on proper money. We knew they'd pay anything to keep that child and the family was wealthy. The husband was a doctor and Frank is always going on and on about the company he used to run. How he had three hundred people working for him before he lost his mind. We'd struck gold."

I close my eyes. What Kathleen said, is that right? Is money the reason most people do most of the things they do? Are ordinary people that shallow? That predictable? That disappointing?

"But before we had a chance to put the plan into action, you turned up," she says, smiling. "Just when I thought life couldn't get any more thrilling!"

Why is she smiling? I killed her child. She *knows* I killed her child.

"You sent Jemma into such a panic, Claire," she says, still smiling. "She was crying when she told me Lucas was missing. She said she'd followed you and Lucas back to your place and that he'd never left. She wanted to go to the police, but I talked her out of it. Explained that if the police found Lucas's briefcase and the stills from that horrible video, she'd get into trouble, and I didn't want Jemma to lose her job. With Lucas gone, that would make my position here very precarious. So Jemma broke into your house to look for the briefcase and that's when she stumbled upon the man drowned in your fish tank. She was quite shaken up by that. It's not what one expects to find in a living room in a decent suburb. Tell me, Claire, who was that man? I've often wondered. What did he do to you?"

"He was a psychiatric nurse who abused my dying father," I say. My mouth is dry. I haven't spoken for a while.

"Well, it sounds like he got what he deserved," says Kathleen. "Is that your thing, Claire? Is that what you do? Hunt down substandard care providers? Very commendable. But what about Lucas? What did he do to you? Owe you money?"

"He short-listed my painting in an art competition," I say. "And then he took the place away."

"And?" she says, sounding confused. "That's it? You killed him for that?"

"It wasn't a good time for me," I offer by way of explanation. "I was upset. I'd just buried my father."

"I see," she says but I don't think she does. "And how did you kill him?"

"Are you sure you want to know?"

"Yes," she says. "I think I do," and this time I believe her.

"I stabbed him," I say.

"Did he die quickly?" she asks, and I think back to that night. Lucas tied to my bed. The screaming and all that blood.

"Quicker than fish tank man," I reply.

"That's good," she says, sitting back in the wheelchair. "That's good."

"That's good?" I say quickly. Too quickly. I start to cough. I need to calm down and catch my breath. There's still enough air in here. Not much but enough. "Is that it?" I ask as my breathing returns to normal. "Is that all you have to say? I killed your only child. Don't you care?"

"Of course I care but I was going to lose him soon anyway," she says, calmly smoothing the blankets once again over her legs. Why is she so emotionless? Maybe this is it, a preview of the punishment that lies ahead—trapped for eternity inside a small box, alongside an ancient version of my mother. "I haven't got long left," she's saying now. "I can feel it happening. I can feel myself dying. Can you imagine what that feels like?" She's silent for a moment and I think about the question. "Maybe you can," she says quietly. "Maybe you feel like you're dying right now. I know I'm dying. I can feel everything shutting down."

Not her voice. I've never heard someone dying talk so much.

"But I don't fear death," she's saying now, "not anymore. Not like I used to. When Lucas was alive I was scared of dying, of leaving him behind. He owed money to so many people. God only knows what trouble he would get into. You saved him from himself and did me a favor. Now he'll be waiting for me when I get there. They'll all be waiting for me. Lucas, Mother, Father, Aladdin."

"Your husband was called Aladdin?" I ask, confused. My tortured mind racing back to the wedding photos in the memory book. The ambassador of decency standing proudly next to his bride. He didn't look like an Aladdin.

"No, my husband was called Gregory. Aladdin was my horse."

"Oh, right."

There's no talking now, just the sound of the alarm as I close my eyes and rest my head against the wall. I should be considering my options. Making a plan. A plan that involves killing Kathleen. But I can't move my head because of the migraine. Can barely open my eyes.

"I wonder how long we've been in here?" she asks. "We've definitely been in here longer than last time, haven't we?"

"Was Jemma coming to see you that day?" I ask, desperate to change the subject. "The day she died?"

"Yes," she says. "She was a ball of excitement. She marched into my room wearing the most extraordinary outfit and told me she had a plan. Said she was going to blackmail you into working for her, that it was perfectly safe because if she didn't turn up at Florence's house at the agreed hour, Florence would point the police in your direction. Poor Jemma. She was so certain her plan was going to work. It didn't seem to occur to her that you would kill Florence too. It occurred to me of course, but not Jemma. She was such a strange character. A hopeless optimist, I suppose, which explains that outfit. Only a hopeless optimist would team wellies with a kilt. Anyway," she says, "I pretended to be interested in her plan, asked her for all the details, memorized Florence's address and wished Jemma luck. I knew there was a good chance I'd never see her again, and I knew that meant I'd lose my link to you. The person who'd killed my baby. But I need to make sure you pay for what you did to my son."

I register the threat but I need to remain focused on my mind. It's turning against me. Telling me the air is running out and

I'm going to suffocate. But I know there's still plenty of air in here. I need to stay calm.

"After Jemma left," she says, "I wheeled myself into the living room and waited for that woman and her child to turn up. She visits her father every day. The woman really needs to get a life. Although," she adds, laughing, "it's a bit late for that now."

I think about my hammer. It's still in my bag in the sitting room on the third floor. This morning I thought there was a chance I'd be using it on Miranda. Never imagined I'd want to use it on Kathleen. But I do. I really do. I imagine holding my hammer above my head and aiming it at her right temple. Swinging it with all my force towards a brain that still works. But I don't have my hammer and, even if I did, I don't think I'd be able to use it. I don't even have the strength to get to my feet and strangle her. Is this how Dad felt in those last two years of his life? How did he cope, trapped inside a living hell?

"Anyway, I was dozing off but half watching *Bargain Hunt* when she turned up. Usual shenanigans, the child started to run around like a demon, and she immediately changed the channel to some nonsense for him. No consideration for anyone other than themselves. Well, what happened next was simply wonderful. I turned towards them and said, 'Excuse me, kidnapping bitch. Would you mind changing the channel back to *Bargain Hunt*. I was enjoying it immensely.' I wish you could have seen it, Claire. She literally jumped up from the sofa! I told her to take a seat and calm down, then got straight to the point. I told her I knew she'd stolen the child and that I'd go to the police unless she did exactly what I said. I gave her the address and told her to take pictures of anyone entering or leaving the house."

"So, it was you," my voice sounds strange. Weak. Ordinary. "You blackmailed Miranda."

"Yes, that's what I just said. Are you having trouble understanding me, Claire? Do you need me to speak slower?"

"All this time I've been coming here," I say more to myself than to Kathleen. "Miranda knew the truth about you. She knew you didn't have dementia."

"Yes, and she kept quiet about it because I told her to. She did exactly what I told her to because she was terrified about losing that awful child. She waited outside Florence's house, took the photographs and when she gave them to me, that was that. At last, I knew what you looked like. I knew the face of the person who had killed my son."

"She made copies of the photographs," I say, my voice reduced to a whisper. Even if I don't die in this lift, my life is over. I'm going to be taken from this box and put in another. It would be better if I die in here.

"Well, I don't know anything about that," she says. "All I know is that she gave me one set and then I had a decision to make. Taking the photographs to the police would mean exposing my sanity and losing my place here. But on the other hand, there was no way I could let you get away with killing my son. Tricky. I was still trying to make up my mind what to do with them when, lo and behold, you appeared in my bedroom! I couldn't believe it. A real-life serial killer coming to visit. And there was me, worried I was going to be bored. Life's been fairly fascinating from that point on. I assumed you were planning to kill that awful Deb and it's been wonderful having a front-row seat. I've loved it. Watching you watching her. Asking questions. Learning about her routine, her life. Marvelous. That's why I delayed reporting you to the police. I wanted you to kill that dreadful woman. My only regret is that you'll never get to kill her now but that's your own fault. You took too long. I'm dying, Claire. I can't wait forever."

Is that why she's telling me all this? I force myself to look at her. She's in her wheelchair, leaning towards me. "I know it's a risk, speaking to you like this," she says, answering my unspoken question. "But when the opportunity presented itself, I thought, what the hell? Might never get another chance! And that look on your face! Well, frankly that's worth dying a thousand times. So, if you're going to kill me, you'd better do it now. Because any second now, those doors will open and then it's all over, Claire. Everyone will know what you are."

I try to stand but my legs have no power, and in any event, I know I can't kill her. She may be ancient, but she doesn't look like a ghost. I close my eyes and let the darkness smother me like a shroud. I think about the darkness Miranda spoke about. The darkness that distorted her mind, turned her into someone she didn't recognize. This darkness isn't like that. Even without a migraine, my mind is already distorted. I've lived with darkness since I was seven years old. Since that first kill. Never acknowledged it but always knew it was there. This darkness is unfamiliar. Final. I sense his approach and I reach out towards him. The waves of grief crash around me, and I let them wash over my head. *I've missed you so much, Dad. Take me with you. I'm ready.*

He's almost here and I'm almost there but then I open my eyes. The lift doors are open and the alarm has stopped. Kathleen is talking and the waves wash away, taking Dad with them and everything else. Everything that made me feel safe.

28

This woman killed my son! She killed Jemma and another woman and a man. She's probably killed other people. She was going to kill you!"

I breathe in the new air and push myself to my feet. Deb and two nurses are staring into the lift and Kathleen is telling them my secrets. Not all my secrets, only the ones she knows about. But frankly that's already too much. Oxygen slowly kick-starts my brain and I think about my options. I don't have any. It's over. This is it.

"This woman is dangerous. She doesn't look it, but she is an extremely dangerous serial killer," Kathleen is saying now. "She's killed four people that I know of, but I suspect she's killed many more. It is imperative you keep her locked up until the police get here."

The nurses look terrified. They stare at me, really stare at me, and suddenly it's my seventh birthday again. I'm in that tiny room, listening to the voices behind the closed door. The man in the horrible brown suit is talking to Daddy and I'm counting down the moments in my mind. Someone is going to open that door and expose the real me. I got away with it that day and many days since. But I'm not getting away with it today.

"She drowned a man in a fish tank," Kathleen is saying now, "and she stabbed my son to death just because she was having a bad day. And Jemma, do you remember Jemma? She made that murder look like suicide."

A frightened glance between the two nurses and then all eyes return to me. The truth is out. When the police dig up my garden, they'll find Lucas. I should have moved him. I should have moved all of them. I close my eyes and think about Dad. Silently talk to him in my final moments of freedom. *I'm so sorry, Dad. I know I've let you down.* I open my eyes. The nurses haven't moved. It's now or never. Have I got enough strength to push past them?

And then one of them speaks in an efficient clipped voice. The words don't make any sense at first. But then they do. They start to make perfect sense.

"How long has she been like this?" the nurse asks me. "This confused and disoriented?"

"About fifteen minutes," I eventually manage to reply. "She became really upset upstairs in her room," I add, as the neurons in my brain fire up. "I thought it might be this bug, affecting her mental state. That's why I brought her downstairs, but I stupidly forgot to bring the doll. Then we got trapped in the lift for quite a while," I say, getting into my stride, "and I think it all got too much for her."

The nurse nods and then walks into the lift and pushes Kathleen out into the reception area.

"What?" shouts Kathleen. "Where are we going? Where are you taking me? There's nothing wrong with me. I'm perfectly sane. You need to get the police!"

"It's OK, Kathleen," murmurs the nurse, wheeling her towards the medical bay. "It must have been nasty being trapped in that lift. I'm going to give you something to help you relax."

"No!" she screams. "You have to listen to me. I've got proof, photographs in my bedroom. Please, you have to believe me. She killed my baby! That woman killed my baby!"

As the screams disappear down the corridor, Deb leads me out of the lift and looks at me with concern. "Listen, Claire," she says, "there's been a terrible incident involving Miranda."

"Miranda?" I say, confused.

"Yes," she says. "It looks as though she jumped from a third-floor window."

I raise my hands to my mouth. "My God!" I say. "How is she?"

"The doctor is out there now, and the ambulance is on the way," she says. "But it doesn't look good. She's completely unresponsive."

"My God," I repeat.

"The police will be here any minute," she says, "and they'll probably want to talk to you."

"Of course," I say. "I'll help in any way I can. But I didn't see or hear anything. Once Kathleen became really upset I called for help but there was nobody around."

"There were no staff upstairs? Are you sure?"

"Yes, positive. I'll mention it to the police."

She's quiet for a few moments. "You look exhausted, Claire," she says eventually. "It must have been really difficult for you being trapped in that lift with Kathleen when she was so distressed."

"Yes, it was awful," I say, "but nothing in comparison to what's happened to Miranda."

She places an arm around my shoulder. "I think you've been through enough today. Get yourself home and have some rest."

"But I need to speak to the police," I say. "I need to tell them what I know."

"But as you just said, Claire, you didn't see or hear anything."

"I don't know . . ." I say, chewing my bottom lip. "I think I should stay here until the police arrive and tell them that I was on the third floor."

"But what will that achieve, Claire?" asks Deb, dropping her arm. "Listen," she says, suddenly abrupt. "As soon as the emergency services arrive, this place is going to be a circus. You saw how distressed Kathleen became just after being trapped in a lift. How do you think the residents are going to cope with sirens and cordons and police officers everywhere? I have a duty of care of our residents so I must insist that only essential personnel remain."

"OK, Deb," I say. "I understand. I hadn't thought about it like that."

"Why should you?" she asks. "It's my job to think about it like that. Now, don't worry about signing out in the visitors' book, I'll do it for you. You just concentrate on getting yourself home."

"Thanks, Deb," I say. "I'll just run up to Kathleen's room to get my bag and then I'll be on my way."

If she says anything in reply, I don't hear it. Her back is already turned and she's writing in the visitors' book. I assume she's falsifying the entry because she doesn't want the police knowing I was here and telling them that there were no staff on the third-floor dementia ward. Deb is still thinking about the Care to Join Us Awards. Which I assume she still believes she's in with a chance of winning. And while I know that assumption has never been a friend of mine, I consider it infinitely more reliable than Deb's delusion.

I take the steps two at a time as I bound up to the third floor. I grab my bag from the eerily icy sitting room and then head towards Kathleen's room. There's not that many places she could have hidden the photographs. As I search, I notice the radio and the reading glasses, the pile of novels and puzzle books on the floor by the armchair. I've noticed those books before. Why did they never strike me as odd? I check the wardrobe, under the mattress, behind the photo frames on the wall, and then my eyes rest upon the memory book. I find the photographs slipped inside the padded cover at the back. Clever. I wouldn't expect anything less.

I stuff the photographs into my bag and take one last look around the room. From the window I see three men walking back from the direction of town. One of the men is wearing a hat and another is holding a small child, whooshing him through the air superhero style. I hear sirens in the distance and head for the door.

As I walk away from Waterbridge Oak Care Home, the sirens become louder, and I find myself thinking about that little boy. For some reason I keep thinking about his shoes with dinosaurs on each side. Then I think about when the whooshing stops. When he's placed back on the ground. Those dinosaurs will be with him but what about the superheroes? Will they still be there?

29

The man buried next to Dad may not have celebrated his sixty-sixth birthday yesterday but that didn't prevent others from marking the occasion. Helium balloons and open cans of Guinness are strewn all over the grave and I'm trying to decide how I feel about this. I want to be more understanding of ordinary people and their peculiar ways, but I can't help thinking this just amounts to littering. Pour the Guinness onto the grave if you must but then put the can into the bin. Is that so much to ask? I'm trying to be nonjudgmental, I really am. I just think consideration is more appropriate than helium balloons when remembering the dead. And I know that's not a cliché. But maybe it should be.

Dad's grave, in contrast to its neighbor, is still looking tidy and stylish. It's still too early for a headstone so I'm focusing on flowers and plants. I planted a rosebush the other week and that seems to be doing quite well. Today I need to clear away the last of the pansies and replace them with white carnations. I like tending to the grave. There's something comforting about being here. Makes it easy to think.

It's been a month since Miranda jumped from that window,

fractured her skull on the sun terrace and died on her way to the hospital. I haven't been back to Waterbridge Oak since. There's no point. Kathleen isn't there anymore. She's somewhere with Lucas, her mother, her father and Aladdin. I hope wherever she is, she's happy. And that there's definitely no cheap lino on the floor.

Ben has got into the habit of calling me two or three times a week. He calls me when there isn't even anything to say. I enjoy our conversations enormously. He told me Kathleen's mental condition deteriorated rapidly before her death, and she had to be moved back to the psychiatric ward where her physical condition worsened and she succumbed to pneumonia. She remained delusional right up until the end, screaming about drownings and shootings and her son being stabbed. He said her death was a kindness.

The big news at Waterbridge Oak Care Home concerns Deb. She was waiting to hear about the Care to Join Us Care Home Awards but instead won notoriety of an entirely different kind. Disturbing video stills were sent anonymously to several tabloids showing Deb, Jemma and another employee abusing elderly residents in their care. Ben told me Deb and Gary (I knew Vampire Smoker looked like a Gary) have been arrested and are awaiting trial. Looks like she'll never win one of those awards now, which is a shame. That would have been quite the achievement.

Ben always catches his breath before he talks about Miranda. I think it's going to take him a while to recover from that. No one properly understands why Miranda did what she did.

Clearly struggling with her father's dementia, Ben thinks maybe she had undiagnosed depression. Sometimes Ben and I talk about grief, and I pass on nuggets of wisdom I learned during the bereavement course. I like easing his grief; it reminds me how far I've come, the five stages I've worked through. The acceptance I feel now. Ben told me Frank doesn't get any visitors anymore. Nicholas turned up once since Miranda's death but hasn't been back since. He had Oscar with him apparently, and a woman wearing even more makeup than Irina. She was a nurse, by all accounts. Probably one of Neonatal Nick's army of angels. Ben says he misses Miranda, and he really misses Oscar. He says the third floor isn't the same anymore without him. I wonder what the future holds for that little boy. The boy with golden curls and blue, saucer-like eyes who pursed his lips together in concentration as he built a tower of building blocks. I wonder whether he'll ever know how much he is missed.

I stand up and look at the white carnations. They look good. Like they've always been there.

I say goodbye to Dad and head towards the car park. The red Mercedes is there, waiting. Helen insisted on driving me here. She said that's what friends do. We're friends now. I have a friend. She thinks I'm funny and I like making her laugh. I get into the car, and she smiles at me.

"OK?" she asks.

"Yes," I answer.

She drives out of the cemetery and down several roads before speaking again. I know what she's doing. Putting a respectful distance between my dad's grave and the rest of our day. She's always respectful, always thinking of others. It's one of the reasons I like her.

"Are you sure you don't mind coming with me today?" she asks.

"Of course not," I say.

"Thanks, Claire," she says. "I know it's a bit weird. It just feels like the right thing to do. I think it might bring me some closure. Does that make sense?"

"Yes," I lie. "It makes perfect sense." It doesn't. But I like being friends with Helen and, as I stare out of the car window, I realize that's probably the most extraordinary thing that's happened to me since Dad died. I never had any interest in being friends with anyone before. Dad was my world. I didn't need anyone else. Now I do. And if that means pretending things make sense when they don't, well, that's fine.

"Thanks, Claire," she says again. "We don't have to stay long. Just pay our respects and leave, then I can treat you to that meal I owe you for looking after me when I got so drunk and making sure I got home safe."

"You don't owe me anything, Helen," I say.

"I do," she says. "You were so kind. When I think about what could have happened—"

"So, how many people do you think will be there today?" I ask, changing the subject as she stops at a red light.

"I'm not sure," she says, turning to face me. "All of Lucas's work colleagues will be there. They're the ones who told me about it. They're such a lovely bunch of people, I think you'll really like them. I still can't believe they invited me to come today. I didn't think they'd want anything to do with me after . . . you know . . ."

"After what?" I ask.

"Well, after what Jemma did," she says, as the light turns green.

"But none of that was your fault," I say.

"I know, but Jemma was my sister," she says, turning onto a dual carriageway. "I can't help feeling a little responsible. I still can't believe she did what she did. I'm so angry at her!" she shouts and bangs her hands on the steering wheel. "How could Jemma have been involved in that abuse? How could she have treated vulnerable people like that? I feel sick when I think about it. Sick with shame."

I look at her profile. Interested to see what an angry, sick-with-shame ordinary person looks like while exceeding the national speed limit.

"Poor Lucas," she says, sounding calmer. "I wonder if we'll ever find out what happened to him?"

"Maybe," I say. "One day."

"The most likely scenario is that he found out his mother was being abused," she says. "Maybe he confronted Jemma and she did something to him."

"Maybe," I say again.

"She must have been involved in his disappearance. Nothing else makes sense. Why else would she have his briefcase? Maybe that's why she killed herself. Maybe she couldn't live with what she'd done."

"Maybe," I say for a third time.

"Maybe the guilt of everything just became too much for her. The abuse . . . and whatever she did to Lucas. Maybe she couldn't think of any other way out."

"Maybe," I say, wondering how many times I can use the word before she notices.

"I wish I'd been closer to Jemma in the last few years," she says, turning off the dual carriageway. "I wish she'd felt able to talk to me."

"You can't blame yourself for what happened, Helen," I say.

"I know," she says. "It just hurts. Knowing I didn't know her as well as I thought I did."

We finish the journey in silence. I know where we are. I've been here before. I pretended to wait for a bus over there. I've sat on that bench and stared into the windows of those shops. She parks and we walk to the bar. A man passes us each a handout as we walk inside and look for a seat. They've hired the whole bar, it's a much bigger event than I was expecting. I stare down at the pamphlet and look at the image of Lucas's beaming face. Funny how photographs never seem to do him justice.

A man wearing a stripy pink shirt and skinny jeans stands up at the front and clears his voice.

"Thank you all so much for coming," he says. "My name is Simon and I worked with Lucas." He takes a pile of cue cards out of his pocket. "As you all know," he says, "we haven't seen Lucas for quite some time now and, the fact is, we don't know whether we're ever going to see him again." A slight pause as he flicks to the next card. "There's been a lot of talk about his disappearance in the media and, indeed, we have a reporter here today. But not much has been said about the man himself. That's why we've organized this informal memorial service today. To remember Lucas. To hopefully press pause on all the intrigue and remember his life."

Press pause? What a prick.

"And that's why we've organized this informal memorial service today," he says. Again. Hasn't he already said that? Is he reading from the same card? "To honor Lucas. To share stories about him. To remember the flamboyant character that he was." He presses pause on his speech and I glance towards Helen. She's wiping a tear away from her eye and nodding. Poor heron. I hope this ridiculous ceremony brings her some closure.

"So, with no further ado," says Simon in the skinny jeans, "I'd like to invite our first speaker to the front."

One by one Lucas's colleagues, school friends, neighbors and anyone else who vaguely drifted into his life traipse up to the front and share increasingly dreary stories about the great man. I'm trying to be nonjudgmental, I really am. But I'm sure most of these people hated Lucas. Weren't they all complaining recently that he never got a round in? Why are they pretending that they care? Are they that desperate to get a mention in the paper?

I glance around the bar. It doesn't seem that long ago that Lucas and I sat over there together. I think back to that night and to everything that's happened since. If I could go back to that moment, knowing everything I know now, would I kill him? When I flirted with him and smiled at his jokes, I had no idea what I was getting into. I think I would have walked away. Killing isn't worth losing everything. I see that now. My heart beats faster every time I think about Kathleen taking my secrets and hurling them from the shadows into the light. All those events that are only alive in my mind, she gave them a voice. I'm so lucky no one believed her, but luck will only get me so far.

Simon in the skinny jeans is introducing the next speaker. She has long brown hair, several facial piercings and a preference for tie-dye fashion. She says she never had the pleasure of meeting Lucas, but she's written him a poem. They're really scraping the bottom of the barrel now. My mind drifts away again and I think about Dad. I think he would approve of my decision. He might even feel proud, and it's never too late to try to make him proud.

I've decided to turn my back on the killing. I'm going to try something different. I'm going to become the kind of person who accompanies her friends to memorial services. I'm going to talk on the phone to people when there's nothing to say. I'm going to try my best to stop judging ordinary people. I'm going to start to live my life as one of them.

Tie-dye girl with the long hair has finished reading her poem. She's saying that even though she never met Lucas, she will always feel grateful to him. He short-listed her painting in an art competition, she says, shortly before he disappeared. She never got the chance to enjoy the benefits of being short-listed because an opportunity arose for her to travel around India, but she will always be grateful to Lucas for the recognition. She sits down now and Simon takes her place at the front.

"Thank you, Claire, for that beautiful poem," he says. "And

for allowing us to print it on the back of the handout, illustrated with your beautiful artwork."

As he introduces the next speaker, I turn the handout over and read the words on the back.

I Never Met You

A POEM BY CLAIRE STOKES

I never met you, but I knew your name
Heard it mentioned again and again.
Where is Lucas? Where has he gone?
Does anyone know when he will be home?
You gave me a chance, despite never knowing me
Made me believe in myself, in what I could be
I hope you're at peace now, wherever you are
I will think of you often, shining bright as a star.

Underneath the words there's a drawing of a boat with a broken mast and suddenly my mind is racing back to the morning after Dad's funeral. The second email from Lucas.

This is the other Claire. The Claire who got the place on the short list. *My* place on the short list. And what did she do with my place? Squandered it. Floated around India in a hippy haze before drawing a dodgy-looking boat to illustrate a stupid poem that doesn't even rhyme properly—or have anything to do with boats. Does it? I read it again. I can't find any hidden nautical theme. Stupid poem.

"Claire?" I turn at the sound of my name. "Are you OK?"

The heron is looking at me with concern. I stare down at my hands. I've scrunched the handout into a little ball. My knuckles are white with the effort.

"I'm fine," I say, forcing a smile and relaxing my hands. "Just feeling a little queasy."

"It is quite warm in here," she says. "I hope there won't be too many more speakers."

There aren't. The ceremony ends soon afterwards. Lucas's colleagues come over to greet Helen and she introduces me to the group. I shake hands and smile, but I'm distracted. I want to see where tie-dye girl is. She's over in the corner talking to someone. She's got her coat on. I think it's a coat. It's long and flowing and covered in flowers and patterns and every color of the rainbow. She's saying goodbye. She's about to leave. I pull Helen to one side.

"Helen, I'm really not feeling that well," I say. "Would you mind if we go out for a meal another time?"

"Of course," she says. "Give me one minute to say goodbye and I'll drive you home."

"Oh no," I say. "You need to stay here and speak to Lucas's colleagues."

"Nonsense!" she says. "I won't hear of it. If you're not well, I'm going to make sure you get home safely. That's what friends do."

"You're such a good friend," I say. "But you need to talk about Lucas with the people who knew him. It will help you move on." She's silent, thinking it over. "I'll be fine," I say with a smile. "I'll call you tomorrow and we can rearrange that meal."

"Well, only if you're sure," she says.

"I am," I say and then we hug goodbye and I walk out of the bar.

The rainbow coat thing is easy to spot. She's heading towards the bus stop. I need to walk this way anyway. Strictly speaking, I'm not following her. We're just walking in the same direction. I think about my recent decision. My determination to turn my back on killing and try something new. But I'm not doing anything wrong at the moment, I'm just walking towards the bus stop. I need to get a bus home. I'm just doing what any ordinary person in my position would do.

I reach the bus stop but she crosses the road and joins a queue for one going in the opposite direction. She's standing at a different bus stop, headed in a different direction to me. I could just wait here at my bus stop. I could watch her get on her bus and disappear from my life. I could go home, work on my painting, speak to Ben on the phone and be ordinary. I could do that. I think I want to do that.

And then her bus approaches and, as she turns towards it, she catches my eye and I see straight through her. And that's when I know. I've always known. Exactly what bus I'm going to get on.

ACKNOWLEDGMENTS

So many thanks to my phenomenal agent, Cathryn Summerhayes, for making everything possible and for effortlessly working her magic while remaining a constant blend of cool, funny and calm.

The brilliant Jeramie Orton—such a wonderful person and a stupendous editor! I'm so grateful to you, the phenomenal Pamela Dorman and all the team at Penguin for giving my book such a wonderful US home. With Miranda Jewess and Viper in the UK, I'm so lucky to be working on both sides of the Atlantic with the best of the best.

Anna Weguelin, Annabel White and Jess Molloy at Curtis Brown—thank you all!

This book would still be a Word document, saved somewhere on my laptop, if it weren't for Jan Moran Neil spotting potential in the earliest of drafts, Cornerstones Literary Consultancy for its excellent feedback, Wanda Whiteley for her superb manuscript critique and Jamie Groves for his editorial input and for helping me get my book noticed. Eternally grateful.

Special thanks to my awesome friend Dan Thompson for "the choir that charisma forgot"—cheers, Dan! And a million mindful thanks to Gayle Creasey for introducing me to the bus analogy and for making me stop talking long enough to meditate.

For reading every draft of everything I have ever written and for never being anything other than unflinchingly positive and encouraging, I say a massive thank-you to my sister Karen. For reminding me about the importance of looking for humor in the darkest of times, and for a lifetime of love and support, I thank Catherine, Kevin and our wonderful mum. You guys are the best.

I'm extremely grateful to be in this world at the same time as so many people I love and admire, and what a perfect opportunity to say so! Thanks to my family and friends, including Pat and Chris Wallace, Mark, Harry, Georgia, Emma, Sinead, Erinn, Ciara, Orla, Matthew, Roxy, Daniel, George Powell, Kylie and Angus Ray, Zoe, Steve, Nikolai and Theia Harris, Susan Mustoe, Marie, Laurence and Eleanor Field, Chrissy French (and Harry and Scarlett!), Mohit Kochar, Clare Holt (thank you for lending your name to my Claire and for being so much nicer than she is), Katie and Tim Rolfe, Pearl Close, Vicki Wanless, Eleanor Parpotta, Katharine Blom, Eve Cinnirella, Will Awad, Dot Hickson, Sarah Baker and Kath Ward.

My husband, Marc, and our children, Grace, Charlie, Lucy and Sam. Thank you (and Star and Wilfred, of course) for being my everything and for never laughing at me—OK, thank you for only laughing a little bit when I kept telling you I was writing a book!

Finally, the biggest thanks go to my dad—for all the inspiration, the memories and the laughter. How I wish he were still here to read this. I miss you so much, Dad, even though—it's strange—you always seem quite near. I guess those who shine so bright never truly disappear.